DRAGON PRINCE

QURILIXEN LORDS: A QURILIXEN WORLD NOVEL

MICHELLE M. PILLOW

MICHELLE M. PILLOW® - MICHELLEPILLOW.COM

ABOUT DRAGON PRINCE

Grier's fiery passion for Salena might be everything his dragon ever wanted but loving her might just lead to the destruction of everything he's trying to save.

With all that is happening in his land, the upcoming shifter mating ceremony is the least of Grier's concerns. Even though he is heir prince of the dragon-shifters, he doesn't have the authority needed to help the humans stranded in dragon territory, nor can he banish those who ruthlessly control them. Yet honor demands he finds an opportunity to intervene, and he hopes that doing so won't start a war the shifters can't win. Discovering his destined mate couldn't have come at a worse time.

Salena knows what it is like to be a pawn of the Federation. They might have kidnapped her and brought her to this strange territory, but she will never do what they want of her... what everyone wants of her. The last thing the fugitive needs is the very public attention of a fierce dragon prince claiming they're fated by the gods—even if the sexy man makes her burn in more ways than one.

FIFTEEN YEARS AGO I PUBLISHED MY FIRST BOOK *The Mists of Midnight* (now titled *Forget Me Not*), a Regency-era ghost romance. However it is my second book that same year, *Dragon Lords: Barbarian Prince*, which became the start of the fan favorite multi-series collection, Qurilixen World.

First, don't let the numbers I'm about to tell you scare you away. Each series installment in the world can be read as a standalone as can each individual book. As the author I do recommend reading series installments from start to finish, but it is not necessary. For help with reading lists, suggested reading orders, and more information please visit my website for the free reading guides.

Not only is this my author anniversary, it is the

fifteen-year anniversary of the *Dragon Lords* series. Though I plan a whole year of celebrating, I'm starting with this book—the 37th title in the Qurilixen World, *Qurilixen Lords Book 1: Dragon Prince*. Fans of my work will instantly recognize that these stories focus on the adult children of the dragon-shifters from *Dragon Lords* series, and their cat-shifter neighbors from the *Lords of the Var®* series. Readers have been asking for these books since book one came out and I cannot wait to hear what you all think!

If you're new to the series, no worries, jump right in! If you enjoy my work, there will be plenty of books for you to choose from.

For the sake of completeness and to make your web searches easier, the Qurilixen World includes the following series: *Dragon Lords, Lords of the Var®, Dynasty Lords, Space Lords, Captured by a Dragon-Shifter, Galaxy Alien Mail Order Brides, Qurilixen Lords, and Galaxy Mates* (The Galaxy Mates shorter stories is currently out of print). You can find out more about each series at https://michellepillow.com/dragonlords.

No mention of my fifteen years would be complete without my heartfelt thank you to the readers and reviewers who have supported me for all these years. I love you all! It has been an amazing journey and I (literally) could not do it without you. I hope you'll come celebrate out with me online and subscribe to the mailing list to be informed of new books, freebies, and all the fun party stuff happening this year!

Thank you,
Michelle M. Pillow

"Filled with intrigue and adventure, Dragon Prince: A Qurilixen World Novel is an exciting new spinoff in a rich and intricate universe. Michelle Pillow creates characters to cheer for, to hope with, while building worlds that are portals for the imagination. Truly, Ms. Pillow is a master of futuristic fantasy."

Yasmine Galenorn, NY Times, Publishers Weekly, & USA TODAY Bestseller (galenorn.com)

"Michelle Pillow weaves a fantastical tale of dragon shifters, full of rich world-building, action and adventure, along with a sexy love story. This entire series is not to be missed!"

Bianca D'Arc, USA TODAY Bestseller (biancadarc.com)

"Sometimes you just need to gobble up the insane goodness that is dragons, and Michelle has been aiding in that addiction for fifteen years."

Eve Langlais, NY Times & USA TODAY Bestseller (evelanglais.com)

"A wonderfully sexy tale filled with romance and dragon-shifters that draws you in from the first page and doesn't let go. The Qurilixen Lords series is one you don't want to miss!"

Mina Carter, NY Times & USA TODAY Bestseller (mina-carter.com)

The Playful Prince
The Bound Prince
The Rogue Prince
The Pirate Prince

Qurilixen Lords

Dragon Prince
Marked Prince
Feral Prince
More Coming Soon!

Captured by a Dragon-Shifter Series

Determined Prince
Rebellious Prince
Stranded with the Cajun
Hunted by the Dragon
Mischievous Prince
Headstrong Prince

MichellePillow.com

Space Lords Series

His Frost Maiden

His Fire Maiden

His Metal Maiden

His Earth Maiden

His Woodland Maiden

Dynasty Lords Series

Seduction of the Phoenix

Temptation of the Butterfly

To learn more about the Qurilixen World series of books and to stay up to date on the latest book list visit www.MichellePillow.com

To the readers who have supported me for the last 15 years, thank you! I'm excited to be sharing my 15 year Author Anniversary and the 15 year Dragon Lords series Anniversary with all of you!

1

HE WAS NOT THE KING, NOT YET.

He could not help the people before him.

He could not banish those who needed to be ejected off his world.

Grier didn't know how to explain to his royal parents and the Draig elders that this wasn't the same world anymore. They clung to the past with an almost delusional need, as if, by willing it hard enough, everything would return to the ways of their youth. Hope and determination did not change reality. Qurilixen was no longer the primitive oasis of farmers and ceffyl herders whose biggest worry was protecting the ore mines from alien attacks or guarding the borderlands against their feral Var neighbors.

If only that were still the reality, when dragon-shifters and cat-shifters were the only kinds on this planet. Such times seemed easy compared to now.

Grier was probably oversimplifying matters. His father had warned him more than once to be careful about minimizing the past. The old days had not been as easy as Grier was wont to believe, and there were many things he did not know. That may be true, but he knew the problems of here and now.

Grier gazed down from the cliffside watchtower at the alien city sprawled over the valley below. There was something calming about sitting on the circular roof, at a height so great that none of the new residents of the planet could reach it. Locals had nicknamed the settlement below Shelter City because they meant it to be a temporary shelter for their visitors. That was over thirty years ago.

The top of the tower that surrounded a spire was flat, wide enough for him to sit, but the roof slats at his feet angled downward. He felt the wind, smelled the fresh air, heard only the barest hint of shouts from below.

The city was not supposed to have lasted as long as it had. Qurilixen was to be a short resting place where the people regained their strength after the destruction of their world and recovered from a virus that killed almost their entire population. His father, King Ualan, and the Var cat-shifting King Kirill, could no longer turn away hundreds of people in need, any more than they could have killed the aliens themselves. When they had agreed to partner with the Federation to save the Cysgodians, there had been invisible strings attached to the deal that had only revealed themselves over time.

Grier gazed over one such string. Until that moment, the shifters had kept their planet from any dealings with the Federation and free of its rules. They did not want to be part of the Federation Alliance. Now they were in a questionable gray area. The Federation claimed squatters' rights because they had dominion over the makeshift city, and the shifters refused to agree that city was anything more than a temporary settlement—to do so would be to accept the alliance.

They were at a standstill. The real victims of this political battle were the people caught in the middle. If the dragon prince could have his way, he'd funnel the people out of the city and allow them to choose their path—whether it was to stay on the planet or leave for space. No one's destiny should be decided by a dictatorship.

The cluster of metal and stone buildings, built in a hurry and falling over time, created the portion of the city that filled the valley. Canvas flapped in the wind, giving shade from the constant daylight of the planet. This is where the Federation kept their poor, which was almost every citizen of the city. Shifters had no say in the alien hierarchy.

Grier wanted to change that. Politics would not let him. He hated these politics.

The shifters did not have poor, or at least they hadn't before the Cysgodians came. Dragon-shifters took care of their own. If a child was orphaned, there was always a family willing to give them a new home. His cousin, Mirek, had not been blessed with children but had more sons than the rest of them combined from taking in those in need of a family. If someone needed food, someone fed them. Everyone worked, and everyone thrived. They considered it a matter of honor.

It was this sentiment that had caused his parents to take in so many off-worlders when they'd known it would strain their resources. Scientists had been convinced the blue radiation from one of Qurilixen's three suns had the healing properties the Cysgodians needed to recover. Besides, at the time, there was nowhere else for the residents to go.

But then, the city grew, too fast to be natural. They discovered others were being brought to the sanctuary— first three more; then twelve; then a shipful dropped off during the one night a year when darkness covered the planet, and the dragons had been occupied with their sacred mating ceremonies. That is how Shelter City now held more than the original Cysgodians, though they still used the term to describe the people there. *Cysgod* meant shelter in the Draig language, so it made sense.

By the time they made the discovery, it was too late. The people had dispersed into Shelter City and to round them up would have meant full-on attacks. None of the shifters wanted a war. What they wanted was the Federation gone as it was their fault this was happening. They had taken advantage of the elders' good-hearted natures and the Cysgodians' desperation.

Grier was not as soft-hearted as the elders. He couldn't be. He knew in order for his people to survive, he would have to make hard choices, ones he did not want to make.

Looking at his hands, he traced an old scar he'd received in battle training as a youth.

"Battles are not meant to be easy. They are meant to be won," had been the lesson his uncle Zoran, commander of the Draig army, wanted them to learn. Zoran was still a hard taskmaster to this day. Grier had received the scar from Zoran's daughter, Grace.

Fights did not scare him. Losing his people did. For better or worse, the Cysgodians were now his people, and they needed freed from the Federation's rule. Only then could the shifters start truly absorbing them into

Qurilixen society if that is what the aliens wanted. As it was, crime and discontentment were escalating.

Above the city of metal and stone were structures of a different nature. They were evenly spaced buildings along the ridge of a mountain, identical and just as they had been since the Federation put them up thirty years earlier.

A large stone building towered over it all, across the valley from his watchtower perch but low enough that he could see the roof. The rectangular structure stretched along the length of the city. Metal arches slashed over the top. That is where the city officials stayed. It was where his parents and ambassador cousin were now, discussing the many issues that arose from this ever-growing nest of malcontents.

Suddenly, a wave of heat hit his back, propelling his body down the side of the roof. A roar of flames filled the sky over his head. He dug his heels against the surface even as his hands flailed to grab something solid. The slats of the roof clattered under his boots as he tried to stop his fall. It didn't work. As he flew over the side of the tower, he managed to grab hold of the edge with one hand. He swung violently so that his back struck the stone side. Another roar of fire filled the air.

He took a deep breath, ignoring the pounding of his heart as he gained control of his body. Kicking the side of the building, he propelled himself around, gripping the roof's edge even as he released his anchored hand long enough to change his hold so that his wrist wouldn't break.

Grier did not hang long. He used his toe to launch from the side and his arm strength to lift his head over the edge of the rooftop to look at his attacker.

Grace peeked at him from the other side of his resting spot, hiding her naked body. Her light brown eyes shone with mischief. His cousin was pretty and would have appeared as regal as any queen if not for the fact she'd just tried to firebomb him off the side of the tower. Her brown hair flew around her head. She grinned down at him. "Let me borrow your shirt."

Grier dropped his weight, kicked off the side of the building a second time and flung his body upward. With much effort, he climbed onto the roof and made his way toward the top. Sitting with his back to his cousin, he took off his shirt and held it behind him. The cooler air hit his naked chest, and he breathed deeply. "Do I even want to ask where you left your clothes?"

He felt Grace take the shirt. Seconds later she was sitting next to him, wearing it. Her bare feet tapped on the roof slats as she propped her arms on her knees. Grier was glad she was his cousin. In any form, she was dangerous. As a fighter, she was fierce. As a dragon, she was terrifying. As a woman, she was stunningly beautiful. As a cousin, she liked to fly up behind him and fireball him off the side of a tower for fun.

"Anything interesting happening in the village of discontent?" she asked, sounding restless.

He ignored her question and instead asked one of his own. "Does Uncle Zoran know you are flying around the forbidden valley?"

Grier already knew the answer.

"My father still thinks of me as I was at twenty years old and wants me to sit where he can see me at all times. He doesn't like me to come here. He thinks it isn't safe." Grace adjusted her position a little. "I don't know what he thinks will happen."

Grier had only known two female dragons in his life —his grandmother and Grace. And his grandmother had died years ago.

Anyone who didn't know the warrior prince would have seen Zoran's treatment of his daughter as contradictory. Perhaps it was because dragons rarely had female children. On the one hand, Grace was a dragon who should be trained for battle like a dragon. And yet, she was also female and dragon males tended to treat females like they were delicate and to be protected—which was funny on many levels. Since Zoran's mother, their grandmother, had also been a rare female dragon he should have known better. And, Zoran's wife, Princess Pia was one tough human.

"Cysgodians could shoot you from the sky. The Federation could capture you and smuggle you off the planet in the dead of night to do experiments on you," Grier listed, mostly to be annoying. "Var marsh farmer could try to mate you and set you up as queen of the stills. The Var prince—"

"Stop agreeing with my father." Grace's eyes flashed gold with warning.

Rare dragon birth, a dragon grandmother, a mother who could kickass with the best of them, four younger brothers, countless male cousins, and a commander father? Yeah, it stood to reason Grace would be a little wild.

"He loves you," Grier said. "His actions all come down to that."

Perhaps Zoran's reactions were something Grier would only understand when he too was a father. And, perhaps still, maybe his uncle's protectiveness had something to do with how his daughter was always rebelling.

"He also doesn't like it when we call Shelter City the forbidden valley." Grace gave a small laugh, clearly wanting to change the subject. "Though, he wouldn't want me saying the village of discontent either."

Grier patted her shoulder. "So, you rebel and fly up

here where he can't reach you? Careful, or he'll have you chained to the ground again."

Grace smiled, not worried. She'd been escaping her father's numerous guards since they were children. "He left my idiot brothers to keep me company. Slipping away from the palace was not difficult."

Grier laughed as he realized what was going on. "The Var princes are coming by the palace today, aren't they?"

"I don't want to talk about it," Grace grumbled.

Grier arched a brow and teased, "I would think you'd be excited to spend time with your future—"

"I *will* throw you off this tower," she warned. "Prince Korbin is not my future anything."

"Careful, little one, that is war talk." Grier wasn't concerned. Grace had been privately ranting about her betrothal to the future cat-shifting king since she could talk. Though, she said nothing publicly. Pia had wanted nothing to do with that part of the shifter peace treaty, and he once overheard his aunt telling Grace that time would dissolve that nonsense. It had not.

"Careful, *bloated* one," she mocked his nickname for her, "or I'll tell Queen Rigan next time I see her that you're planning on hiding from the mating festival again this year. You know the people would feel better if the future king settled and began the next generation. Such security in the future would go a long way toward keeping the peace our parents fought so hard to secure. There are factions on both sides keen on restarting the old wars to decide once and for all who is the superior shifter race—cats or dragons."

Grier took a deep breath. She was not wrong. Add to that the political unrest surrounding the intruders below, and it wouldn't take much to incite some battle over this or that.

"I don't know why you resist," Grace teased. "You would have such cute little dragon babies."

Grier picked at the crystal sewn into the thick leather bracelet on his arm. When he met his mate, the stone was supposed to glow and let him know that fate had arrived. It kept the guesswork out of marrying, and for that he was grateful. Who had time to test out relationships? Frankly, the alien method of dating multiple people sounded tiring.

"I am not like my parents," Grier said when she continued to look at him expectantly. "I do not wish to marry. It is too much of a distraction, and I need my mind focused elsewhere."

It wasn't the complete truth. He didn't go to the mating ceremonies because he didn't want the gods to bless him yet. Of course, he wanted to marry. Who didn't want to find the other half of their soul? But if a battle were to come, in any of its many threatening forms, a wife would be a weakness he couldn't afford. There were stories of how some of his aunts had been kidnapped by the previous Var king to be used as leverage, but that was decades ago.

"On that we can agree," Grace said. She did not wear her crystal. They never spoke of it, but he assumed it was because her fate had been sealed since she was born, and to know anything else would have been too much for her heart to bear. "We are definitely not our parents."

"Besides, if anything happens to me, I have plenty of cousins who can take the throne." He nudged her arm.

"Don't trust your brothers to do the job?"

Grier laughed. "Do you want Creed ruling this planet?"

"Fair point," Grace said of Grier's youngest brother. "Though Altair might—"

"Order all dragons from the sky to live like the old ways?" he inserted.

"Right, never mind." Grace held up her hands. "It's settled. You have to marry and have many children."

"Or you could take the job. What do you say? Queen Grace and King Korbin could unite the shifter people once and for all. You have Grandmother Mede's fierce dragon heart. You will be the first to rule both dragons and cat-shifters."

"Not on your life." She closed her eyes and lifted her face toward the two yellow suns. The blue sun wasn't high in the sky at the moment. She gave a wistful sigh. "Do you remember our parents' faces when they realized all their dragon babies could fly and spout flames? I think our grandmother was the only excited one."

Before their generation, only the rare female dragons flew and breathed flames, and only under extreme duress.

"That's because Queen Mede was the only dragon who had ever flown or breathed fire in Qurilixen's history before we came along." Grier smiled as he remembered their shared past. It had been what felt like a hundred years ago, but the memory was a fond one. "Rune panicked and became stuck in that tree, and you tried to help him but ended up setting the tree on fire, which lit up the barracks and took out the palace guards' housing. Half of them bunked in the palace dining hall and the other half slept on the practice field."

Grace laughed. "Then they caught us trying to set dried solarflowers on fire."

"You and Kane were trying to set fire to them," he corrected. "The rest of us were wrongfully blamed."

"Don't complain. Grandfather pretended to punish us, but really let us camp out in the royal offices all night as he told us scary stories about the portal travels our ancestors took to leave the evil persecutors." Grace closed her eyes and smiled. "He stole those biscuit things from our grandmother, and a tray of chocolate. We ate so much we had upset stomachs for two days."

"Great-grandmother's sugar biscuit recipe that she brought with her from the Florencian moons. I haven't had those for years." The wind whipped through Grier's hair, tousling it around his head.

"I miss them," Grace admitted. King Llyr and Queen Mede were not only missed by their grandchildren, but by their people. "No matter what happened, they always defended us. Grandmother was the only one who could understand what is inside me."

Silence came over them, and he followed her gaze upward to the sky. The wide open space called to something deep inside him. It stirred his blood with excitement and tempted him with the freedom it offered.

"Do you remember when Jaxx convinced us we could fly into space if we went high enough?" he asked.

Grace again laughed. "We thought we were so tough. Maxen passed out and free fell to the ground. It was a miracle Lantos caught him. Then Aunt Nadja grounded us all to the castle while she tried to figure out how our shifting abilities had mutated so differently from our parents'. I think they wanted to temper them back to keep us safe."

"You can't hold back evolution," Grier said. "We are what nature and the blue sun intended us to be."

"What do you think the radiation will do to their genetics?" Grace nodded down to the city.

The blue sun gave the shifters strength and a long life; it also had made the odds of having a female baby extremely rare. It had taken generations before the dragon gene had mutated into what they were now.

"What do you think their grandchildren will become?" she continued to muse.

"Space explorers?" Grier hoped. "Then they could fly off this planet for good and finally be free of the Federation Military."

"Perhaps." Grace laughed. Then, gesturing toward the rectangular buildings, she said, "What do you think they do all day in there? I want to freeze time and walk around those buildings to see all their horrible secrets."

"Nothing useful." Unable to stop himself, he grinned at her and again patted her shoulder. "Kind of like you."

He slid his hand from her shoulder down to the small of her back and launched her from the tower with one push. She screamed in surprise, flailing her arms as her body sailed over the edge of the roof before dropping. The sound of her voice became smaller as she fell down the side of the cliff.

Grier settled into his original spot, overlooking the

city. It was almost a shame to lose the shirt. He liked the fit of that one.

A whoosh of air sounded from below and then another, the rhythm steadily growing louder before his cousin's dragon form appeared. She was a slender creature in shifted form, smaller than her male counterparts, but what she lacked in brute strength she made up for in gracefulness. Her wings flapped slowly, holding her body suspended in air.

Grace roared fire into the sky in a show of mock anger before turning her mouth toward him. He braced himself for the flames, ready to shift if he had to protect his fragile human skin. She inhaled a deep breath, but instead of flames, a playful ring of smoke came from her mouth to drift around him. Part of the circle broke apart as it hit the tower.

She propelled herself backward, circling in the air before diving away from him. He could tell by the way she flew that she had only come here to waste the hours until the Var princes returned home. The royal family couldn't expect her to entertain if she was nowhere to be found.

Shouts sounded from below. Grier narrowed his gaze to focus his vision as his eyes shifted to make out the details. A mob of people flowed through the central street of the city, clashing with a second mob. The people converged like two swollen streams, spilling over into the side streets.

He sighed heavily. The fighting was not unusual.

Grier resisted the urge to swoop down and drag them apart with his talons. Instead, he went to the side of the roof, grabbed a knob that had been placed at the edge, and then dropped over the side. He swung around into an opening at the top of the tower and landed on the stone floor. There, he pulled off his boots and pants. Once naked, he went to the window and dove from the tower. His body fell for a few seconds before he let the shift have him. The transformation was painful, but it was an old pain that he had long ago learned to disregard.

Grier's bones cracked as his body extended, and his skin hardened with protective brown armor. Wings ripped out of his back, lifting him before he hit the ground. The transformation finished as he was suspended in the air. A long tail grew from the bottom of his spine only to have a spade sharpen the end. Deadly talons replaced his nails. His beard disappeared, and his jaw popped, making room for sharp teeth.

The wind caressed the full length of his form. For a moment, the feeling of freedom rushed through him, the animal instinct desperate to take over his reason. The beast was as much a part of him as the man. He pushed the feeling down, concentrating on what needed to be done.

Grier dove toward the fight in the street, roaring before sending a burst of flames into the sky. He was careful not to hit any of the structures, but it was enough to get the people's attention. He swooped over the epicenter of the hostility. Screams pierced the air as people ran away from him to take cover.

Grier roared once in warning before lifting himself higher and flying away. Then, because the freedom of flight felt so damned good, he circled the entire city a few times before heading back to the tower. He wanted to keep soaring but forced himself to land on the roof.

His body contracted as he shifted halfway back to his human form to stand as a dragon-man. It was in this half shift that he looked like his father's dragon. The tail disappeared as did the talons on his feet. The talons on his fingers shortened, still sharp and deadly but more like fingernails. In this form, the dragon impulses were easier to control. He used his dragon vision to look down at the valley below. The fighting had dispersed, and the streets cleared of both mobs. The fray was over.

The thick armor of Grier's skin protected his naked body as he slid down the side of the roof. He again grabbed the knob and swung down into the tower window. His clothes were piled on the floor. Now safely inside, the armored flesh softened into human skin, and he again stood as a man.

The tight pants felt a little constrictive after a shift. His sensitive skin tingled. Grier leaned against the partition wall as he tugged on his boots before rounding the corner to the other side. The wall acted like a windshield for the landing room.

Stacks of plain linen shirts and pants had little by way of style but were cheap to make. They served as replacement clothes for the flyers, and he took a shirt from the top of the pile. Their full dragon bodies expanded beyond the confines of clothing. It was a little hard to fit a giant pair of wings into a tunic shirt, and they'd kept ending up naked in inopportune situations.

His aunt Olena had been the one to suggest the caches around the kingdom. Out of all the elders, she alone never tried to curb their wild ways. It wasn't a secret in their family that she'd been somewhat of a space pirate in her youth. She used to hide treasures in the forest for them to hunt down.

Grace had set his thoughts toward the past when he needed to think about the present. The tension in Shelter City had already spilled over into the rest of the planet. The little skirmish below was bad, but it was hardly the worst. Some of the residents were trying to migrate, especially those who'd been born since their arrival.

The Federation didn't like that. In fact, they had forbidden Cysgodians from leaving the city limits.

The Cysgodians' desire to be part of the Qurilixian culture wasn't an issue for the shifters. Dragons would always do the honorable thing and these people needed a place to live.

He gripped the shirt in his hands as he took the winding path down the stairs. There was little light to see by, but his shifted eyes didn't need help to navigate the way down. Even though the fight was broken up, he should go to the city and find out what had started it.

A soft glow caught his attention, and he turned around to see who followed him. No one was there. He looked down the steps—again, nothing unusual. It was then he realized what caused the glow.

The crystal on his wrist had begun to pulsate with a soft light.

Grier held very still, unable to believe what was happening. He took another step down, then stopped, unsure what he should do. How could his mating crystal be glowing if he was alone in the tower?

He was alone, wasn't he?

Did he really want to find the answer to that question?

"Show yourself," he ordered.

Silence.

His crystal was only meant to glow if he was close to his mate. It was the belief of his people. When they were born, their fathers dove to the bottom of Crystal Lake and chose a crystal. That stone stayed with them until they married. No one was one hundred percent sure how it worked, but they knew that it did. There was no questioning the will of the gods.

"By order of the prince, show yourself," he commanded.

His heartbeat quickened. Had the gods heard him tell his cousin he had no wish to marry? Had they taken offense to his rejection of their gifts and this was their answer to his blasphemy?

Grier ran down the stairs. He couldn't be alone with a glowing crystal. It would mean he was cursed. There was no other explanation.

"Who is there?" Desperation made the dragon's gruff nature enter his voice.

He rushed out the tower, hearing the weight of the wood door slam shut behind him. The rocky landscape was empty as Grier ran around the base of the tower to see if a woman hid from him. His feet slipped as he came close to the edge of the cliff. Pebbles fell down the side, clanking to punctuate how alone he was.

"Please, someone be there," he whispered into the wind. "Where are you? Show yourself."

The glow of his crystal faded. He lifted his arm, pointing the bracelet in every direction to see if the crystal would reactivate. It was over.

In those brief seconds, everything changed.

Grier forgot about the village squabble. How could he think of such things now? He'd received an answer to his offhanded comment to Grace. He would be forever alone.

The gods had cursed him for his arrogance.

2

"By order of the prince, show yourself!"

Salena had run from the tower the moment she heard someone rummaging around above her. She had no clue who was coming or what they would do to her if they caught her trespassing. In fact, she knew little about this planet beyond the desire she had to be off it.

The red and gray stones could have been on any thousands of planets. The three suns—two yellow and one blue—were a little more unique, but her knowledge of planetary geology was nonexistent so that information was of no help. Then there was the city—part overcrowded market, part Federation base, part political house overlooking it all. None of those elements looked as if they belonged together.

Whatever alien cohabitation experiment was

happening in the city below, she wanted no part of it. If they thought she wouldn't fight because she was merely a human, well, they might actually be right about that. But she would run, and she would hide.

And she might starve.

Her stomach had moved from growling noises to sharp, shooting pains. There was nothing she could do about it now. The headache had become her constant companion. She'd waited for night, hoping to sneak down into the village to forage, but either night didn't come, or this was the longest day ever. Both could have been a reality. She had lost all concept of time.

"By order of the prince, show yourself!" The hard voice inspired fear.

Salena went to the cliff's edge and lowered herself onto a narrow walkway. She'd seen the cave from the ground and had explored it as a place to hide from the authorities below. It had not been ideal, and she'd opted for sleeping in the tower instead.

"Who is there?" the angry voice demanded from inside the tower, louder than before. The prince was close.

Her foot slipped, and her weakened limbs shook. She held on to the stone and climbing took more effort than it usually would have. She felt around with her foot, finding the notch she needed. She lowered her body into the dark inlet. The space wasn't overly large, but it would hide her from the man shouting above. It wasn't hard to connect that the officials probably used the tower over-looking the city to keep an eye on things. If the man caught her, he'd bring her back.

That could never happen.

Salena took a deep breath, not bothering to stop the hot tears that streamed down her face. Starving in a cave would be better than what her captors had planned for her. And at the moment, she didn't have much of a choice.

"Just a little sleep," she whispered, closing her eyes. "I'll be able to climb out once I have some rest."

It was a lie, and she knew it. She would not be leaving this cave. There was nowhere to go, and no food when she arrived there. All she could hope for now was not to wake up.

"Let it be over," she mumbled. "I give up."

3

"What is this I hear from your mother that you plan to skip the ceremonies?" King Ualan strode into his royal office and began looking over the spines of antique books. Some were electronic, some on parchment, and many so old they had been sealed to preserve them from decay. None of them seemed to be what the king wanted. He tapped his finger along the shelf as if noting and dismissing each one.

Things had significantly changed since his father had taken the throne. Grier had watched the man transform over the last fifty years as the stress of being king weighed heavier and heavier. It showed around his tired eyes and in his smile, and there was a tension in his stance that only faded when he was with the queen. In all their years of marriage, his parents' love for each other had never wavered. Yes, there had been fights, but never wars between them.

The king glanced at him when he didn't respond.

"Grace spoke to her?" Grier averted his gaze. An electronic clipboard rested on the wood surface of the desk. The antiquated technology scrolled through a list of data. He stared at the upside-down Old Star language words, reading them without paying attention.

His father chuckled. "I do not know what you did to your cousin, but she informed your mother of your aversion to your duties."

"Who says I did anything?"

The king arched a brow at his son.

"Fine. I threw her off the Shelter City watchtower." Grier shrugged. "But only after she tried to roast me."

The king laughed. "I consider myself lucky that we did not have the fire breath when I was young. It would have been too tempting to spit fireballs at your uncle Zoran when he made us trudge waist deep through the shadowed marshes while we trained with the other soldiers."

There was no false modesty in the king's tone. He might be a different kind of shifter from his sons, but he was still a ferocious dragon—one Grier would not want to face in battle.

"That was discussed on many occasions." Grier gave

a small smile. There was something about this time of year that brought everyone's thoughts around to the past. Perhaps the one night of darkness caused the elders to look back at their own weddings. For the unmarried, it represented a momentous change. If they were lucky, the end of singlehood. Dragon-shifters wanted to be mated, but that didn't mean they ignored the change such an event would bring to their lives.

Grier glanced to the crystal on his wrist. A sick feeling came over him. He might never get a chance to find out. Dropping his arm over the side of the chair, he hid the crystal from view. "Grace is one to talk about duty. I hear Prince Korbin was at the palace this morning."

"Sometimes I look at you children and marvel at how much you have grown, and then you tattle on each other." King Ualan bent over and pulled a bound stack of papers off the shelf and dropped them on his desk.

Curious, Grier leaned forward to look at what his father chose. "Lithor Republic negotiations documents? Those look to be a thousand years old. Don't you have an electronic version?"

"Careful, son, they are only a little older than you. And the electronic version was lost when we had that unfortunate mishap with the new palace databases. A new Lithorian dignitary replaced Barun Monke, and he insists we return to the old ways." The king gestured at the stack on his desk. "These are the old ways."

Grier frowned. "Why are you worried about chocolate supplies with everything else going on? Who cares if they sell to us? Chocolate is a luxury we don't need."

"Everything else going on? Do you mean that flying stunt you pulled in the city today?" The king lifted the stack of papers and held it toward his son. "And wait until you are married, and your wife is with child. I'll wager you'll care about chocolate supplies then. Your mother could take any dragon on during the months she was pregnant with you and your brothers."

The queen was human and had come to the planet with a shipment of brides. To hear his father tell it, she didn't come for marriage, but one look at him and she couldn't resist his many charms.

Grier *did not* want to hear his father tell it. No matter how old he was, there were some things a son did not want to hear about his parents' love life.

"I remember the first night I saw your mother," the king said.

Gods' bones, here it comes. Grier tried not to flinch.

King Ualan closed his eyes and smiled softly. "In many ways, you are lucky. Back when I married, the ceremonial gown was," he gave a small moan, "something of great beauty meant to tempt the sexual desires of the grooms. It made the tests of the wedding night as difficult as possible to pass, and your mother was—"

"Oh, please stop." Grier lifted his hands. "Don't need to know about your wedding night with my mother. I'm still scarred from the last time you told me about the old ceremonies."

The king laughed.

Grier again looked at his wrist. It had not glowed again since his time in the tower. "What if I don't marry?"

"Don't say such ridiculous things," his father dismissed. "Of course you will marry. Never make such a statement again. You are the future king, and you will set an example for the Draig." He shook the stack of papers. "Take this to Kane."

The quick dismissal kept Grier from saying more. Even though he joked about their ability to lead, either of his two brothers could provide an heir to the throne. He could take comfort in that.

Grier nodded, took the papers, and stood to do as he was told. As he turned to leave, his father added, "And by royal decree, you will be at the mating ceremony this year, even if I have to make you stand between your mother's and my thrones during the event."

The king could never know how the order caused an ache inside his son's chest. Grier thought of the tower, of going back, of moving every stone in case he'd missed something.

"Oh, and Grier, no more stunts like today. Several complaints were filed that a dragon attacked and nearly killed three people."

"What makes you think I did it?" he asked.

"I think I know what my son looks like. I saw you from the window during my meeting with General Sten. Things are in a delicate state with Shelter City. They wish to police their own streets and we must let them. They must stand on their own."

Grier wanted to remind the king that it had been roughly thirty years, and that Shelter City might never stand on its own.

"The Cysgodians or the Federation wish to police the city?" Grier shouldn't have spoken, and he wished to take the words back the second they were out. He kept his eyes on the door, not turning around to face the king.

"I know you have your reservations about the alien visitors, and some factions are of concern, but the Cysgodians are not bad by default." The stern tone of his father's voice was not surprising. "We cannot keep interrupting in their affairs, or the Federation will use it as an excuse to set up an official base here."

Grier finally turned to look at his father. "The Federation should never have been allowed to remain on this world."

"This is a delicate political matter that will take time to resolve. You have not had the dealings your elders have had with the Federation. They have been trying to force our hand into an alliance since before I married your mother. When we allowed the Federation Military to bring the people under their protection here to recover, they believed that gave them grounds to remain with their charges and to build a small base. The disease might have been stopped, but the Cysgodians' shortened lifespan creates an argument for their further recovery. As long as they stay within the confines of that base, we have no cause to force them to leave. To do so would anger the Federation. Not agreeing to be a part of the Federation Alliance is one thing. Declaring war on the Federation is quite another." His father came from around the desk and put a hand on his shoulder. "We cannot win that war. So, no more interfering."

Grier hated it, but he knew it was true. The Federation was too big and the politics too complicated. He nodded. "I understand. But for the record, I didn't almost kill anyone. If I wanted someone dead, there would be no almost."

"Go." The king gestured toward the door. "I have much to do."

"As you so command, my king," Grier said with a formal bow. The answer caused his father to suppress a small smile but not before Grier saw it.

He had lived in the mountain palace his entire life and the old halls had seen few changes during that time. The home was carved into the red stone of a mountain, the fortress hidden in the natural façade of the rock. It was the stone that determined the color of the walls and floor. Markers had been carved near each turn in the hall to indicate directions. Outsiders could not read the encoded maps, and the endless hallways could easily get a person lost.

Sculptures and paintings decorated the palace. The painting he currently walked past was inscribed with the title *Captured by a Dragon-Shifter,* by an artist named Princess Beth of the Var. In it, an incredibly terrifying dragon-man ran from a cave carrying a woman over his shoulder. It depicted the shifter myth from long ago, during a time his ancestors had reopened portals to travel across space to find brides.

Every alien race he'd ever met had a creation story, and this was part of theirs. It was said his shifter ances-tors escaped a planet of persecution and fear by coming through the portals to Qurilixen. They sealed the way to keep from being followed but out of desperation, had to reopen the portals. Something happened and, after a few trips, they had to be sealed off again.

Though the stories might have been based in fact, Grier assumed they were more to teach children a lesson —the stars might seem brighter around another planet, but there was no comparing it to the safety of home. Or maybe it was, respect the gods when it comes to marriage. Going out and forcing it will only lead to trouble.

Grier touched his crystal. Maybe if he apologized to the gods, they'd lift the curse.

Then again, maybe it had glowed the one time it was meant to, and it was too late.

Duty. That is what he had left. That is what he had foolishly told Grace he wanted to focus on.

Draig believed strongly in family, and they liked to stay close to home. The mountain palace had been expanded to accommodate Grier, his brothers, and a few of the cousins.

Like Grier, his cousin Kane still lived at the palace. Prince Olek had been training his son to be the next royal ambassador. It was uncertain if that was what his cousin wanted, but like Grier, he knew his duty to his people. Looking at the bound papers, he doubted anyone would want to read the tedious document.

Kane was stepping out of his home when Grier

approached. His cousin arched a brow in question before seeing the papers. He sighed and nodded while holding out his hand. "I was coming to retrieve those. Apparently, I have until the morning of the mating ceremony to memorize the etiquettes or the bridal tents will have no chocolate. I don't suppose you came to help me, did—"

Grier's gaze turned toward the floor. The idea of the wedding ceremony sent a wave of anguish through him.

"What is it?" Kane pushed the door and held it open to urge his cousin inside. "Is this about your attacking the people of Shelter City?"

"I didn't attack them," he dismissed.

Kane smirked. "I know. I saw the mobs. They were lucky to have you break up the fight."

"At least someone thinks that. The king was not pleased," Grier answered.

"Are you joking? Your father was trying not to laugh the entire time you were swooping them." Kane carried the papers to a table and dropped them on the surface with a heavy *thud*. "General Sten was less than amused, but then I think there is something wrong with that man. He's like a black hole that sucks the pleasure out of any situation."

"I think the gods have cursed me," Grier stated, unable to keep the words to himself.

Kane's expression instantly changed. He motioned to a chair at the table.

Grier began to pace, not taking the offered seat. "My crystal glowed."

Kane laughed. "You worried me for a moment. That is not a curse. Unless you're going to tell me that you're destined to marry a Corge or a Syog. Then I might feel sorry for you."

"No one."

"No one what?" Kane slid the papers before him and pulled at the tie binding them together.

Grier sat and placed his hands on the table. "No one was there when my crystal glowed. I was alone. That can only mean one thing."

"Maybe you didn't see her. Maybe she was on the other side of a wall, or on the floor below you."

"I was in the cliffside watchtower. There is no other side of the wall or bottom floor. There was an empty tower and the surrounding rocks."

"Someone down in Shelter City perhaps?" Kane seemed skeptical, and for a good reason.

"That distance is too great for the crystal to be affected, and it stopped when I ran to the cliff's edge." Grier leaned his forehead down onto his folded hands and stared at the grain of the tabletop.

"This makes no sense. Why would the gods curse

you?" The sound of paper flipping disrupted Kane's words.

"I said I didn't want a bride," Grier mumbled.

"Are you speaking to me or the table?" Kane asked.

Grier lifted his head just high enough to look up and said, "I told Grace I didn't want to be married. I think the gods heard and..." He lifted his braceleted wrist. "Wish granted."

Kane tried to pretend he was unconcerned, but there was no hiding the expression in his eyes as he turned his gaze downward to study the papers. "Maybe it was not a curse, but a warning?"

"Have you ever heard of any such thing happening?" Grier asked.

Kane hesitated before shaking his head in denial. "No. To my knowledge, the path from the gods is usually fairly straightforward. You see your mate, your crystal glows. You don't see your mate, no glow." Kane quickly added, "But that doesn't mean it couldn't be a warning this time."

The assurance gave little comfort.

"Do you know what I think you should do?" Kane asked.

"What?"

"Take your mind off your worries by helping me

learn these rules." Kane placed his hand on the stack of papers.

Grier gave a small laugh. "You wish me to do penance?"

"No, I think you should show the gods you are committed to making a wife happy by giving her chocolate." Kane grinned.

"So penance." Grier scrunched up his nose at the idea but remained where he was. "Give me the top half. What is it we are looking for exactly?"

Kane split the stack in two and handed part of it over. "Supposedly, we'll know it when we see it."

4

SALENA WOULD HAVE CRIED IF SHE HAD ANYTHING left inside her. As it was, the severe exhaustion only released her into consciousness for brief glimpses.

Glimpse one: the window of the cave showing the green tint of the alien sky. The view was more isolating than safe.

Glimpse two: a fierce beast blocking that sky with sharp teeth and an angry growl. She tried to hide, but only managed to fall over onto the stone floor.

Glimpse three: being pulled from the cave by her ankle, lifeless arms dragging over the rocks before falling toward the ground. She waited for a crash that never came.

Glimpse four: dangling in the air like fresh-caught prey being taken for dinner. Blast it all, anyway. At this point, one death was as good as any other, she supposed, as long as she died free.

She was unable to fight throughout the entire ordeal. Maybe it wasn't even real. The dangling sensation could have been her dizzy head. The growl could have been her empty stomach. Perhaps her nightmares were trying to make sense of her reality. Then again, maybe her nightmares were coming to life.

Her body swayed, surrounded by the cold swoosh of wind. It flooded her ears and made everything else sound far away. She felt herself falling and refused to open her eyes for the moment of impact.

All of a sudden, the hold on her ankle jerked, and she was lowered onto a soft bed.

She finally opened her eyes to see the fierce beast standing over her. He panted hard, blasts of heat coming from each breath as it hit her face. The dark brown of his armored flesh appeared almost black. She gave him a small smile and whispered, "Greetings, Death, took you long enough to find me," before falling into the blackness of eternity.

Eternity might have been an overstatement.

Glimpse...what number was she on? Well, whatever glimpse of consciousness this was, it wasn't a cave, or a beast, or a prison hold. There were softness and warmth, both of which led to a feeling of hope, and as false as that feeling might turn out to be, Salena kept her mind focused on it for as long as she could.

In the cocoon of that moment, she heard whispers from her past, the sound of her mother's voice, a mere tone of indecipherable words. They were muffled by the pacing thud of footsteps as her father moved back and forth, back and forth, over the slats forming the ceiling above her room. If she could be locked in any moment of time, that was the one she would choose—when the darkness of night hid the monsters of the world, when the sound of her sisters' breaths lifted and fell in tiny sighs, when her parents were close, and the smell of clay permeated from the walls of the room dug into the ground.

If she didn't open her eyes, she would stay forever small, safe from the dangers of the universe.

Slowly, hope was replaced by reality. There was no traveling back to that moment. The world was no longer safe. Her father's boots and her mother's words could no longer protect her. The universe did not care about the hopes of three sisters from a poor family, digging clay from the ground with their bare hands. The universe was vast and cold, and those within it only cared about what they could take.

"We have to wake up now," Fiora's soft voice insisted.

The pain inside Salena caused the memory to slip, and she had no choice but to let it. She opened her eyes, knowing Fiora was gone. Her sister would not be there to greet her. Never again.

Dying hope turned to fear, and it looked like she might be right back where she'd started—in the grips of the Federation.

The room might be comfortable and well appointed, but it was more dangerous than the cliffside cave. It didn't appear to belong to the makeshift homes she'd seen in the valley, nor was it military issue. That could only mean she was in the stronghold. They would not risk letting her escape again.

Salena scurried out of bed. She felt better than she should have for not having eaten. She checked her arms, seeing two small red dots where someone had injected her from a handheld medic device.

A blue dressing gown had replaced the tunic shirt she'd stolen from the tower. The shapeless folds hung from her shoulders, leaving her arms exposed. The idea of someone taking her clothing while she slept caused her to hug her arms to her waist in a protective gesture. Were they watching her even now?

Windowless walls surrounded her, stained to an uneven brown. A light tube formed a large circle in the ceiling and cast a soft glow.

Salena moved toward a wall and pressed the tips of her fingers to it. Segments of the paneling moved, parting to reveal hidden compartments. Seeing a figure, she jolted in surprise and stepped back. It was only her reflection staring at her from a mirrored surface. It had been a long while since she'd seen herself. Her hair was a wavy brunette mess around her head. Red surrounded the brown irises of her eyes. A scrape ran from below her ear, down her neck, into the front of the gown. It was odd that the Federation would have used a handheld medic to treat her instead of a fancy medical booth—not that she'd ever had access to a medical booth.

Her mother had a word for creatures that looked like she did now.

One of the compartments had a variety of dispensers and glasses, and another one held a folded stack of clothes. She disturbed none of it.

Salena went toward the door, not expecting it to open. They rarely did for her. Before she made contact, the door swung inward. She stepped out of the way before it smacked her.

"I thought I heard you up," a woman said as she appeared in the doorway. Flaming red hair was piled high on her head. Her tight pants and loose green tunic shirt were not what Salena would have expected of a prison guard. "I admit I was concerned after my son brought you here from one of the cliffside caves."

Salena recalled the feeling of falling. Had this woman's son pulled her from her hiding spot? Before she could stop herself, she asked, "Why?"

The sound of her voice was more of a croak than a word.

"Because you were dying," the woman answered. "How did you get in there? Please tell me that's not some new form of Federation punishment."

Salena coughed to clear her throat, hoping it would make her voice stronger. "Who are you?"

"I'm a princess," the woman said with a small laugh. "But you can call me Olena."

A princess? This planet had royalty?

"I can tell you don't believe me by your expression," the woman said. "That's all right. I never dress the part."

"No, I know you speak the truth." Salena leaned to look behind the princess. This didn't make sense. She was in a home, not a Federation hold. "How did your son find me?"

"Jaxx was dropping supplies off to some of our

contacts in Shelter City and happened to see you as he flew by." Olena frowned.

Salena could easily guess the woman's thoughts. Right now, the princess was wondering why she'd admitted as much to a stranger, but the woman wouldn't be able to help herself. It was the same with everyone— first confusion, then fear, then either fascination or scheming, and finally avoidance. But regardless, everyone told Salena the truth whether they wanted to or not.

"What supplies was he dropping off?" Salena asked.

"Food." Olena pressed her finger to her temple, frowning.

Salena stepped slowly around the woman, watching to see if she'd try to stop her. Olena moved out of the way.

"You're looking much better," Olena offered. "I thought you would need sleep more than anything else, but now that you're awake I can see to that scrape on your face and you're welcome to take a water bath or use a decontaminator, whichever method you prefer."

"Thank you," Salena mumbled.

The home was not what Salena would have expected of a palace. Black accented the dark wood. Curtains were pulled open over a dome in the ceiling to let in light. Giant logs had been sawed in half to form the walls. She imagined the trees they came from would have been gigantic. A contained fire burned in a stone fireplace. Carved figures decorated the mantel and rugs draped over couches. There was none of the decadence one would expect from royalty.

"Why do you need to bring the people at Shelter City food?" Salena asked, keeping her body angled so she could see the woman. Though there were no guards in the vicinity, but that did not mean she wasn't being watched.

"The Federation refuses to let the citizens have food simulators to materialize food because their scientists believe exposure to the minuscule radiation from the units will make them sick. The whole situation is a diplomatic mess, but people need to eat. Since the leaders of Shelter City won't take care of their people, we smuggle in what we can." Olena's expression did not lighten. "I need you to stop asking me question—"

"What do you want with me?"

"I want to feed you and get rid of that ugly cut on your face," Olena answered, before pressing her fingers over her mouth.

"Feed me?" Very rarely did things surprise her. That did. "Then what?"

"If you don't want to find a partner at the mating ceremony tonight, then we'll deliver you back to Shelter

City before they take a census and realize you're missing. We can't be caught interfering with the city." Olena held up her hands. "Please, stop whatever you're doing to me."

Salena opened her mouth to speak.

Olena plugged her ears and backed away. "No. Stop it."

Salena pressed her lips together and nodded.

Olena lowered her hands. "How are you making me tell you everything?"

Instead of answering, Salena asked, "Do you mean to hurt me?"

"No."

Salena nodded. "All right. Then I thank you for your hospitality and respectfully decline your offer to mate with anyone. Promiscuity is fine for some, but it is not in my nature."

"Promiscuity?" Olena gave a small laugh. "No, you misunderstood. The mating ceremony is for marriage, not sex."

"What kind of marriage is sexless?" Salena questioned, not sure she needed to know the answer. She might not be promiscuous, but she was no prude. And what kind of marriage was decided in one ceremony?

"Of course our marriages have sex, but it's not allowed the first night. It's a tradition dating back centuries, to ensure the choice is the woman's and no one is forced, and at dawn the women give their decisions. But I'm not sure why I'm telling you about the ceremony. I wasn't planning on bringing it up until later when we were walking by on our way to take you home in case you were interested in stopping to look for a husband. The choice would be yours, of course."

"Shelter City isn't my home. I can't go back there." Now that she knew the woman didn't intend to harm her, Salena turned her back on her and made her way through the home.

There was an Old Earth look to the place, which was strange for what she'd seen of the planet so far. Curtains hung over a large window, with smaller windows on the opposite side of the house. The house was divided into two levels, the upper where she stood, and the slightly lower level with the fireplace and common space with seating and a food preparation area. A monstrous beast's head had been carved into the wall over the food counter, where the ceiling was higher. Sharp teeth flashed in her memory causing her to stumble.

"Sit down," Olena ordered. "You're clearly too weak to walk. Let me get the medical unit and check your levels."

"No," Salena denied. "I can't stay here."

She could not risk them sending her back to the

Federation. Yet she wasn't sure how she would find a way off this planet. She couldn't stay. She didn't have the space credits needed to leave.

"I can't let you wander around like that," Olena said.

"Yes, you can. You won't hurt me," Salena answered.

"Are you always so trusting? How do you know? I could be lying to you." Olena frowned. "Even if you weren't swaying on your feet, I'm afraid you are too innocent for this place. Someone will take advantage if they haven't already. I can't let you go."

Salena gave a small laugh. No one had ever called her innocent. From a young age, she had known more than anyone should. People gave her their secrets whether she wanted them or not. Most often, she did not. Her father had warned his three girls about telling people what they could do. Their abilities received two reactions from people—fear that the sisters would share their confessions with others, or they would attempt to use the sisters' abilities for their own personal gain.

"I thank you for your concern, but I know enough of the universes to protect myself." Salena moved toward what looked to be a glass door. She felt more than heard Olena moving behind her.

Broken yellow stones formed a patio surrounded by trees. The trunks of some were as wide as a small space vessel. The constant daylight clearly affected their growth.

Salena reached to slide the glass open but hesitated. She stopped herself from leaving. People might not be able to lie to her, but she could lie to them...and to herself. She clearly couldn't protect herself, and she was terrified. She knew nothing of this planet, of where to go. It was easy enough to ask someone if they meant her harm and to receive an honest answer, but by then it was often too late and didn't stop them from attacking.

"I need a ride," she whispered, looking at Olena's reflection in the glass. It wasn't easy asking for help. Her parents had raised them to be self-sufficient. Too bad they hadn't raised them to survive off their homeworld of Noire. She cleared her throat, and said louder, "I need to find a ship that can take me off this planet. Do you know of one that will be safe?"

"There will be a ship landing tonight under the cover of the Galaxy Brides' vessel when it brings potential brides for the ceremonies. I'm required to be at the celebration, but Jaxx can take you when he goes to meet them. It's flown by my old pirate crew, and they can smuggle you off-world. I trust them because I know they'll adhere to the Pirate Code. And I shouldn't have told you I used to be a pirate, or that we're sneaking in ships, or that my son is involved. Oh, wow, you're a dangerous one, aren't you? I'm going to need to know who you are and how you came to be here before I can help you do anything." Olena lightly touched her shoulder. "Come, sit, let me feed you and we'll talk."

"I can't afford to pay for the passage." Salena focused on the woman's hand. The touch was the most contact she'd had with another person in...well, she couldn't remember how long. She became afraid to move, which would break the connection.

"No one is asking you to pay for anything." Olena let go of her and walked toward the kitchen. "Do you like blue bread? I just made a batch."

Salena again peered around the home, unsure what she should do. The offer of kindness scared her almost as much as the Federation's captivity. She'd been alone for so long.

You have to wake up now, Salena, Fiora's soft voice whispered through her memory. The words prompted her out of the growing haze around her thoughts. It was then she realized she'd been about to walk outside barefoot, and in a dressing gown. She was not making good decisions.

"You're not used to talking about yourself," Olena observed. "Well, I'm afraid I'm going to have to insist. There is too much at stake. If I'm going to go up against the Federation, I need to know who I'm helping and why."

"You can't send me back to the Federation." Salena felt lightheaded and swayed. She reached out for support but only found air. The moment was quick, but it was enough to convince her to join Olena in the food preparation area.

A smaller window revealed more forest. It was above the wooden table with rounded seats. Whereas her room had been modernized with hi-tech compartments, the kitchen's cabinets were wooden and opened manually.

"What did they do to you?" Olena asked, as she began taking items from the cabinets and placing them on an island countertop.

"They brought me here. I don't want to be here. I need to go." Salena sat on a stool by the counter and rested her hand on the smooth surface. She pressed her hands flat as another wave of dizziness washed over her. Her arm slid, and she found her forehead pressed against the counter. Mumbling, she insisted, "I need to go."

She closed her eyes, trying to make the dizziness stop, and found she couldn't reopen them. All she needed was a few seconds of rest.

Just a few seconds...

5

"Make sure your uncles see you tonight before you leave the festival," Olena instructed her son as she slid a gold band up his arm. The intricate design only drew attention to the fact the man was all muscle. The sky had darkened, and it looked like night would finally fall. The princess looked more like royalty in the full-length black gown with a shimmering overlay. She had undoubtedly dressed for the occasion.

"I know. I will." Jaxx was nothing like the hallucination she remembered. For starters, he was a man not a beast. Actually, more correctly, he was a half-naked man in a black loincloth...and only a loincloth. He didn't even have shoes. Black markings wound up his arm and covered his shoulder. A glow from inside the house shone on his oiled skin.

"Do you have your mask?" Olena asked, reaching to straighten his hair. The man stood a foot above her and was way past the age for a mother to fuss over.

Jaxx held up his hand to show a leather mask. "It's right here."

"And did you get your crystal back from your cousin?" Olena dropped her hand when her son shifted his stance and refused to answer. "Gods' bones, Jaxx. If you won't do it, I'll make Grace hand it over. I still don't understand how she came into possession of it. At least pretend to care about finding a mate."

Jaxx's green eyes turned to Salena, acknowledging her presence for the first time. "Do you want to marry me?"

Salena nearly choked in surprise, and managed, "N-*no*."

The questioned caused her to stiffen and avert her gaze. She'd tried to have relationships in the past, but they always ended quickly and poorly. A woman did not want to hear about how the man she was with fantasized about other women, or when he wished she'd shut up, or leave, or she looked terrible, or any number of things a man thought and was not meant to say out loud. One had confessed he was going to rob her in the middle of the night. The idea of signing on for a lifetime of that kind of heartache was unimaginable.

To his mother, Jaxx said, "Now you can tell the family I tried. This was not my year to be blessed by the gods."

"Leave Salena alone." Olena laughed and swatted his arm. "You know that you're making your elders crazy, all of you children. None of them could wait to find a bride. Your father—"

"Was so lucky to have met you during his very first ceremony," Jaxx droned with a roll of his eyes. "But they forget, they are the ones who taught us you can't rush the will of the gods. If I am meant to marry, I will know, crystal or not. Until then, there is nothing I can do about it. So, I might as well make myself useful by smuggling women off the planet while Galaxy Brides is bringing them on."

"Women? There will be others?" Salena asked, finding some comfort in thinking she wasn't going to go alone on a pirate ship.

"Woman," Jaxx corrected. The teasing light on his face faded, and he gave her a kind smile. "I'm glad to see you have recovered. I wasn't sure you would after you greeted me as Death."

"Thank you for saving me," Salena managed. She found the size of him intimidating, though she supposed if he had meant to harm her, he would have done it already. "I'm sorry I cannot repay you for the trouble."

"Why would you pay me for saving you?" Jaxx winked at her.

"I need to go. Your father is waiting for me and has probably already started drinking with your uncles. If I don't stop him, he will spend the entire night serenading me. It used to be romantic until I made the mistake of teaching him songs about plundering and sailing the high skies." Olena searched a pocket hidden in her skirt before reaching to take Salena's hand in hers. She felt the woman press something soft against her fingers. "Safe travels. Be careful with your gift on the ship. I trust them with my life, but they are space pirates, after all."

Salena knew the princess wasn't talking about the gift the woman had left in her hand.

"See you there." Olena lifted on her toes to kiss her son's cheek before disappearing into the trees.

"It's not too late if you want to throw on a bridal gown and try your hand at the mating festivities," Jaxx offered. He nodded at the simple blue gown Olena had given her to wear. "You never know, you might make someone's crystal glow and can avoid the crusty pirate ship altogether."

"I really hope crystal glow is not a euphemism," Salena said. She'd pulled her hair away from her face, knotting it in a bun at the back of her head in preparation for travel.

Olena had given her the use of a decontaminator before she healed Salena's face and neck with a hand-held medic.

"Go ahead, ask me if I mean you harm." Jaxx crossed his arms over his chest and waited. The gesture only drew attention to his strong body. Salena furrowed her brow in confusion. "My mother said you're some kind of a truth-speaker."

"No." That wasn't how Salena would explain her abilities. She was more of a truth-listener.

"So you're a liar?" Jaxx teased. For the briefest moment, she thought she saw his eyes flash with an inner yellow light.

Salena chuckled. "I am quickly getting the impression you take very little seriously."

"Not true," he said. "There are plenty of responsibilities I take seriously, but to quote Lord Vladan, if I took everything seriously, life would be nothing but endless tasks and battles."

"Never heard of him," she admitted.

"No reason you should have," Jaxx answered with a resigned sigh as he gestured for her to walk with him.

"Do you mean me harm?" she asked.

"No."

Salena fell into step beside him as he led her into the forest, keeping enough distance between them so they didn't touch. The sky had darkened and the oversized leaves on the giant trees began to droop on their branches. A subtle smell emitted from them, like leaves dying in anticipation of the cold season. They cast shadows over the worn path of red dirt. Hints of yellow plants dotted places among the forest floor.

"Is it annoying that you have to watch over me tonight?" she asked, instantly wishing she hadn't.

"A little," he admitted.

She stopped. "I'm sorry. If you point me in the right direction, I can find my own way to the ship."

Jaxx furrowed his brow. "This truth power of yours is strangely fascinating, and highly unusual. Let me clarify —the only annoyance comes from the fullness of this night. There are many burdens, and now you are also a worry." He hummed softly. "That is not how I intended to clarify. I'm sorry."

"Don't apologize, I'm used to blunt honesty." Oh, what she would give to have someone lie to her, just once to have to wonder if she was being told the truth. And if not that, to have them hold something back, to keep a secret.

It's not like she could turn the ability on and off at will. It was always on. If she asked a direct question, the other person felt compelled to answer. If she didn't ask a question, any number of confessions could be forthcoming, depending on the person and the situation. Her head was full of too many of the universes' secrets. Most of them she wished she could forget.

"Protecting you is not a burden," he said.

"Only that you have many other responsibilities tonight," she finished for him.

"Yes."

"I understand." She nodded.

"Ask me about something else. This conversation became awkward." Jaxx lifted the mask he carried and rubbed his thumb along what looked to be an eyehole.

Streams of blue light came from above, and she glanced up to find one of the largest moons she'd ever seen peeking through the treetops. "What planet are we on?"

That clearly surprised him. "Qurilixen. How do you not know that?"

She didn't answer, but instead asked, "What quadrant?"

"Outer edge of the Y quadrant," he said.

"Y? So far," she whispered. She'd been on the Zibi fueling docks when they'd caught up to her.

"I know the Var did not kidnap you. They would never have let you starve, and you were by Shelter City. Am I to believe that the Federation brought you here unwillingly?"

She slowly nodded. Nothing they had said indicated she couldn't trust them.

"*Argh,*" Jaxx growled, the sound causing her to stumble away from him. His eyes began to glow and this time the change was unmistakable. Tiny hints of armor formed over the skin on his forehead. "I want to round all of those Federation creeps into that facility they constructed, scoop it from the planet's surface, and blast it into the nearest star. Then there would be no more sneaking around, trying to feed people. The situation is beyond absurd. And now they are capturing people and bringing them here? Unacceptable."

"I did nothing wrong." It wasn't a hallucination. This man shifted forms. She'd heard stories when she was little but had never seen it happen. He was half man, half monster.

He looked at her questioningly before the skin around his eyes softened. The eyes still glowed, but with less intensity. He held out his hand to her. That's when she realized she'd stepped off the path into the trees. "I told you, I won't hurt you, and that goes for my dragon form as well."

"Dragon? Is that what you call the monster?"

"I'd prefer you didn't call me a monster. I think my treatment of you has been quite the opposite."

"It has been." Salena rejoined him on the path. She

heard a shout of laughter carry over the distance and knew they were getting close to the celebration. "I'm not good with people. I tend to avoid talking to them."

"I can imagine why the Federation wants you. Someone with your talents would be valuable. And I can see why you would want to leave here. I'll take you to the ship." He nodded to the small gift she wrung in her hands. "What did my mother give you?"

Salena had forgotten about it. "Oh, um..." It was a small cloth bag. She pulled at the string, drawing it open, and dumped the contents onto her hand. Tiny stones gleamed in the moonlight. In many ways, they were better currency than space credits.

She instantly poured them from her hand back into the bag and pulled it shut. She tried to give it to him. "I can't take these."

"What do you want me to do with them?" He gestured at his only clothing, the loincloth. "I'm already carrying one set of jewels, not sure I have anywhere to put a second."

Salena tried not to laugh, and the sound came out like a snort.

Jaxx lifted the mask to his face, covering himself from his forehead to upper lip. He tied it behind his head to hold it in place. "I'll show you where you can wait for me. I have to make an appearance at the Procession of Finding and then I'll be back."

She detected an orange glow on the trees before she saw the large bonfires dotting a hillside. The smell of burning wood fragranced the air. Her view was partially blocked by a sea of pyramid tents that had been erected over an open field. Their many colors and placements had no discernable pattern but created paths like the mini-streets of a village. Small ribbons and metals had been pinned to their sides like tokens. Torchlight glowed, illuminating where the bonfires did not reach. Banners, mostly with monster—*dragon*—symbols, fluttered above the tents in the breeze.

"Salena?" Jaxx questioned.

She looked in his direction.

"Everyone is distracted by the ceremony. If you remain hidden in the trees over there," he pointed behind the tents, "no one should bother you. However, if something does happen, find the black tent and go inside. I will come for you there."

Salena nodded. He cut through the tent paths and she made her way behind them. She slowed each time she caught a glimpse of the crowd. She found Olena sitting in a throne beside a man, presumably her husband by the way he kissed her wrist. Other couples were also in the place of honor, set high above the boisterous crowd below. The royals had longer hair, very unlike the Federation leaders, and tunic-style clothing, and she saw glints from the metal crowns that rested on their heads.

The gathered men below the royals had shorter hairstyles and more variety of clothing, from tunic shirts to tight leather pants with cross-laces up the side. Loin-clothed men mingled through the crowd. There was something all dragon men had in common—they were tall and strong and carried themselves like warriors.

Salena found herself frozen in place, partly exposed as she stared at the narrow view she had of the celebration.

You have to wake up now, Salena, Fiora's soft voice whispered from somewhere far away.

Salena blinked, coming out of her trance, as she ducked into hiding. She knew the voice wasn't real, only a memory, but still it gave her some sense that she wasn't alone. It was only dumb luck that she hadn't been seen by one of the celebrators.

Salena clutched the bag of jewels, determined to repay every piece she had to borrow from it. She had no idea where she was going, or what she would do when she arrived there. All she knew was if she stayed on Qurilixen, it was only a matter of time before the Federation had her locked in an interrogation room, forcing people to give up their secrets.

6

GRIER LIFTED HIS HAND TO GREET HIS PARENTS AND forced a smile as he looked up from his place in the festival crowd. The mask and beard hid most of his expression. The king lifted a mug of what he guessed to be rum. The queen grinned, clearly happy at her son's appearance at the mating ceremony.

When he was younger he loved the festival, even before he was of age to come as a potential groom. They had been a time of drinking and laughter, of mischief and pranks. With darkness only coming one night a year, it brought with it a sense of freedom. He also had a feeling the festival started long ago as a way to gather all the dragons in one location for safety. In the old wars, the cat-shifters would have been foolish to attack a crowd of dragons during the night.

Seeing a Var citizen passing by him in the traditional cat-shifter garb of cross-laced pants and shirts for easy removal during a shift, Grier laughed. Things had changed a lot from those days. Now even some cat-shifters had found wives during the festival—after the dragons had a chance to make sure the women didn't light their crystals first, of course.

"Another prince is here," Ascelin, one of the palace guards, shouted over the crowd. The man's face mask was pulled up to rest on his head and his eyes had the glazed look of too much drink. He gave a half grin. "We might as well find our clothes and go home, dragons, too much competition this year."

The taunt caused a round of laughter. That was not how the pairings worked and they all knew it. In the mating ceremony, all men were equal. The crystal showed the bearer their future, but it was up to the man to convince the bride to accept the marriage offer. And, as if to make things more difficult, the grooms were only permitted to say one word, "come," to communicate that the bride was to follow them to the tent to be wooed.

The sound of his uncle Yusef as he began to sing a loud, bawdy song caused the musicians to join in. The lively music of the gittern dominated the other instruments. Grier made his way through the crowd, ensuring that his people would see him.

During his first festivals as a groom, he had worn the traditional fur loincloth. What no one talked about was the fact that, with oil on their skin, the edges of fur tended to stick to the thighs. Now he wore leather. It was much more comfortable.

Someone shoved a goblet into his hand. He saw the head of one of the servers walking away. Without much thought, he tipped the cup back, smelling the thick liquor before the taste hit his mouth. He gulped the contents before dropping his arm to his side holding the empty goblet.

He glanced at the inert crystal on his wrist. He'd been staring at it for the last couple of days for a sign that somewhere out there was his mate. The obsession frustrated him.

He should be focusing on escaping the ceremony to fly out to Shelter City to watch for Federation activity. This was the time of year they usually had a new influx of citizens. Grier had been trying to catch them in the act of smuggling people onto the planet. The Federation wasn't properly caring for the citizens for whom they'd already taken responsibility.

As a royal, it made him seethe with fury. Ruling was not just a birthright. It was responsibility, duty, an honor. The needs of the Draig came before anything he felt or wanted. The Cysgodians lived on Draig land, and that made their well-being his concern. Not being able to do something caused anger to bubble inside him.

The blast of a horn sounded and was met with cheers. Though he couldn't hear it, he knew his father would shout, "Grooms to the lines!"

"To the brides," a man yelled, inciting a round of cheers.

Grier looked for another drink. When he found no servants nearby, he handed the empty goblet to a man too young to participate before walking toward where the luxury spacecraft would have docked. He didn't expect his crystal to glow a second time for a woman who had just arrived on his planet.

"Let's go, prince!" Someone slapped him hard on the back. The crowd began to flow around him, like he was a stone in the current of a river.

"I caught one," a guard teased as he swept his wife into his arms. Her shout of delight rang out as he carted her away from the tents.

"Careful, that one looks feisty," a friend warned.

"That she is, dragons, but that is also why I pick her again every year," the guard answered, eliciting laughter. "I advise all the grooms to find a woman with spirit. Life won't be easy, but it's never boring!"

"Watch yourself or you'll be sleeping with the ceffyl herd," the wife warned from where she draped over his shoulder. She gave her husband's ass a hard smack. The guard walked faster.

The husband and wife would not be the only married couple planning to relive their wedding night while the new grooms hoped for a future.

Grier felt the friendly pats on his shoulders as people passed. He heard their shouts at the hissing sound of the spacecraft doors opening. He couldn't see the ship but knew where to find it.

Grier took a step to the side, moving toward the tents. He couldn't do it, knowing that his future would not be stepping off that ship. He started to push the mask up from his face, only to stop as his wrist passed his vision. The crystal did not glow, but it was a sufficient reminder to keep up appearances long enough to disappear from the crowd. His parents would most likely notice his absence, but hopefully the people would be too focused on the incoming bridal shipment.

He moved into the village of tents. They were constructed each year as a symbol of hope. Many would remain empty and unused.

Pain rushed into his chest, choking him. He knew that out of all the moments of his very long life this one would be the worst. Maybe it was facing with the mating ceremony without any hope that forced him to accept the truth. He was not meant to marry. Love was not in his future.

His logical mind tried to whisper that in time, it would not matter. He had his duty, his people and his love for them. He had his family.

He had...

He had...

The pain became worse. His nose burned with the threat of tears. It tried to manifest itself in a roar from his throat. He grabbed his wrist, watching as the dragon clawed its way to the surface. His flesh beneath the crystal changed, hardening. As much as he wanted to let the beast inside take over, he knew that it would burn down the entire forest.

The animal nature did not reason like a man. If threatened, the dragon protected itself. If scared, the dragon flew high or hid. If heartbroken, the dragon would set fire to the planet as it screamed in agony.

The prince cradled his shifting hand to his chest and held it tight, focusing on stopping the transformation. His mouth opened in a silent scream as his jaw cracked and his beard disappeared. The panting of his breaths, each one filled with agony, cut through any other sound. Sharp teeth pushed from his gums. His eyesight sharpened so that each granule of the red dirt became well defined.

Grier fell to his knees. It was too late to stop what was happening. He was shifting.

"*Ah-hh!*"

The startled exclamation came from the direction of the forest.

His head snapped to the side to see a woman staring at him. Her parted lips and frozen stance reminded him of a beautiful statue. Only her blue gown moved. It was not the dress of a bride. Her brunette hair had been pulled back, revealing the soft brown of her eyes. She couldn't have appeared at a worse time.

Energy shot through his legs, propelling him upward so that he leapt in her direction. The half-shift of his body turned him into a man-dragon, running on two legs but covered in the protective armor of his shifted form.

The woman screamed and took off through the tents.

Grier ran after her, the hunter in him overtaking all reason. He chased her as she wove around the structures in a haphazard pattern as if to throw him off. Coming to a yellow tent, he paused. The sound of her feet had stopped.

Grier panted, though he was hardly out of breath from the minor excursion. Light glowed on the yellow tent wall and he lifted his hand to the flap so he may enter. The light moved with him.

It didn't come from inside. The crystal on his wrist glowed.

Desire surged, tempered only by the fact he was half-shifted and Draig did not mate in dragon form. A tingling spread from his wrist, up his arm, as if he could feel a physical change happening. The pulsating glow was a beacon of hope. The gods forgave him for his careless words. He would not doubt their wisdom again.

As soon as the woman agreed to give him a chance, he would go to the temple and give thanks, as was the tradition. Then he would spend the night in a tent, convincing his bride of his worth. He would do all the traditions—every single one—if that meant he could have her. If the gods wanted him here and not at Shelter City that is what he'd do.

First, he needed to find her.

His taloned fingers ripped the material of the tent flap as he charged inside. Heat pushed out with every breath. He turned in circles, but it didn't take long to realize the tent was empty. Mindless and desperate, he clawed through the sidewall material. He could not lose her again. He needed to find his woman.

7

WHAT IN ALL THE UNIVERSES...

Salena stood in the dark tent, made more so by the black walls. Strands of her hair had fallen free, and she pushed them behind her ears. She saw the shadow of a figure run by the outside of the tent and watched as the beast-man passed her.

Salena had never seen anything like him. She'd heard a strange noise and had gone to look, only to discover the transmutation of man to man-dragon. The hardening of skin and the growing of talons had been intimidating, but they were nothing when compared to the yellow of his eyes when he looked at her. She'd been held captive in place, unable to move. In that extraordinary second, she'd not been scared of him.

Then he'd tried to pounce on her.

Jaxx did not want the dragon to be called a monster, but what else was she to think of the man who pursued her? Even now her heart pounded, and her throat felt like it was closing. A ridge protruded down his forehead to his nose, thickening his brow over his eyes. Fangs filled his mouth and deadly talons stretched in place of fingernails. It was the thing of nightmares.

Jaxx had said to come here if she got into any trouble. She would say being hunted by a man clearly going through a painful metamorphosis counted as trouble. Jaxx might not be a monster, he had saved her, but she couldn't say the same for the creature chasing her like prey through a forest of canvas.

Jaxx's proposed hiding spot did not feel safe. As her eyes adjusted to the darker light, she detected a bed, a table with empty serving trays, and a bathing tub. A thick rug covered the ground, cushioning her as she walked. She moved toward the trays and lifted one to swing it through the air. The test only convinced her that she couldn't strike hard enough to stop the man chasing her if it came to it. She set the tray back down.

"Think, Salena," she whispered. "What should you do?"

You have to wake—

"Oh, shut up." She cut off her own thoughts. Her

sister's voice really wasn't helpful in this situation. Her eyes fell onto a knife. She grabbed it.

Salena forced a calming breath and repeated to herself, *The darkness will protect me from monsters. The darkness will protect me from monsters. If they can't see me, they can't get me. The darkness will protect me...*

She heard material rip from the direction the dragon had gone. He was too close.

Salena ran to the opposite side of the tent and sliced an opening. Still carrying the knife, she crawled out and made a run for the dark forest. Without really consulting her brain, her feet chose speed over stealth, and she pushed her body as fast as it could go.

A figure leapt out from behind a tent, and she screamed, stumbling to a stop before backing away. The dragon-man stared at her. His chest lifted and fell with harsh breaths. His mouth shifted and, she couldn't be sure, but he looked like he was smiling. He towered over her, just like the others she'd seen at the festival. Sounds from the celebration were so close, and yet the people there felt so far away.

The man was dressed like a groom, with a mask and loincloth. There were hints of muscles beneath the armored flesh. The ground did not appear to bother his bare feet.

There was something primal about the way he

focused on her. Energy seemed to jump off of him toward her. It pulsed so thick that the air became heavy with it. Already she was breathing hard from her run and the sensation made her lightheaded.

"What do you want?" she managed, unsure he could understand her. Her hand shook as she held up the knife in warning.

"Come." The one guttural word barely sounded like the Old Star language most aliens spoke, but the passionate intent was clear.

A shiver worked over her body. He wanted her to follow him? She could only guess at the purpose of that trip. "No, thanks."

He lifted a hand as if to point a glowing device at her. She flinched, not taking her eyes from his sharpened fingertips as they twitched to beckon her forward. "Come."

"Not happening, scary man." Salena darted to the side, tripping on a rope tethered to the ground. The knife slipped from her fingers, and a hand wrapped around her upper arm from behind to keep her from falling. The heat of the touch caused her to call out in alarm. "Let go!"

Surprisingly, he obeyed the command.

Salena caught hold of the rope and righted herself before backing away from him. She glanced to the side just enough to make sure she didn't back into a tent. Seeing the knife, she snatched it from the ground and held the blade before her.

"I heard a scream. This way," a deep voice announced, the words followed by the thundering of feet.

The noise prompted her to run again. She turned, bursting from the village of tents onto the festival grounds. The crowd had thinned, but those remaining parted, giving her space. Salena skidded to a stop. She pressed her knife hand against her skirt in an effort to hide the weapon. Eyes moved from her toward the man chasing her.

Salena turned to see a human figure standing in a loincloth. The dragon had disappeared from his features to be replaced by an incredibly handsome man. Her heart continued to beat fast, the adrenaline flowing full force. It didn't take much to feel the excitement coursing through her. She instantly wished he'd turn back into dragon form. It was less intimidating.

Liquid-hot eyes gazed at her from beneath the mask. Firm lips were framed by a trimmed beard and proud jaw, which led to a strong neck. He was as fit as the rest of them, and she could assume shifting burned a lot of energy, which would account for the muscles...so many muscles.

Salena wasn't sure how long they stood, staring at each other, before someone yelled, "His crystal glows!"

"Many blessings," another voice added, joined by a chorus of shouts.

"Take her to feast with the other brides!"

"To the feast!"

"Come." Her pursuer's one word sounded odd against the shouts of his people.

"Someone is overeager to start the wedding night," a man teased, causing laughter to erupt.

"To the tent!" came the new cries.

"Take her to the tent!"

"Stop it," Salena ordered.

"I don't understand what we are supposed to stop." A woman leaned into the arm of the man next to her.

"I wish you would stop trying to cook wilddeor stew," the man answered, looking momentarily stunned at the confession that came out of nowhere.

"You said you loved it," the woman said.

"No, I said I love you." The man lifted her up and kissed her.

Salena knew that was just the first of the unprompted confessions to come, and they generally became much worse. The fact everyone had been drinking made her effect on them worse. For obvious reasons, she hated crowds.

"Come." The man held out his hand, and she realized the glow came from a bracelet.

"Go to him!"

"Go!"

"Put him out of his misery, my lady!"

"No." She shook her head in denial. The cheers were meant in good fun, but their focused attention made her want to run. The voices didn't stop with their endless suggestions, ones that were becoming increasingly bawdier. "No!"

She held up her hands to get them to stop shouting, but the gesture revealed her weapon. Her hand shook violently. Silence fell over the grounds like a wave where she was the epicenter, and like a ripple, murmurs returned as those farther away sent questions back as they tried to figure out what was happening.

"You threaten him?"

"How dare you say no to a Draig prince," a woman's voice shot, the words slurred, "as if he had no honor and was not worthy of you!"

The honesty kept coming and she would not be able to stop it.

"Why come to marry if you do not agree to such a fine husband?" a man demanded.

"Why are you here?" another asked. "Who are you?"

"It's as if you mock us," yet another concluded.

"The gods would never set a match like this."

"Someone should get her out of here."

Salena stared at the man with the glowing crystal. Why in the world had he picked her? She wasn't dressed as a bride. She wasn't with the other...

Wait. Did they say prince?

A large hand seized her wrist, instantly disarming her before she even saw who'd touched her. The blade fell to the ground. She followed the hand up a thick forearm littered with scars only to land on a face that had clearly seen its fair share of fights.

"Halt! Farvald, release her!" Her would-be mate commanded.

Farvald obeyed.

The crowd instantly turned to watch the prince, pressing in on itself as those in back tried to move closer. Gradually, he raised his hand and pulled the mask from his features. Gasps sounded at the gesture.

"No, you mustn't. Don't lose hope. Not all brides decide quickly." The man who spoke pushed through the crowd. He was older, with long black hair streaked with silver. "Put your mask on."

"We're scaring her. Can't you see she's terrified?" The prince dropped his mask on the ground and tried to move toward her.

"Salena?" Olena appeared at her side. She pulled at her arm. "What are you doing here...?"

"She carried this." Farvald handed the knife to the princess.

Olena took the blade. Her eyes went toward the groom prince and widened. She stepped past Salena toward him, only to stop and glance back. "Oh, no."

"My love?" the man with long black hair asked. He reached to pick up the discarded mask.

"Maiden's Last Breath! Calms even the most skittish," Olena yelled. A round of cheering went up over the crowd. She hooked Salena's arm and whispered, "Come with me. Now."

The words were not a request, and Salena wasn't given much of a choice. Since it would get her out of the crowd, she didn't protest.

She glanced back to see the man with black hair thrusting the mask at the prince. "By all the gods, boy, put this on."

The prince's eyes met hers. She wasn't frightened of him in this form, but more of what she felt when she looked at him. Attraction was the last thing she'd expected, considering the crazy man had chased her down to propose.

Olena cut through the crowd toward the tents, angling their path slightly away from the prince. As they made it to the edge of the crowd, she waved a man over to them. He wore the same style of tunic Salena had seen on men stationed around the festival, and she assumed him to be security. He rushed to their side.

"Find my son," Olena ordered. "He is with the grooms. Send him to his tent."

"Yes, princess." The man bowed his head before running to do as she bid.

Olena led her through the tents until they reached the black one. Lifting the flap, she pushed Salena in. The men followed, the older one carrying a torch which he slid into a sconce to cast light over the area. Her suiter once again wore the mask.

Olena tossed the knife onto the bed. "Yusef, this is Salena. Salena, my husband."

"I am glad to see you have recovered from your ordeal," Yusef said.

Salena nodded at the man. She started to speak, but in the end felt it best to stay quiet.

"And Prince Grier, my nephew," Olena finished. "He—"

"My lady?" a voice called from outside.

"What is it?" Yusef answered.

A servant entered carrying a decorative goblet on a tray. She wore a loose-fitted tunic and her hair was slicked back from her face. The woman walked the cup to Salena. "Your drink."

"Thank...you?" Salena's hands shook as she took it. She was parched. The servant left as quickly as she'd arrived. She lifted the goblet to her lips.

Olena swiped it from her and the liquid sloshed onto Salena's hand.

"Don't drink that," Olena said. "You were not part of the bride orientation, so trust me on this. Maiden's Last Breath has side effects, and I think clear heads are required at present."

"What will happen now?" Salena looked around the tent.

What was scarier than anything they could have said was the fact they said nothing. They didn't know.

"I suppose we will go speak to my brother before he hears what has happened," Yusef said after some deliberation.

"Good plan." Olena nodded. "The last thing we need is palace guards sent to look for them. They'd assuredly send a few to the forest to search, and we took great pains to ensure what we do does not reach the elders."

"That," Yusef said, his tone a little wry, "and the fact Rigan will worry about her son."

"Well, of course, that," Olena dismissed. "I meant that as well."

"We should go," Yusef said to his wife. "These two have much to sort out." To Grier, he instructed, "Use this tent. We do not need it. Jaxx did not find a bride."

"I'm not a bride." Salena looked meaningfully at Olena. "Tell them I am not here to marry. Tell them I'm leaving."

"The Federation is after her," Olena said. "Jaxx was going to smuggle her to my old ship and secure her a ride off-world."

"Was?" Salena inserted. "Don't you mean he *is* going to smuggle me?"

But the woman didn't mean that. Everyone always told her what they meant whether they wanted to or not.

"No." Olena looked at her nephew. "I'm sorry, Salena. Things have changed. I can no longer help you leave."

The small hope, her only hope really, slipped away with that admission. Why was she saved if only to watch liberation slip from her grasp? It was a question no one could answer. The world did not need a reason to be the world. It just was. People just were. She was nothing in the scheme of everything.

A tear slipped down her cheek. All her life, nothing had been in her control, not beyond the briefest of instances. The ache of that knowledge filled her. Maybe fighting was useless. If she remained on this world, the Federation would track her down eventually. They had pursued her through space, a little bit of planetary terrain would hardly be a challenge.

She went to Olena, clutching the woman's hands in hers. "You can't change your mind. I don't want to be a prisoner. The things they will ask of me. Jaxx should have left me in the cave."

"What cave?" Grier had pulled the mask off his head.

"Grier, you can't..." Yusef reached for the mask as if to force it back on his nephew.

"Leave him be, Yusef," Olena said, before answering Grier. "By the Shelter City watchtower. She was in hiding in one of the cliffside caves."

"You were hiding from the Federation?" As a man, Grier had a kind voice, one filled with concern. He sounded nothing like the dragon who had chased her through the tents. She glanced at the slit she had made in the canvas. It was like a completely different person faced her now.

"Yes," Salena answered.

"In a cave?" he asked.

"Yes."

"By the watchtower overlooking Shelter City?" he persisted.

"Yes."

That answer seemed to relieve him, and he let loose a short sigh. "And why do they want you?"

"She has something they want," Olena answered for her.

"Can we return it to them?" Grier asked.

"What they want is part of her," Olena said.

Not wanting Olena to speak on her behalf as if she were a child, Salena broke in, "I have a talent for extracting the truth out of people."

"An interrogator?" Grier eyed her but did not seem to doubt her words.

She nodded.

"She is able to pull the truth out of people whether they want to tell it or not," Olena said.

"Mother?" Jaxx came through the opening. He glanced in surprise at those gathered. "Shall we be off? Payton will be waiting for me, and we all know how much patience cat-shifter women have. Grier, I didn't realize you'd be here. Are you coming with us to the drop-off? We will be glad for the help transport—"

Grier held up his glowing wrist and cut off Jaxx's words.

Jaxx smiled, instantly turning to Salena. "I thought

you said you didn't want to marry? I suppose I should thank you for turning me down gently." When no one laughed at his joke, he straightened his posture and crossed his arms over his chest. "What is it?"

"We should leave these two alone," Yusef said. "Jaxx, go see to the shipment of food simulators and make sure they're stashed safely before dawn. We don't want this batch to be raided like that last one."

Jaxx nodded and left. She heard him running away from the tent.

"I should go too," Salena said.

"Please stay." Grier moved closer but stopped before he reached her. "I give you my word no harm will come to you. Besides, it's dark, and the forest is filled with people. There is nowhere for you to go tonight.

"He's right," Olena said. "Things have changed. The pirate ship is not an option right now. You need to stay here for the night."

Salena glanced at the single bed in the room.

"I will sleep on the floor," Grier offered.

Thankfully, her ability did not compel her to speak the truth, otherwise she'd have blurted out how disappointing she found that statement to be. Who wouldn't want a sexy loinclothed lover in their bed?

"I can't stay," Salena said.

"You must," Olena insisted. "We will figure out the new plan in the morning, whatever form it may take."

"No one wants their elders hovering at such a time. Come, my love, back to the celebration, where I will serenade you. We can check on the children in the morning." Yusef pulled his wife from the tent to leave them alone.

"Please, no more pirate songs." Olena's voice became smaller as they left. "Is that a hole in Jaxx's tent?"

The emptier the tent became, the smaller the space felt. Now it was only the two of them embraced by an awkward silence. She felt him staring at her, and she pointedly looked everywhere but at him.

"Servants will bring food if you're hungry," Grier said after a while, "and it appears my cousin chose a tub for his tent, so there will be heated water for a bath."

"It is too bad the servants have to work with such a celebration going on," she said.

"Why is that bad? It is a job of honor, and they all volunteer to do it," he answered. "I served a few years before I was of age to marry."

"You did? A prince serving drinks and carrying bathwater?"

"Yes, as did my cousins and brothers. How else were we going to get a peek inside all these tents?" He chuckled. "When we were children, it all seemed so secretive and mystical."

She found the glow from his wrist to be a distraction. "Does that shut off?"

"No." He untied the leather strap from his wrist and carried the bracelet toward the bed. He slid it under a pillow. "But I can hide it, so the glow doesn't bother you."

"If you want to rejoin the celebration, I should be fine here," she said, though she didn't want to be alone. Ironically, the scare he gave her during the chase was what prompted her emotional need to talk to someone.

"I can't leave until the morning." Grier walked toward the table and took the goblet of wine. He looked at the contents before setting it back down without drinking. She studied his naked back, watching the muscles move hypnotically beneath the flesh. "I must apologize for my first impression. I cannot explain what came over me, other than to say I saw you and had to have you."

Well there was a dose of honest if she ever heard it. This was one of those instances where her ability compelled too much of a confession. She knew she shouldn't pry deeper, and still she couldn't stop herself. What woman wouldn't want to hear how the primitive sexy-man was attracted to her? "Does that happen often to you?"

"Never before tonight." Grier didn't turn to her, and she had plenty of time to let her eyes roam over the loincloth that showed teasing peeks of flesh. When he shifted his weight, the material lifted by the back of his upper thigh to expose the beginning curve of his ass.

Salena had never been more grateful that her ability couldn't be turned around on her than she was in that moment. If she'd blurted what was going through her mind when she looked at him, she'd have to fling herself in a deep hole because she'd die of embarrassment. The loincloth shifted again as he moved, and her eyes darted upward to meet his before quickly turning toward the hole she'd cut in the side of the tent.

"You may look all you like," Grier said.

"I wondered…" Salena swallowed nervously and began picking at a chip in her fingernail. "I mean, what's the significance of the loincloth?"

"Tradition. It is all part of the ceremony."

"Is that…?" She glanced toward his waist, and then at her finger with a renewed determination not to peek at his naked flesh. "Is it like…? Did your people traditionally wear loincloths as normal clothing for daily life?"

Not the most articulate of inquiries, but it'll do, she thought.

"Not that I have heard. Some say it's a symbol of exposure, no barriers," he said. "You appear preoccupied with my loincloth."

No, only what's underneath it.

While we're on the topic, I should ask him for a closer look. For anthropological reasons of course.

Shut up, stupid brain.

"Shut up—*what did you call me*?" His legs were spread shoulder-width apart, and he crossed his arms over his chest. For as unthreatened as she felt for the time being that didn't mean his primal energy put her at ease.

Oh, blast of space fire, how much of that did I just mumble out loud?

"I was saying, my brain was stupid for asking dumb questions," she explained, trying to cover up her muttering.

"You do not appear stupid to me." He moved closer.

"So the..." She glanced around. "Masks."

"What about them?" He kept distance between them but was close enough she could touch him if she reached out. It was tempting.

"Why do you wear them?"

"All men are equal in the search for happiness." Grier's gaze dipped over her, and he did not attempt to hide his sexual interest. Yellow glinted in his eyes, raw with emotion. "When our crystal glows, it tells us who the gods will for us. Then it is up to us to prove our worth. We have one night to do so. This night. We are not allowed to speak until our woman removes our mask and permits us to do so. It is a symbol of her acceptance, and proof that her decision is made freely."

"Then what happens?" She was acutely aware of where the bed was behind her.

"There is exploring." He grinned, coming closer. His jaw lowered, and she had the impression he wanted to kiss her.

"What kind of exploring?" And, evidently, she wanted to be kissed.

"Whatever we want, so long as we do not consummate the union until the bond is cemented before the elders."

She stiffened. "You have sex in front of the elders?"

That was a line she wouldn't cross.

He recoiled at the question. "Gods' bones, no, woman!"

"But you said—"

"The couple declares their decision and they break the crystal. People cheer. Then they can have sex, but not in front of anyone. Usually they go spend a week in the privacy of their own homes."

"You already broke a rule. You took off your own mask," she said.

"As much as I tell myself I am going to behave in accordance with tradition, I seem always to be messing up with the gods." His expression didn't change, and she didn't know if he was joking. "I hope you can forgive me."

He inched closer.

"That is not mine to forgive." Her voice was not as strong as before. She met his gaze. If she leaned in and lifted on her toes, they'd be close enough to kiss. She glanced at his lips and felt drawn forward to be closer to him. She wondered if his beard would tickle or scratch.

"My prince, forgive us. We did not know you had returned to the tent."

The sound of the intruder's voice stopped her from doing something foolish. This was not the time for seduction. She pulled away from Grier, walking around to the other side of the bed to put distance between them.

The servant appeared young, no more than eighteen by human standards. His tunic was simple, a creamy white with blue stripes down the arms. The pants were baggy, and he wore shoes that cut off at the ankles.

"Come in, Ketill." Grier gestured toward the table.

Ketill went to set down his tray of meats. Two similarly dressed boys appeared behind him. The second carried another tray of food, and the last, two pitchers and matching goblets. The second boy paused, looking openly at the mask on the ground and then at Salena. He gave her a small smile. The third ran into the smiling boy's back, causing the liquid in his pitchers to splash over onto the tray. Slices of blue bread dropped onto the ground. It was almost comedic to watch them fumble around.

"My apologies," one of them mumbled but she couldn't see which one. Ketill went to pick up the bread, and they finally managed to arrange the food table...somewhat.

"You're beautiful." The second server watched her more than what he was doing at the food table. "Much prettier than some of the others who came tonight."

"Timon, that will be all," Grier said, his tone holding a small warning.

"I don't know why I said that," Timon answered.

"Because she is beautiful," the third answered as he set the drink on the table. He kept his eyes averted.

"It seems you have admirers," Grier stated. Gesturing to the boys, he said, "Ketill, Timon, and Alfarr." Then gesturing at her, he said, "Lady Salena."

"My lady," the three boys said in unison, grinning excitedly as if they awaited her approval.

"Thank you for bringing food," Salena answered. They kept smiling and staring. She wasn't sure what they expected from her. "Are you enjoying the festivities?"

"I can't wait until my ceremony. I had a dream once that I found a woman with your color of hair," Timon said. "I think it was the gods saying they will bless me."

"I think it was the Galaxy Playmate hologram you found." Alfarr snickered.

"You're not supposed to talk about that in front of a lady," Ketill scolded. "She's our future qu—"

"Out," Grier ordered, the sound of his voice leaving no room for argument. "Now."

Ketill and Timon rushed from the tent.

"But we are to bring you chocolate." Alfarr stood holding the flap open. "The Lithorians delivered it late and the carvers are still chiseling off the bits to put on the trays."

Grier glanced at her.

Salena shook her head. "I don't eat chocolate. I never developed a taste for it."

"No chocolate." Grier motioned his hand in a decisive gesture.

The servant gave her one last look before leaving.

"I don't know what came over them. They are usually well behaved," Grier said.

"No need to apologize. I'm used to it," Salena answered.

"I imagine you would be. They were right. You are beautiful. I'm not surprised that you have been told that often." His tone dropped, becoming a little husky.

"That's not what I meant." Salena tried not to let the

pleasure of his compliment show on her face. Rarely did conversations turn to how she looked.

"You should eat something. Come." He moved toward the food and poured two goblets, leaving the Maiden's Last Breath on the table. "This is strong, so I am going to have to insist you drink slowly."

She took the goblet from him. His finger caressed her, and there was no denying the fire stoking between them. She saw it in the liquid swirling of his eyes, felt it in the heat of his skin. If they hadn't been interrupted, who knows what they'd be doing now? Definitely not talking about the potency of liquor.

"That is sweet of you to be concerned." Her tone dropped, and she found it hard to breathe. His finger fell away from hers, severing the connection.

Grier smirked. She heard him suppressing a laugh as he turned from her.

"Did I say something that amused you?"

"The last person to call me sweet was my grandmother when I was nine. I'm sure her opinion changed when she discovered the flowers I gave her were a distraction so that my cousins could sneak out of the mountain palace."

"You really are a prince, aren't you?" The title separated them, making whatever she felt an impossibility. There was nothing more visible on a planet than royalty.

Everyone watched them, everyone spoke of them. That included everyone the royals were with. The man before her represented the kind of notice she did not want. Not only would the Federation eventually track her down, but the dragon people would also begin confessing their secrets to the royal family anytime they saw her with Grier.

She realized he hadn't answered, at least not that she had heard.

"I think I need to go." She set the goblet on the table, the contents untouched.

"You were not supposed to know who I was before you accepted me," Grier said.

"And I haven't accepted you. There will be other nights for you to try. I am sure the next bride will be—"

"There is no next bride. Tonight was my only chance."

Blasted stars! No pressure there. Her thoughts came out sarcastic, and she had to remind herself that she was the alien on this planet, not him. She needed to respect his ways even if she couldn't participate in them.

She picked up his mask and held it out to him. "Maybe if you go back, you can find someone else to bring to your tent."

"Our ways do not work like that." There was pain in

his eyes as he looked at the mask as if that single gaze could set the material on fire as she held it.

"Please." She arranged it in her hands and lifted it to tie around his face. He didn't move to stop her. "Don't make me responsible for your unhappiness. I don't know you, and you know nothing of me. I cannot stay on this planet."

She couldn't manage to tie the mask and it dropped from her fingers to the floor.

When she would have stepped back, he grabbed her arm to stop her. The grip was firm but didn't hurt. "What does the Federation want with you, really? Is it just because you compel the truth in interrogations? Or is there more? Whatever the reason, I can protect you. As my wife—"

"Protection is the last thing I would marry for," she interrupted. "The universes use all of us in many ways. I refuse to enter a marriage based on usefulness and nothing else."

"There is attraction." He admitted it easily, taking a drink.

"You have known me less than an evening. I can see you are not a simpleminded man, so I know you understand that attraction fades."

At that, his eyes narrowed slightly. "I do not understand that way of thinking. Marriage is for life, and there is nothing more attractive than a mate. That feeling should grow in time, not fade. I feel sorry for those cultures that rely on less sophisticated methods of finding a partner."

She arched a brow and couldn't help her sarcastic response to his superior tone. "You dress in a loincloth, get drunk, and pick a bride at random. How is that any more sophisticated than—?"

"The grooms are not drunk," he broke in. "And I've told you, there is nothing random about the will of the gods."

His expression stayed neutral, but she felt the shift in his mood. She'd angered him.

"I should go," she said.

"Where? It's dark outside."

"Maybe I can find a ship to take me off-world." Her hands strayed to her skirt pocket as she felt the jewels. She started toward the tent flap.

Grier sighed heavily and sat on the bed. His voice stopped her. "I am cursed. I don't know what the gods are trying to tell me. First, I think I am destined to be alone, then I discover you were there, only hiding in a cave by the tower, and now I find you and everything should be perfect but..."

She wasn't entirely sure where he was going with this speech. "But it's not perfect."

"No. It's not," he agreed. "And whereas this should have been the simplest decision of my life, it has now become a complication. Tomorrow, I will be explaining this failure to my people instead of trying to determine if Shelter City had an influx of citizens because I was unable to watch the skies for landing ships."

"If you have somewhere to be, I'll cover for you," she said.

"I need to be here." He closed his eyes. "And I need to be there."

"For what it's worth, if you're watching for ships landing at Shelter City, I don't think you will find them. When they brought me here, we traveled by land craft for about a day and a half. I think we passed by a few people, but we did not go through any settlements, if that helps narrow down a location." She pushed at the flap, wondering if he would command her not to leave. "Maybe that is why your gods wanted you to find me tonight, so I could tell you that you are going to look in the wrong place."

8

IT WAS HIS WEDDING NIGHT, SUPPOSEDLY THE MOST blessed, happiest time, and he was...talking about Federation smuggling routes? And that was only after he'd chased his bride around like a beast after prey.

Grier silently berated himself. It was as if every romantic notion and daydream he'd had about being with his bride never existed. Instead of slow seduction and teasing brushes of flesh, he was inarticulate and argumentative. Instead of coaxing her onto the bed so he could worship her, he had chased her out the door. He literally had to be the worst groom in Draig history.

Salena ducked out of the tent.

"Don't leave me. I need you."

They were not the words he would have chosen if he had time to think about it, but they were honest.

Grier stood and set his goblet on the table. Every fiber of his being pulled in her direction. He'd felt it the moment he saw her outside the tents, had known it before he even realized his crystal glowed. She was a piece of him, a piece that fit into an empty cavern inside his chest, one that he hadn't known was there. When he looked into her eyes, he was breathless.

The rest were just details that he would gladly spend his life learning.

He wasn't sure she had heard him, but finally, she stepped back inside.

"In the morning, I will help you explain the situation to the royals in charge." Her eyes drifted from him, to the food, to finally land on the bed. "You're a prince. Surely, they will have to let you take another attempt at a future. I can't believe the gods would want a life of loneliness for you. And I can't believe you would be punished for a mistake. Tell me it's possible to fix this somehow. There has to be a way around the will of your gods. I'm sure this is not the first time a bride was chosen by mistake."

She sounded so hopeful even though he knew he'd already explained the crystal to her.

"No," he whispered. What she suggested was not possible.

By all the fires that had ever burned, she was lovely. The torchlight caressed her skin, casting shadows to accentuate her perfect curves. The gown was plain, but that didn't matter. Nothing could detract from the creature before him. Her lips had an almost hypnotic quality. The graceful flow of her limbs reminded him of those of a dancer. None of those things compared to the soulful brown depths of her eyes. Those were her weapon. All she would have to do is blink in his direction and he would do whatever she wanted.

Grier had thought married men were exaggerating about the effect their wives had on them, like hunting stories told around the campfire, each one trying to outdo the other.

"Grier?" she asked. "Can I speak to them on your behalf? Can I try?"

"That won't be necessary. They will know your decision when you do not go to announce your acceptance." Grier took a piece of blue bread and a slice of meat, folding them together before dipping it in a small bowl of broth. He held it out to her.

She moved slowly toward him. He would give anything to start this night over.

"Do you have somewhere safe to go once you leave here?" Grier watched as she took the food from him and tried a small bite. "I take it your silence means you do not. I want to propose something."

"I already told you, I won't marry you to protect

myself."

"Then marry me to protect *me*." It didn't occur to him to try to lie. This was the one person the gods told him he could trust, and he would listen. He might have failed to perform every tradition when it came to marriage, but he would not fail his marriage.

"Protect you? How?"

There were many honest ways he could answer that question.

As the future king, I need to set an example for the people.

It will make my family happy. It will make my people happy. It will make me happy.

I wish to be a father someday.

You are more things than I, a mere dragon, can put into words. The gods would not lead me down the wrong path.

"I don't want to spend eternity without my wife," he said.

"We're not married."

"We could be."

Salena closed her eyes and took a deep breath. "I do not know all the details, but from what I can gather, the dragon people—"

"Draig," he supplied.

Her eyes opened, and she nodded. "The Draig and the Federation do not share a harmonious relationship."

He chuckled. "That is the nicest way I've ever heard it said. Yes, it is a delicate balance. They are guests here who have overstayed their welcome."

"But they are the Federation, and you cannot kick them off without hurting their feelings," she said.

Grier noticed her eyes kept wandering to his chest before quickly darting away. The interest in his physical form gave him some hope. She felt the attraction between them.

Her gaze met his, and he had the impression she was digging into his thoughts. It was said mates developed telepathy between them. Is that what this was?

"And what do you think they would do if they thought you had betrayed them somehow? If they thought you had stolen from them?"

"It would start a war that we shifters could not win. We could easily take out those governing Shelter City, but they would only send more to replace them. It is the Federation. They could send armies if only we gave them an excuse to force their will upon us."

"That is my point. I am the last thing you need disrupting the precarious balance. They would not care that you are a prince, or that you married me. They made my value to them perfectly clear. They will come for me, they will find me, and they will do whatever they have to in order to get me back. And they would not be above hurting those I come to care for."

He saw the earnestness of that belief and hoped to dissuade her fears. "It is my duty to protect you."

"If that is true, then is it not my duty to protect you? I cannot repay your aunt's kindness, or your cousin's mercy, or your generosity by causing a war. Do not ask me to put that much death and pain on your doorstep."

It was his turn to close his eyes. He held back the pain that tried to wrench from his chest.

It was one of the few arguments she could have made to stop his begging. He could risk his life a thousand times over to protect her. His people would do the same without question, for she would be their queen. But the cost she ascribed to herself was more than he could ask of her. There were worse things than an honorable death and being to blame for those deaths was one of them.

She moved toward him. He felt her as sure as he felt the breath entering his lungs. Already, he felt their connection deepening. Knowing her an hour, a day, a year, a lifetime, that was inconsequential to how he felt. The pain would not get easier with time.

He would do as she asked.

He would let her go.

"Even if you say it wouldn't be my fault, it will have been my doing. I can't pretend I do not know the cost of such a decision. I need to leave. It's my only chance." Her voice had fallen to a whisper. The words were punctuated by a soft touch against his cheek. "But I will never forget your offer. If there is any way I can repay your family—"

"There is." He forced the dragon from his gaze before he looked at her. "I need to know where the Federation is landing, and how they are getting people into the city. The more reasons I can find to prove they're breaking their treaty, the better chance we have of negotiating them off our world."

"I don't know the terrain. I told you, we traveled by land craft for—at my best guess, gauging by food intake— a day and a half. Perhaps three times that if we had been walking by foot, judging by our speed. There were no cities or villages, only pockets of voices of other travelers. They never let me look out when the others were around. Beyond that, I saw trees so dense that the branches sometimes blacked out the sky. I hope that helps."

"That is a wide territory. If you help me narrow it down the best you can, I will help you leave and will make sure you are set up somewhere safe, and nice—not at the mercy of Aunt Olena's pirates."

"That is the best I can describe it." Her hand moved from his face, smoothing over his beard before moving down his neck. "But if it will help you and your family, I will go there with you and try to recognize what I can. That is the least I can do for saving my life...twice. First from the cave, then from this planet."

"I will protect you," he swore. The plan bought him more time with her. That is all he could ask for.

"I know."

He liked that she accepted him at his word. "We'll leave in the morning. There is no point in searching the woods in the dark."

"Agreed." She dropped her hand from him. "I am sorry tonight did not work out the way you had hoped."

"I met you. That is more than I have hoped." He grinned, trying to hide the feelings churning inside him. Hot desire fueled his need for her. He wanted to kiss her, to keep kissing her. He wanted to bring her onto the bed and hold her until the universes ended.

His physical body strained with longing, which pooled in his hips to lift his arousal against the confines of the loincloth.

"Now what?" she asked.

"Sit on the bed," he requested.

She gave him a quizzical look but did as he asked.

Grier took the trays from the food table and brought them to her. He placed them in the middle of the bed before sitting across from her. "If you don't like what is offered, I'll have the servants bring something else."

She smiled, took some bread, wrapped meat in it and gave it to him. "I think this feast will do just fine."

9

Salena stretched out on the bed and watched as Grier placed the half-empty trays on the food table. She knew the deal they had in place was not the one he'd wanted to come from this night, but it was the best she could agree to. Having him secure her safe passage sounded better than being smuggled by space pirates. And, truthfully, she also wanted to get to know him better—maybe not married at first sight, but perhaps a memory or two that she could daydream about later.

When he wasn't chasing her like a dragon, or asking her to be his bride, she found Grier to be enjoyable company. He didn't appear to mind the effect her ability had on him. It was a nice change for once. She didn't expect it to last, but it was nice.

Then there was the loincloth. For all intents and

purposes, he might as well have been naked. Very little was left to the imagination...including the telltale bulge trapped in leather. Not that she stared. Correction, not that she *tried* to stare.

"You were saying you had two brothers," Salena prompted.

"Prince Altair and Prince Creed."

"And you're a prince," she said.

"Yes. You know this." He came back toward the bed and returned to his seat across from her. Only now, there were no trays between them.

"And Jaxx is a prince," she added. "Yusef is a prince, and Olena a princess."

"Yes."

"How many cousins do you have?" Salena tilted her head to the side.

"First cousins, or extended as well? There are eight first cousins, and more than I have ever cared to count beyond that. Why are you asking?" He came closer, sliding forward on the bed.

"And you're all royalty, so this planet has like—*what?* —twenty princes and princesses? I thought only the children of kings and queens had those titles, so you have multiple kings and queens as well?" She leaned on her arm, bracing herself as she closed a little bit of the distance between them. "That is complicated."

"No, one dragon king and queen. We all have the title because our grandmother decided that we were all her princes and princesses. The cat-shifters have one king and queen. There is a family chart in the palace if you are interested in Draig and Var lineages." He slid a little closer. "What about you? Any family?"

"My parents died. I have two sisters. We were very close. They're gone now." Salena didn't want to talk about herself.

"I'm sorry, what happened to—"

"Would you mind handing me a drink?" She pointed at the table.

"Of course." He nodded, going to fetch a goblet.

Salena pulled at the covers, slipping her legs underneath. He returned, handing her the drink. The stout liquor wasn't one she was used to, but she managed to swallow it. She nodded her thanks and gave it back.

Grier set the goblet down, then took the torch from its sconce and carried it outside. The tent was cast in darkness. The silhouette of his figure showed in the entryway as he returned. "I will sleep on the floor."

She saw him kneel.

"You don't have to do that. This bed is big enough for both of us." Salena wasn't sure what prompted the offer. Sleeping close to him would be a temptation she might not be able to resist. Then again, she was an adult. Who said she had to resist?

"My lady, I might not be the best at keeping traditions, but that is one offer I will have to decline. I don't think my body can take being that close to you without acting on what I feel, and I have disappointed the gods enough for one night."

Salena took one of the pillows and slid off the bed to give it to him. She looked down at him kneeling on the rug. "It doesn't feel right having you sleep on the ground. Are you sure you won't sleep on the bed?" Instead of handing it over, she held it up. "We can put this between us. I promise not to breach the pillow wall."

"If you insist." Grier placed his hands on the floor and hopped to his feet. He took the pillow from her and said, "But I can't promise the same thing."

Salena hid her smile. It would seem he didn't need much convincing after all.

10

Salena imagined she could hear breathing coming from the other side of the bed. The sound was so soft that it was difficult to tell if it was real or her imagination. She kept her eyes closed and reached her hand to her side. Her fingers hit the pillow before sliding under it.

As if he'd been thinking the same thing, she found Grier's hand was also beneath the barrier. Her fingers rested against his, not taking it any further.

An electrical current seemed to run up her arm. It tickled its way across her chest and down her stomach. If the brush of his hand made her feel such awareness, she wondered what his kiss would do. There had been a couple of times where she'd thought he might kiss her, but the moments always passed.

Those thoughts led to others. What would it be like to have someone, to wake up next to him each morning and go to bed with him each night? To never be alone.

She waited for her sister's voice to tell her to wake up from the fantasy. For once her head was silent.

For a brief time, Salena let herself imagine the possibilities.

The sound of someone slipping a package through the tent flap forced her to open her eyes. With the morning came the end of the dream, dispelled by the light of day.

"It's a change of clothes," Grier said, his voice sleepy. His finger twitched next to hers, but he did not hold her hand. "Next they'll come around with food."

"Does that mean it's time for us to go?" She kept her voice soft as she looked at the light coming through the side of the tent. Soft noises of the morning came from beyond, the shuffling of feet and the various songs of nature.

"Soon." He rested a few seconds longer before finally rolling forward. He pushed his hair back and then scratched his beard. "They didn't deliver bathwater last night, but there should be a handheld decontaminator with the clothes."

Salena pulled her hand from beneath the pillow barrier and covered her mouth as she yawned. Though his nearness at night had been comforting, she felt a sting in her body as she moved. It ached for attention, from her tingling lips down to her toes. Attraction could be very inconvenient at times.

She watched as Grier ran the handheld decontaminator over his body. Any shiny remnants of oil disappeared under the caress of the green light. It moved over his chest and to his stomach, down a calf and up a thigh.

Before she thought to stop herself, she stood and went to Grier. He appeared surprised when her hand moved over his to take the decontaminator, but he let her have it. She ran the light over his back, watching it make a slow trip down the length of his spine. She touched his skin where the light cleaned, feeling the warmth against the tip of her finger. His breath caught.

"I wish we could have met under different circumstances." Salena completed his back and dropped her hand away from him. She handed him the decontaminator, so he could finish.

"I wish the same," he answered.

She turned her back when he reached for the loincloth, not needing the sight of his naked form haunting her thoughts.

Well, maybe just one peek.

She slowly turned her head. Her gaze met his, and she whipped her eyes away. Maybe not.

The sound of material sliding against skin held her attention. She licked her lips, trying to control the quickening of her heart.

"I'll step out so you can dress," he said. She glanced to see he wore a green tunic shirt that fit snug along the waist, black pants, and a pair of boots. A dragon emblem had been stitched on the chest. "We should leave before the other couples begin to wake up. I don't want to explain what is happening. We should be able to catch up to Jaxx."

Salena pulled off the wrinkled dress she'd slept in and quickly cleaned herself. The gown they provided for her was too fancy for a trip through the forest. The green material was soft and well stitched. The same dragon had been sewn into the bodice. She left it folded on the bed. Instead, she ran the decontaminator over her blue dress to clean it the best she could before putting it back on. Then, before she thought to stop herself, she'd made the bed and arranged the trays on the food table.

"You don't have to do that," Grier said. "They'll come to dismantle the tent."

"My mother always said to make sure you left a place looking as if you had never been there," Salena answered.

"If it is within our power, I think we should leave places better than we found them," Grier said.

"I'm guessing we had very different childhoods," Salena observed.

"How so?" He glanced over her gown.

She wasn't about to tell that story to a prince. "I'm ready to go."

Grier nodded and lifted the flap so she could step out into the sunlight.

Outside, the party had raged on, the aftermath of which was a field of sleeping men. Several tents had been dismantled, leaving the area open. The bonfire had all but burnt out, the soft orange glow of embers all that remained of their former glory. The festival grounds looked a lot less daunting in the daytime.

Grier led her away from the tents toward the trees where a path cut through the forest. The worn walkway made it easy to navigate their way. "You didn't answer about your childhood."

"No, I didn't." She reached to pull a yellow plant with small leaves growing off a center stem.

"You mustn't pick the yellow." He touched her hand to stop her.

"Why, what is it?"

"It's called the yellow," he chuckled. "My ancestors were not very inventive. The pollen causes whoever sniffs it to fall into a deep sleep. It used to be an issue before my aunt Nadja developed a shot that inoculated the population from its effects."

"She must be intelligent to have come up with that."

"Yes." He nodded. "You said you had two sisters? What happened to them?"

She stopped walking. "I won't talk about it. Please stop asking."

Grier's expression fell, and he nodded. "As you wish."

"It's not something I'm comfortable discussing."

"I understand," he said.

"After my parents died, we were separated," Salena explained. She didn't know why she kept talking; only she hated that his small smile had disappeared. "There is not much else to tell."

"I understand," he repeated.

"I don't think you can understand. Your family is right here. You know where to find them if you wish to." She stared at the path, watching the toes of her short boots as she walked. This must be what everyone else felt around her, the strange need to speak even when she knew she should keep quiet.

"I understand you don't wish to speak of it. I will not ask you to again," he clarified.

"They were...are...were called Piera and Fiora. We

were born at the same time and looking at them was like gazing into a mirror."

"It must be tough for you to be without them," Grier said.

She nodded, saying no more on the subject. "Is it far?"

"Not to reach my cousin, though it is a fair distance to Shelter City. I might suggest that we fly there." With each step, he seemed to move closer to her. Her hand brushed against him.

The night spent lying beside him had clouded her thinking. Each tickle of the breeze was pronounced against her sensitive skin. She should be trying to remember what she could of the path the Federation took. Instead, she focused on how close his hand was to hers and whether each gentle swing of their limbs would cause them to touch. The ache was terrible and tried to consume her thoughts. It made her want to cry and act rashly at the same time.

She wanted to kiss him.

She wanted to touch him.

She wanted more of him.

Her breath came out in a tremble and she'd forgotten what they had been saying. She stopped on the path, trying to calm her racing heart.

He took two steps before moving to look at her. "What is it?"

"I don't trust my judgment."

"In what way? Are you scared to go to Shelter City?" He came back to her, his head tilted in question and his eyes concerned. "I won't let anything happen to you."

"I don't trust my judgment around you, Prince." Salena lifted her trembling hand to touch his cheek. "Maybe we should keep our distance when we travel."

"I can't protect you from a distance," he denied.

"Then I'm afraid I cannot be trusted to use good sense." She stroked his cheek, feeling the texture of his beard against her palm. The heat of him soaked into her fingers. "You almost kissed me last night before we were interrupted."

"I almost kissed you many times last night, and this morning," he answered. "I am almost kissing you right now."

She licked her lips. "I wish you would."

Where did that admission come from?

His lips curled up at the side. Her fingers stayed with him as he leaned forward. At the first light contact, her eyes drifted closed. She held her breath and waited. The soft pressure began to increase.

"Don't you dragons have tents for this kind of thing?" a woman asked, her tone wry.

The kiss did not deepen. Grier sighed against her, not turning as he stated, "Good morning, Princess Payton."

"Welcome the dawn, Prince Grier," the woman returned with a laugh.

Grier appeared apologetic.

Payton was the name of the cat-shifter Jaxx was supposed to meet the night before.

Salena leaned to the side to see past him. A young woman stood, hands on hips, grinning at them. She wore the same tall boots and tight pants with cross-laces up the side of each leg that Salena had seen at the festival grounds. Her shirt fit her frame, the red leather having laces down the front. It provided borderline coverage without being completely immodest. Like the dragons, she appeared fully human.

"I assume blessings are in order." Payton gave a slight nod.

"No." Grier finally turned his back on her and faced the princess. "We've come to speak to Jaxx."

"I just left him," Payton said.

"You are going the wrong way if you wish to get back to the Var palace." Grier pointed in the direction they were walking.

"I'm avoiding my father," Payton said. "I did not attend a certain ambassadorial dinner last night, and it's best to let his anger cool before I show myself. I thought it would be entertaining to watch the dragons announce their marriages."

Grier slipped his hand on Salena's elbow and escorted her forward as if to pass the cat-shifter princess. "If you hurry, there are plenty of men who did not find brides. You never know."

Payton's face scrunched up in disgust. "May the flames burn off your tongue for that, Grier. I have no intention of marrying. It's the one thing my father and I agree on, though for different reasons. He thinks I'm too young and I think the prospect too boring."

Grier tried to leave, but Payton fell into step beside them.

"What are you up to?" Payton asked. "I feel an adventure brewing."

"You always feel that," Grier dismissed.

"I'm right, aren't I?" Payton dropped back and reappeared in line next to Salena. "Tell me. Where are you going?"

Salena glanced at Grier and didn't answer.

"Does it have anything to do with last night?" Payton asked. "If you tell me, I'll tell you where Jaxx is. He's not where you think he is."

"We're not playing games. You should go home," Grier said.

Payton gave a little rumble in the back of her throat. Grier answered with a louder growl of his own.

Salena stopped walking, so that she was no longer between them. "Where is Jaxx?"

"Fine." Payton screwed up her face and rolled her eyes. "He's with Roderic. We had to change the location of the drop-off last night. Marsh farmers were blocking the way to the original spot, so we stashed the units inside one of the old storage trees. After half of the last shipment was stolen, we're not going to risk it."

Both of them turned to look at Salena.

"You *are* an interrogator. I've never seen her cave that fast." Grier smiled and nodded in approval.

"What did you do?" Payton looked down over her body as if searching for a device that pulled the truth out of her before turning back to Salena. "Are you a *gwiddon*?"

"She's not a witch," Grier denied. Then, arching his brow in her direction, he asked, "Are you?"

"I don't think so." Salena wasn't sure what a *gwiddon* witch was.

"Hey, can you ask her who really stole the clothes from the Var border watchtower, causing my brothers and I to appear at the interplanetary dignitary dinner naked?" Grier asked.

"That was like thirty years ago. I told you Roderic did it," Payton answered.

"That is what you said, but..." Grier arched a brow.

"How old are you? Thirty years ago, you must have been a baby." Salena moved closer to them.

"I'm seventy-two by the Old Star charts," Grier answered.

"I'm a few years younger," Payton said.

Shifters apparently aged very well.

"I feel like a baby next to you two. I'm twenty-eight." Salena fell into step between them. "So what happened at the dinner?"

"I did it," Payton blurted. She gasped, covering her mouth.

"I knew it!" Grier pointed a finger at her.

"Well, you shaved my fur while I was sleeping," Payton countered.

"We only clipped a little of it," Grier said.

"Off my ass," Payton exclaimed. "I ran around with a bald spot for a week."

Grier laughed. "It was funny."

"So was your naked appearance at the dinner. The Klennup dignitary seemed to enjoy the show." Payton eyed Salena. "I'm going to have to watch myself around you."

"Do you have a lot of secrets you don't want to confess?" Grier asked.

"Yes," Payton answered. "As do you, I am sure. Oh, hey, Salena, ask Grier who told the Grug pilot I was available and had a hair fetish?"

Salena had never had quite this reaction to her ability before. She glanced at Grier but didn't try to force him to speak.

"What? You two would have had adorable furballs together." Grier grinned, clearly not sorry for the incident.

"Yes, as you apparently pointed out to him when you said I was interested. The creep kept trying to get me to shift into tiger form so he could..." Payton shivered and made a sound of disgust. "Actually, Salena looks like a lady, and I'm not going to repeat the offer in front of her."

"What?" Salena asked curiously.

"He wanted to put on a dress, mount me from behind, and ride me into submission." Payton again gave a dramatic shiver.

"Sorry I asked," Salena said.

"Ugh, I'm sorry you asked too," Grier added. "That is an image I didn't want in my head."

"Serves you right," Payton answered.

It was clear the two were close, having grown up as friends. Salena was a little jealous of that fact. Not so much that she thought something was going on between them, but because they had the kind of familiarity that developed by having a shared history.

Payton led them off the path and into the woods. Old trees had rotted out, now standing as broken, hollow shells. The musky smell hung thick on the air. Plant life had invaded the trunks, covering it like a fine blue fur. The forest became dense as if they were the first to disturb it in years.

"Would you like me to carry you?" Grier offered as they came to a cluster of rocks blocking the path.

Salena almost said yes, but it wasn't because she couldn't make the small climb. She wanted to feel Grier pressed against her.

"I'll be fine," she managed, her voice a little raspy.

11

"THERE, NOW YOU DON'T LOOK LIKE YOU'RE GOING to a royal reception," Jaxx told Grier, as he tossed the prince's embroidered tunic on the couch. It landed on Payton's head. She grumbled in protest as she yanked it from her head and threw it on the cushion next to her.

They were in Jaxx's home, waiting while he had something to eat after his long night. The home was an addition to his parents' house.

Jaxx had not done much by way of decorating, not because the family couldn't afford it, but because he was hardly ever home and saw no need. There was a couch, the cloth seats a little worn but so comfortable no one suggested replacing it. A royal banner was rolled up and resting against a corner, waiting to be hung. It had been waiting for close to a decade. Since Olena lacked any semblance of a homemaker gene, she didn't push her son to change his ways. However, it drove Nadja to distraction. She threatened to break in and take over. Jaxx never locked his door so it wouldn't be hard.

Payton covered her mouth as she yawned. Like Jaxx and Roderic, she'd been up all night unloading food simulators and sneaking the units around the forest and had yet to sleep. It wasn't that the equipment was illegal, just that they couldn't risk anyone questioning why they had acquired so many of them. The fewer who knew about what they were doing, the better.

"When I was traveling through some of the Var villages this last fortnight, I could feel the tension hanging heavy on the air. Whispers of attacks on shifters are spreading," Roderic said. He sat on the back of the couch facing them. The cougar-shifter had light brown hair and blue eyes.

Roderic's father was an ambassador, but he didn't appear to be following that path. He hated the inaction of diplomatic talks, often saying things like, *"Political conversations are a test of strength and will. Whoever gets tired of talking in half-truths and circles loses. And, sadly, punching your opponent for being a slargnot is often not allowed."*

Salena kept several paces from the group, not saying anything but also not turning her back on them. Her distrust was clear, not so much of Grier but of every-thing. Just as his royal duties had been taught to him since childhood until they became a part of him, so appeared to be her mistrust of others.

Roderic eyed Salena.

"You may speak in front of her. I vouch for her," Grier said. He met her gaze and gave her a small smile "She is here to help us."

Roderic seemed to hesitate a few more seconds before saying, "Have there been any confirmed reports with the Draig? Or is it still only rumors?"

"Rumors," Jaxx said in between bites of bread. "But still disturbing to consider."

"I thought this had to do with feeding the people of Shelter City because the Federation was not taking proper care of them," Salena said. "Are they attacking shifters as well? Is it because you are trying to help the people and are getting caught in the process?"

"Welcome to our complicated political mess," Payton mumbled. "If only it were that simple."

Grier took a deep breath, trying to think of the best way to explain.

"Honor is in short supply in Shelter City," Jaxx cleared his throat before pointing a piece of meat in the general direction of the group to punctuate his point, "and I blame the Federation for that. They have not made life in the settlement easy. Their strict laws have created a tense atmosphere and make little sense."

"The alien citizens are mostly good, but it is not the same with the Cysgod as it is with shifters," Grier said.

"That is because they have no old code, and much about their ways clash with Draig culture." Jaxx shoved the meat into his mouth, taking a large bite as he tried to hurry.

"It is hard to worry about things like honor when children are going hungry," Grier said.

"I didn't mean to imply they are bad. They handle things differently." Jaxx looked at Salena. "We would never let our neighbors starve. Since we can't set up food simulators in the city because the Federation would be able to detect them, that doesn't mean we can't take the food to the city after it is materialized."

Salena's brow had furrowed as if she tried to piece together the story.

"I think it will be less confusing if I explain from the beginning," Grier said.

Salena nodded.

"The Cysgodians were brought here because they were at the wrong end of a biological attack...not that there is a right end to be on in such a situation," Grier explained. "The radiation from our blue sun helps give us strength and longer lives, with some side effects."

"That would be me. I'm the side effect," Payton inserted with a small lift of her hand. "Female shifter births have become an anomaly, so I'm special."

"Don't you have female cousins?" Grier inserted, though he knew the answer.

"I didn't say I was the only special one," Payton defended.

"You're a pain in the special furry ass," Roderic mumbled.

"Not when that furry ass is shaved." Jaxx chuckled.

Grier ignored the banter. "The Federation asked if we could take in our alien neighbors so that they may benefit from the blue radiation. Their doctors believed it was their only hope of survival. After much negotiation, it was determined the virus was not a threat to shifters or our mates, so we allowed them to set up camp in a valley that received plenty of direct blue sunlight. How could we not?"

"*Temporarily* allowed," Jaxx corrected, walking toward the small kitchen area to drop off his now-empty tray.

"We couldn't let them die," Roderic said.

"That temporary camp became Shelter City," Payton added. "They kept adding to it and then, suddenly, structures were erected."

"What does this have to do with the shifter attacks?" Salena asked.

"I'm getting to that," Grier said. "The blue radiation worked. It essentially eradicated the virus. However, a new problem has emerged in recent years. The blue radiation helped stopped the virus, but it did not add years to the Cysgodians' life spans. Many of them are dying before their natural lifespan should have ended."

"Because they had the virus," Salena concluded. "It damaged them somehow? Left them weak or susceptible to other illnesses?"

Grier found himself drawn closer to her. He watched to see if she would back away from him. She did not.

"Possibly," Grier answered, "but the Federation won't let us test the population, and we'd need their cooperation to carry out such a task since technically they are visitors and under Federation protection."

"They claim the illness is why they won't let the Cysgodians have food simulators—because of the fear of more radiation from the devices—they also won't let us do any independent tests regarding the blue radiation. They claim ESC scientists are investigating the situation and our primitive medical experience will only sabotage their efforts and expose the population to unknown factors."

"We have no proof any of this radiation scare is true,"

Jaxx said. "And in the meantime, they're going hungry. It's difficult to save a population if they all starved before you could figure it out."

"And, let me guess, they are working off one of their top secret, *not-so-secret*, analyses of the shifter populations, and have concluded you are good-hearted people. They want to force you to accept the Cysgodians as citizens in order to help save them, which will let this planet officially become part of the Federation Alliance. Since you let them build the settlement, they know you are not the type to turn away those in need." Salena gave a long sigh and closed her eyes briefly in irritation. "Am I close? Become an official part of the Alliance or they won't allow you to run tests and save Cysgodian lives? It sounds like the faulty logic of the Federation to me."

"She's not stupid," Payton told Roderic, who nodded in agreement.

"And that is why in the midst of this mess the shifters are being attacked by Cysgodians?" Salena furrowed her brow and gave a small shiver of disgust. "I'm not sure I understand. They're not hunting you for food, are they?"

"I should hope not. What I'm telling you is the beginning of the reason things are the way they are," Grier said. "Cysgodians were cured of their initial illnesses, but they're still dying before their natural time. They had expected to live longer because that is what happened to shifters when our ancestors came here."

"Death causes fear," Roderic said. "Fear causes irrational actions and jealousy."

"We should go." Payton motioned at the door, prompting them to leave as they talked. She lifted a bag of supplies she had packed while Jaxx made food.

Salena fell into step next to him. Grier wanted nothing more than to lift his arm around her and pull her close. He wondered if there was a reason the gods kept allowing them to be interrupted every time he tried to kiss her.

"Those irrational actions are beginning to increase because of rumors that shifter blood holds the key to a long life." Grier did not want to see his people attacked and drained of blood due to a cultish myth. Draining a dragon of blood would do only one thing—kill the dragon. The same thing went for cat-shifters. "And how do you obtain shifter blood? Direct from the source."

"I understand now." Salena nodded. "The Federation is a slippery foe."

"We have resisted joining the alliance for generations." Grier let her pass through the door before him as they went toward the forest. "It is believed that—"

"It is a fact that," Jaxx inserted.

"—if we joined, the Federation would try to take over

and regulate our ore mining. It is the only reason they want Qurilixen in their alliance."

"What ore?" Salena's arm brushed against his. Her eyes caught his and for a moment everything else faded. He opened his mouth to tell her how beautiful she was.

"*Galaxa-promethium,*" Jaxx said when his cousin didn't answer the question. "It is used to make fuel for long-distance space travel. We like to call it liquid space credit."

They walked at a steady pace, moving quietly through the woods. Salena appeared to be considering what she had learned. Jaxx, Roderic, and Payton just looked exhausted. No one complained. They were all considered leaders to their people, and this was part of their responsibilities even if no one would ever know what they had been up to.

"So, I don't get it. Are you two married or not married?" Jaxx asked. "I saw the glowing crystal myself, but you arrived at my home a little too early to have gone to the official announcement ceremonies before the elders this morning."

Grier thought of the softly glowing crystal on the bracelet hidden in his pocket and couldn't answer.

"It was a kind offer, but my staying here would only complicate the shifters' situation with the Federation more," Salena answered.

He was both hurt by the truth and relieved that he was saved from forming a response.

"It is going to take too long traveling like this." Payton gave Salena a pointed look and almost tripped on a low branch.

"You two should run. Grier and I will fly. Grier, you carry Salena. I can carry the pack." Jaxx's tone didn't exactly sound like a suggestion.

Salena's eyes rounded and she looked up.

"You did all right with me," Jaxx said.

"Didn't you dangle me by an ankle while I was mostly passed out?" Salena returned.

"But you're unharmed." Jaxx smiled.

"I will leave the decision to you," Grier told her, having no desire to force her to do anything, "but you would be able to get a better look at the terrain to see if anything is recognizable. We won't be able to fly the area too long, since I was told to stop flying over the city, but we should be able to get a decent look."

"I heard you tried to roast some of the citizens," Jaxx said.

Grier frowned at how the small deed had been embellished by rumor. "I swooped them to break up two mobs that were starting to fight in the streets."

"I heard that you tried to steal two children," Roderic put forth, "but their parents bravely fought you off."

"I heard they cornered him in an alleyway and he cried like a baby," Payton said. His friends laughed. Salena suppressed a smile.

Grier grumbled under his breath. "Stop making up stories."

They laughed harder.

"I'll do it," Salena said. "I'll...*fly*."

"Wonderful!" Payton dropped the bag on the ground. "Let's get naked."

"Wait, what?" Salena unconsciously placed her hand over her neckline as if to stop the naked plan.

"To shift," Roderic clarified, pulling on the cross-laces of his shirt. "Please be so kind as to pack our clothing for us."

Salena nodded.

Roderic, Payton, and Jaxx stepped behind some trees. After a few moments, articles of clothing were flung in her direction. She gathered them up and shoved them into the pack.

A roar sounded, and Payton leapt from behind a bush in the form of a large white tiger. She landed in a predator's crouch.

Salena yelped in fright and instantly pressed against Grier, grabbing his arm.

Payton made a strange noise that sounded like a laugh. She looked to have gained an extra two hundred pounds. Her fur was a light cream with gray stripes, setting off her blue eyes and pink nose. Thick fur covered her limbs. She may have been a rare beauty, but she had the ferocious spirit that surpassed that of many of her peers.

"Payton, behave," Grier ordered, "or next time we'll shave both of your furry ass cheeks."

She slashed her claws at him, whipped her head around, and turned her butt toward them. Her tail swished before she took off running into the woods. The sound of her roar filled the forest, and he knew the freedom she felt in that moment as the animal inside surged through her.

"She's being a brat," Grier said. "She has complete control over the shifting and won't hurt you. She knows what she is doing."

Roderic appeared in a much more civilized manner. The cougar came from the trees with his head down. He paused before Salena, letting her see his sleek body. Tawny fur faded to a lighter shade along his neck and chest. Yellow entered his shifted eyes, masking his human blue. Salena's hand shook as she slowly reached out to touch his head, but she instantly snatched it away when he moved. Roderic looked up at her, made a small noise in the back of his throat, and then took off after his cousin.

"That's..." Salena whispered.

"I'm worried about, if you're scared of the cats, what you'll think of the dragon. I promise I won't—"

"That was remarkable," she exclaimed. "And they can do that whenever they want? Just turn into an animal?"

"Not any animal. Only their big cat form." Grier buried the ping of jealousy he felt at her amazement over the Var. "I can half-shift into a dragon-man, or—"

Salena gave a small laugh. "Yeah, I remember. Now that was terrifying."

He thought of the crystal in his pocket and wondered if it still glowed, or if it had given up now that the ceremony night was over. He was too afraid to look.

Tree limbs rustled, and he saw a glimpse of Jaxx as he shot up into the sky, not bothering to come back to the small clearing where Grier waited with Salena.

Salena looked up, but Jaxx could not be seen through the tops of the trees. "And I take it the full shift is the flying dragon. I take back my first comment. From what I remember of Jaxx when he saved me, *that* was truly terrifying—oh, wait, he forgot the bag."

She went to pick it up from the ground.

"No, he left it on purpose," Grier said. "Even though he *can* carry the pack, doesn't mean he intended to. I would have done the same thing to him."

Salena stopped mid-action and eyed him.

He didn't move.

She gave him a small smile.

"What?" Grier wasn't sure what she was doing.

If he followed his instincts, he would cross over to her and start kissing her, and this time he wouldn't stop. He wanted her too badly—wanted to touch her, beg for her, make demands. He wanted to marry her. He would give her everything, anything, whatever she so desired.

The ache he felt only deepened with each passing second. Here she was, so close, and yet he couldn't have her. This was the cruelest punishment from the gods, for what else could this be? To have the only woman he would ever want, he would risk a war with the Federation and the death of his people. It was a choice no one should have to make, but he wasn't just anyone. He was a Draig prince. His wants would never come first.

"Can I watch?"

It took him a moment to process what she was asking him. She wanted him to strip out of his clothes while she watched? The very thought sent a heat wave of desire down his body, pooling in his already oversensitive regions.

How could he say no?

His gut tightened.

How could he say yes?

Thankfully, he couldn't mate in dragon form so he could half-shift before disrobing. That might help him control his desires.

"I won't hurt you," he said.

"I know." She nodded. "I trust you."

"When you're ready, climb on my back and grab hold at the base of my wings. I'll try to fly slow and steady. Keep your head down while I'm going forward so the wind does not take you. When I hover, you can lift to get a better look. If you get scared, kick me with your knee. If you fall, I will catch you. No harm will come to you. I give you the word of a prince."

"I understand," she said, her hands shaking a little. He couldn't blame her. If he didn't have wings he'd be terrified of being so high in the air. Her bravery humbled him a little.

He reached for his shirt and pulled it over his head. As he went to the pack, he made sure to wrap his crystal in it so that no one would see it. The stone still glowed softly. He put his boots in as well. "You will put the rest of my clothes in the pack for me?"

Salena moved closer and again nodded. Her eyes strayed to his pants, but he did not remove them. Already the arousal would be unmistakable.

Grier knew he could not let the wild nature take over like the night before. Though heartbroken, his dragon would have to behave and prove he was worthy to the gods. Maybe then they would forgive him and let him have her.

Maybe.

Hopefully.

Somehow.

The prince was acutely aware of how he must look to her as the hard armor of his shift started along his neck and hands. His vision became focused, and he looked past her to the trees. The familiar pain pulled at his jaw and gums, reshaping his face. Though he was fully protected by the armor of his shift, she could still pierce him with just a look. Nothing could protect him from her.

Even now his need for her swirled in his blood, but the arousal had been covered so that it would no longer show his desperation. It took the edge off his desires and allowed him to concentrate. Barely.

He was being selfish, thinking of how this affected him. Salena was a fugitive. Cysgodians were starving and their city could not take another influx of people brought in during the darkness of night. It might already be too late to stop another shipment. They all needed the Federation gone from their planet, peacefully and willingly.

The last part was proving to be impossible.

When he didn't shift further, she came to him and touched his face. He felt the pressure of her fingers, but not in the same way his man flesh did. They brushed over his cheek and down the center ridge of his forehead to his nose. The smell of her filled him, and he memorized her scent so that he may always track her. He observed her face for signs of fear or repulsion. There only seemed to be a fascination. That was good. He didn't want her to be frightened of him.

Her exploration continued down his neck to his naked chest, only to stop over his heart. He wondered if she would be able to feel just how fast it was beating. Probably not with the armor of flesh protecting it.

"You are captivating." She lifted one of his hands in hers and touched a taloned finger. "The progression of man to man-dragon in such a short span of time, so seamless a transition. I have never seen anything like it."

His communication would be gruff in his current form, so he said nothing—not that he could form words if he wanted to with her standing so near. The dragon part of him wanted to yell "Mine," and the man part of him wanted to beg "Please have me, I can't imagine a life without you."

She dropped his hand and stepped back. He took her silent meaning and turned partly to the side to push the pants from his hips. He tossed them toward the pack and, as she went to shove his pants inside and tie it closed, he let the full shift overtake him.

Grier tried not to let her see how painful it was to transform. The cracking of his bones and popping of his extending jaw sounded loud in the quiet forest. Wings tore out of his back, ripping their way free. His feet lifted slightly off the ground before he fell forward onto all fours. His tail extended from the base of his spine and he realized he should have warned her to stay away from the spade at the end. The talons grew longer on all four limbs. His mouth made room for more sharp teeth.

Salena was slower to approach him this time. She stared at his face, eyeing the protrusions that grew like spikes from his head. Instead of touching him, she reached to pick up the pack.

Grier stepped forward, and she paused mid-reach. He took the bag in a taloned fist, not wanting her to add extra weight to her body. It would be easier for her to hold on without worry about a bag of clothes and food.

Now that he'd come closer, she lifted a trembling hand to once again touch his face, this time as a full dragon. It hovered by his mouth as if testing the heat of his breath. He lifted his head and spouted a little stream of fire so that she could see it. Grier should have warned her about that as well. He didn't want her panicking in the sky if he needed to use it.

He thought about changing back so he could explain everything better, but her look stopped him. She nodded, as if to say she understood. Her hand skimmed his face, patting his cheek, before she moved along his side. She ran her hand over his flesh. He lifted his wings, and she ducked beneath one.

Grier lowered himself toward the ground and leaned in her direction. He felt the slight weight of her body moving on top of him. She inched around, as if trying to find a position with her legs, before finally straddling his sides and taking his wings. He felt her fast breaths and pounding heart as she lay her chest flat against him.

Salena tapped his shoulder a couple of times before again gripping his wing. "I'm ready."

Grier moved his wings slowly a few times, letting her feel the movement before he pushed harder to lift off the ground. He hovered for a little while until she tapped him again. He rose up into the trees. Her legs tightened as they reached the top of the branches. His hearing picked up a little noise of what sounded like panic. Again, he hovered, concerned as he gave her time to adjust. They had given rides to the cat-shifters before, but normally the goal had been to scare them.

She tapped his wing really fast before gripping it tight to get him to move.

Grier propelled them forward at a slow pace, but still

much faster than they could have walked. He didn't take her high into the clouds. He found no reason for it. Her hand and legs held on tight, but he felt her head move from side to side as if she looked over the treetops at the distant landscape. The mountain palace was within eyesight, built into the cliff face of a small red mountain. From the distance it looked like any other cliff, crafted that way to hide what it carried within.

Grier focused on keeping a steady path, and on the movements of his passenger. The soft green light of morning had grown stronger. Jaxx had gone on ahead and he could not see him in the sky. Somewhere below the Var shifters ran to meet them.

Slow and steady, Grier repeated to himself, his body tense. *Slow and steady.*

By all the stars, she was flying.

In the air.

On a dragon.

Salena had to be crazy. Insanity was a viable explanation as to why she'd agreed to this.

Her heart pounded so hard that she found it difficult to draw a satisfying breath. The cold of the wind whipped around her, causing her to shiver. It never occurred to her that flying would feel so cold. Or that they would be going so fast. The trees moved in a blur, almost nauseating to stare at directly. It was entirely possible she would have chosen Jaxx's unconscious ride dangling by her foot over this complete awareness.

Her eyes dried from the rush of air and she closed

them. Not seeing was almost worse than seeing, so she opened them again and dealt with the discomfort.

Grier's powerful body flexed. Each beat of his wings rippled the muscles beneath her. Her fingers became numb from gripping him so tightly, and from the cold. They ached, but she didn't dare let go.

If insanity ever hit her again and she did this a next time, she would wear more clothes. And she'd also tell him to go slower.

She focused on a distant cliff jutting out of the trees. His wing blocked her vision in steady beats. It helped the nausea to watch something that didn't appear to be flying by at a breakneck pace. The faint shape of a tower appeared to peek up from the top.

Qurilixen was a beautiful planet. The air was clear, with no dark trails of smoke like she'd seen on Rayvik, whose industrial sectors forced everyone to wear filters over their faces. It also lacked the overpopulated streets of Quazer and the constant sound of pampered voices. If she could choose a place to stay, this would have been high on her list. The red clay would make for fine pots if she were to take up the family business...and if the clay deposits were manageable. She'd have to build a kiln. Though strange with their rounded bark that looked as if it had bubbled up over the trunks, there were plenty of trees. She had seen bonfires burning so it could be done.

Why was she even thinking about it?

You have to wake up now, Salena.

"I know, Fiora, I know," she whispered. "I miss you."

After what felt like an eternity, Grier slowed and hovered in place. She had a hard time sitting up. Her limbs shook as she saw more of the land below. Shelter City covered the valley like a speck in the distance, so small she could conceal it from view with her hand. The Federation had not brought her by the tower, nor down the cliff stretching beyond the tower. From this angle, she could tell they had not passed too close to the city. She would have known it. And, since they hadn't climbed too far uphill, she could only guess they came from the trees stretching behind the structure with strange arches on the roof that overlooked the city.

A darker dragon than Grier's brown came up from the watchtower as if to see what they were doing. She assumed it was Jaxx waiting on them.

Her hand shook as she forced herself to let go. With her numb fingers, Salena tried tapping Grier on the shoulder. The experience had reduced her to a ragdoll. Stretching her arm out fully, Salena pointed in the direction of the Federation stronghold.

As he turned them in the sky, she saw Jaxx dive from the watchtower in the direction they had come.

He dropped out of sight. Moments later, he

reemerged and soared through the air toward them, only to come to fly beside Grier.

Salena gasped to see his speed, and it occurred to her then that Grier had not been flying fast at all.

Jaxx's eyes found her and he nodded his head slightly as if to say hello. She tried to smile but was sure the look was as frozen as she felt.

Grier avoided flying over the city as he took her in the direction she had indicated. He hovered again, and she pushed up to look around. Pointing away from the arch-covered fortress, she leaned back down. He followed her direction, moving past the city. This time, when he stopped, she tapped her knee against him. He continued to hover, so she struck harder.

Grier made a small crackling noise, communicating what he was doing to Jaxx. He stayed parallel to the ground. She leaned to the side while keeping her body pressed down to see where they went. He slowly lowered them toward a clearing.

Jaxx dove back the way he'd come, and she could only guess he was telling the cat-shifters where to go. He disappeared from view, only to return, flying ahead of them to dive at the ground, rotating at the last minute to land.

Salena rocked as they touched down. Her legs were weak, and she slid more than climbed from his back. She

landed with a stumble and moved toward his face.
Lifting her hands, she felt his warm breath against them.
He could set her on fire right now and she would be
grateful.

As the feeling gradually came back, she dropped her
hands and turned to see Jaxx standing naked. He'd
covered his manhood with his hands to hide it from
view. Smiling, he asked, "Mind throwing me my
clothes?"

Grier had released the bag. His body trembled and
contracted as he shifted.

Salena opened the bag and dug through it. Grier's
shirt unrolled, and she saw a soft glow. It was the crystal
he'd been wearing.

She glanced at him to see his limbs lengthening. The
transformation process looked like it hurt, and yet neither
dragon acted as if it bothered them. She couldn't imagine
her bones breaking and her body expanding to create a
new form.

She quickly rewrapped the crystal. A feeling of
regret filled her. He clearly hadn't wanted anyone to
know he carried it.

Salena found Jaxx's clothes and tossed them toward
him while keeping her eyes averted. She picked up
Grier's shirt, careful to keep it rolled, and the rest of his
clothing and carried it to him.

She couldn't meet his eyes as she handed him the clothing.

"They must be landing in Var territory and crossing the border," Jaxx said, looking around. "There is nothing in this direction but trees and marsh farmers. That's why no one reported anything or took it seriously if they did. Marsh farmers are a strange lot, passed out drunk around their stills more often than not."

"Roderic mentioned something once about off-world nef trade picking up." Grier had dressed and was pulling on his boots. "He said they've been getting a lot more space traffic than usual. I wouldn't be surprised if the Federation lands at the same time as trade ships to mask their entry. No one would detect the extra ship if they weren't paying close attention."

"Or if they were paid not to notice." Salena averted her eyes as she observed the bulge of the bracelet in his pocket. What wasn't noticeable before was glaringly obvious now. "What's nef? Another ore?"

"No, nef is a specialized drink the cat-shifter marsh farmers make. It has a calming effect," Grier said.

"I hear rustling," Jaxx said. "That must be Payton and Roderic. I'll see if I can find them. Stay here."

When his cousin left, Grier moved in front of Salena. He stood close, forcing her to look at him. "I scared you."

"No," she answered, only to tell the truth. "Well, a

little."

"I am sorry for that." Heat radiated off him, causing her to shiver. Pheromones seemed to drift from him, real or imagined it didn't matter. Her skin tingled. Seeing his many powerful forms had an effect on her.

"I thought you were going super-fast until I saw Jaxx whiz by." She gave a nervous laugh, trying not to think of his crystal. Or his eyes. Or the warmth drawing her in. Or the memory of his kiss. Or... "Now I must thank you for taking it slow."

Her eyes dipped again to his pocket and then away. She'd meant flying slowly, but the words seemed to have a different connotation.

"What do we have here, boys? I'd call this a jackpot." A raspy laugh followed the words.

Grier grabbed Salena and flung her behind him so fast that she nearly fell.

"Why don't you shift for us, animal?" the raspy man continued. "We don't eat human."

Salena gagged. She leaned to the side to see what they were up against. Three men in tattered clothing spread out before them. It looked as if it had been a while since they'd had access to a decontaminator. The natural discoloration that came down their temples in stripes gave away that they were from Cysgod. Two carried a long, curved knife each and the third a bow and arrow.

"Put the kukris and bow down, and leave," Grier ordered. "I don't want to shift and hurt you."

The men laughed. "All right, shifter, we'll go, but only if you show us what you're hiding behind your back."

"No," Grier denied.

Salena stepped out and lifted her hands to the side, hoping she had been close enough to force them to speak the truth. She doubted it. At a distance it could take a moment for the ability to take effect. But it was worth a try. "You've seen me. Now go."

"We lied," the man answered, his eyes fixed on her. His two buddies didn't speak. "We're going to kill your friends and take you home with us. There's money in both prospects, and we aim to collect."

And there it was. Sometimes she really hated her ability.

"Friends?" Salena asked.

"Salena, go." Grier didn't give them time to answer as he tried to jerk her out of harm's way. He tossed her behind him. "Run!"

An arrow buzzed her arm. She ran into the woods but stopped when she realized Grier wasn't running with her. The thud of loud contact caused her to look back. She'd gone too far and couldn't see him.

Seeing a large branch hanging by a sliver of wood

from an old tree, she kicked at it several times until it broke free. Lifting it like a club, she returned to the fray. Two of the men surrounded Grier in his dragon-man form. They wielded the knives, striking at him, the blades hitting the armor of his dragon skin.

"Get him," the raspy man ordered when it became clear that they were not going to win against the dragon. He swung his weapon, but Grier deflected the blow. "Shoot him."

The attacker with the arrow drew back the bow and took aim. Grier struck the silent knife wielder with his arm, sending the man flying across the clearing into a cluster of low branches. His head and limbs became lodged in the tree at a strange angle. If he was dead, Salena thought it an appropriate ending for such an unsavory character.

Salena lifted her club and ran at the man with the bow. She swung as she neared him. He turned at the last moment and his arrow shot wide. The club landed in his side, doubling him over. She lifted it again, and swung downward, screaming as she landed another blow on top of him. She repeated the swing, crying out each time she felt the thud of wood against flesh.

"Let him go," a voice ordered.

The man lay unconscious beneath her. His bow was broken by her swings. She breathed hard, still clutching the weapon. Grier had the leader by the throat. The Cysgodian kicked in the air as he unsuccessfully clawed at the dragon-man's hand.

Salena lifted the club and ran to where the third attacker had landed in the trees. By the sounds, he was not dead. He was trying to fight his way out of the thick branches.

"I said let him go!" The sound came from her left. She stopped mid-swing, but kept her club aimed at the man in the branches.

Salena found the fourth man. He had Jaxx before him with a knife to his human throat.

"Did they hurt you?" Jaxx's eyes shifted color, but he did not change into a dragon. She wondered why. He could have certainly escaped the man's hold.

Grier growled. He threw the man by his throat toward his fallen comrade struggling in the trees. They made a sickening thud as they crashed into each other and then fell into a tangled mass in the branches.

"Salena?" Jaxx called.

Salena still held the club in mid-air.

"Stop talking," the attacker ordered Jaxx. He had stringy brown hair and was just as dirty as his fallen friends. Two scars crossed over his cheek to create an X. To Salena, he ordered, "Put down the stick."

"Jaxx?" Grier asked.

"There are more in the forest," Jaxx warned.

Salena breathed hard. She forced her hands to open, so the branch fell to the ground. Blood stained the end of it where she'd hit the archer.

"Shift back," X ordered Grier. "Or I cut him."

Salena stared at Jaxx, willing him to shift and end this.

When Grier didn't listen, X pressed the knife to Jaxx's throat. Blood trailed down his neck to stain his shirt. Grier let the hard armor of his body return to human flesh.

"Raimon, Partha, get out of that tree." X withdrew his knife slightly, but Jaxx's wound continued to bleed. "Pick up Bharath."

Salena flexed her hands. She wished she was fast enough to grab the branch and disarm the man holding Jaxx hostage. She looked toward Grier for a sign of what he was thinking. The trees rustled as Raimon and Partha freed themselves. Red marks that would most likely form into horrible bruises marred their features.

"Why are you doing this?" Salena demanded. "We haven't done anything to you?"

Raimon and Partha lifted Bharath from the ground and dragged him between them as they moved to stand behind X. They lowered the fallen man to the ground.

Salena felt guilty for her part in his injuries, but not for trying to protect Grier from attack.

X made a strange noise, the sound a half laugh, half grumble. "People do what they must to each other. And what we must do is take care of our own. If that means harming others, so be it."

"If it's food you want, we can get you food," Grier said. "There is a better way."

"We want a lot of things," X exclaimed, as if he spoke to an entire congregation of invisible people. "To eat, to live, to leave, to be free of this hell that we're trapped in. We want our planet back, our homes. Not all of us asked to come here to be lorded over by soldiers and taunted by shifters. We want what we were promised. We want what all of you refuse to give us. What we don't need is more empty assurances. Our families can't eat promises."

Raimon and Partha grunted in agreement.

The second X's knife hand wavered, Jaxx punched his fist back over his shoulder and struck the man's nose. "Well, we tried."

The blade sliced through Jaxx's arm as he pivoted to be free. X Fumbled the knife and instantly dove to pick it back up. Within seconds, the cousins shifted into dragon form, ready to fight. Salena scrambled for her branch and lifted it, prepared if the opportunity provided itself.

The Cysgodians had lost the advantage. They could not fight two dragon-men. Jaxx swept his leg and knocked X off his feet when the man tried to stab him with the blade.

Grier leapt over the heads of the other two, disrupting whatever thoughts had been going on in their heads. He punched both fists at once, hitting Raimon and Partha at the same time. They crumbled to the ground, dazed but not unconscious.

"Enough," one of the men mumbled from the ground. "No more, please, no more."

"What do you want to do?" Jaxx asked Grier, holding X up by the back of his shirt. That man, too, was dazed.

"Feed them," Grier stated. "It should have never come to this."

Salena dropped her branch.

"Leave them where aid can find them," Grier continued. "These men cannot be blamed for their desperation, and the beating they received will be a fitting lesson. I bet they'll think twice before taking on dragons in the future."

"Grab your friend," Jaxx ordered Raimon and Partha. "Let's go. March."

The sound of running feet prompted Salena to retrieve her weapon. Payton and Roderic burst from the trees. Salena sighed in relief to see it wasn't another threat.

Payton stopped when she saw Jaxx with his prisoner. She roared.

"I'd do what she says," Jaxx warned.

Raimon and Partha scrambled to grab hold of Bharath.

Payton lowered her tiger head as she stalked behind them. She gave a low growl in the back of her throat as if ordering them to walk.

Bharath came too and mumbled, "Did we win?"

Salena hurried to Grier. He shifted to human form and pulled her close.

"Are you injured?" he asked.

"Are you?" She tried to search him for wounds.

He cupped her cheek, turning her face toward him to focus her attention. "I told you to run."

"And you stayed behind." Salena furrowed her brow. "That makes no sense. Either we both run, or we both fight."

"If I didn't know better, I would think you were a dragon." He leaned closer as if to kiss her. Salena's eyes began to drift closed.

"I'll just grab my clothes," Roderic said behind her. "Ignore the naked man. Carry on."

The interruption ruined the moment. Her body

stung with frustration. Grier's hand dropped from her cheek.

"What was that all about?" Roderic asked. "They couldn't have gotten here from the city so fast. They had to be in the woods already. What were they doing out here?"

"My best guess? Hunting for food," Grier said.

Salena kept her back to him, not wanting to turn too early and catch Roderic naked. Her hands shook in the aftermath of what had happened. First flying and then being attacked. She had thought the Federation was the only thing she needed to worry about.

"Why didn't Jaxx shift and stop them sooner?" she asked. "Why didn't you? They were no match for the dragon."

Grier sighed. "I wanted you to run, so you'd be safe because neither Jaxx nor I wanted to hurt those men. The fact they are out here and willing to take on a shifter speaks to their desperation. Jaxx knew shifting would only escalate the fight as did I. We wanted a chance to reason with them before we hurt them."

"Another byproduct of the Federation complications," Roderic added. "This situation cannot hold much longer. One tilt of this delicate scale and I'm afraid we'll be at war."

13

A MAN WHO HAD NOTHING TO LOSE WAS A dangerous creature indeed.

Grier had suspected for a long time that the tension building over Shelter City would soon reach a bursting point. This attack appeared to be the first seepage of something bigger. He imagined there to be a giant pustule, throbbing over the city with invisible anger and fear. He had seen the desperation in those men's faces. They had a wildness to their eyes, the kind of mindless, helpless rage people felt when nothing in life was under their control.

"I always miss the fun. You couldn't have left one of them for me to play with?" Payton walked ahead of them next to Jaxx and Roderic. Grier knew she joked.

His cousin had a strip torn off the bottom of his

tunic. It had been bound around his arm to stop the bleeding. It wasn't a severe wound and would heal fast. The cut on his neck had already closed. One of the benefits of shifting was fast healing times for external injuries. Shifter bodies were used to changing, and that appeared to speed up recovery times when compared to other humanoids.

"Does any of this look familiar, Salena?" Payton asked.

Salena turned in a slow circle before catching up with Grier. She shook her head. "It's hard to say. All the trees look the same."

"You pointed for me to come this way. What made you think this was the place? Start there and work your way back through the trip." Grier put his hand on her shoulder and locked eyes with her.

"I know we had to come from this direction because of where we entered the facility. It's why I went toward the watchtower when I escaped. I didn't want to go in the direction I knew they had come from in case there were more of them traveling through there."

"Before you reached the building, what were you doing?" He kept his gaze on hers, willing her to remember, but also mesmerized by the color of her eyes. He found himself focusing on them, taking in each tiny line of color in their depths.

"We traveled for about a day and a half. The land craft flew relatively straight for maybe a fourth of the day before we reached the end of the journey. Before that we were winding along a path that looked flat and worn, but an old worn, like it hadn't been walked on for some time and small plants were beginning to overtake it. Before that I heard some roaring, but I can't tell you what it was, maybe machinery, maybe a ship, maybe water on stone, wind in a cave? I couldn't see much. They had me sitting on the floor of the craft most of the time, but I felt the swaying and heard the roar. I'm not sure before that. When we first landed, I slept hard. They might have given me a tranquilizer before I left the ship."

"What type of land craft was it?" Payton asked.

"Basic. Open top so I could see the trees and feel the air, but deep so when I sat down I couldn't look over the sides," Salena answered.

"We're near Var territory," Payton said. "A day and a half of land craft travel would be well across the border. Someone might have seen them traveling through."

"I was thinking the same thing," Roderic said. "With the production of nef on the rise, the marsh farmers are expanding operations beyond the shadowed marshes."

"Unfortunately, marsh farmers do not make the most reliable lookouts." Payton flung her arm around her cousin's shoulders. "But they do make reliable liquor."

"Don't let Prince Falke hear that," Jaxx warned. "He'll ban all liquor on the planet if he thinks his baby girl is partying with the farmers."

"She's telling stories," Roderic said, dismissing Payton's claim. "Payton, you've never drank in the marshes."

Payton snorted.

"What are the shadowed marshes?" Salena asked.

"Essentially swampland," Jaxx said. "Marshes with trees. I think our ancestors were confused when they first translated the word to the Old Star language."

"Close enough." Payton gave a small wave of dismissal. "Our planet. We can call it whatever we want."

"So marsh farmers are just people who come from the marshlands?" Salena asked.

"Whose families have farmed the marshes for centuries," Payton corrected.

"We never knew him, but by all accounts, our grand-father was a bit of a..." Roderic paused.

"Slargnot?" Payton offered.

"Yeah, that." Roderic gave a small laugh. "King Attor commissioned a biological weapon that nearly killed the shadowed marshes and the farmers began to migrate. It's how my parents met. My mother an ESC scientist who came to clean up the mess.

But that's old history, and the land has since recovered."

"Mostly," Payton mumbled.

"Yeah, mostly," Roderic agreed.

"Attor was the late Var king," Grier explained.

"And what is a slargnot?" Salena asked.

"Um, blackhole, waste of air, space cadet," Roderic tried to explain.

"And insult," Grier said.

"Someone who might as well be wearing their ass on their head because they're an idiot," Payton added.

"Got it," Salena said.

"The farmers are still a little bitter about it all," Roderic continued. "They don't like royals in their business. I guess my point is, if we're crossing into Var territory here, we need to be on the lookout for the farmers. They're usually drunk, ornery, and overly protective of their stills. We should avoid them if possible."

"Want us to airlift you?" Jaxx offered.

"No," Roderic and Payton answered in unison.

"I don't think I'd recognize anything from the air," Salena said.

"Then we walk." Grier tried to give her an encouraging smile. He'd felt her trembling against his back as they flew and did not want to frighten her unnecessarily by making her go back up.

"Do you think that man I hit will be all right?" Salena asked, her voice lower than before. She focused her eyes on the ground in front of her.

Grier didn't like that she'd run back to help him. Yes, he liked the fact she cared for him enough to do it, but not that she was put in harm's way. He was supposed to be the one protecting her. Not the other way around.

"I don't know, but he was waking up so that is a good sign," Grier answered. "If they're smart, they'll take him to the Federation facility to use the medical booth."

"Does the Federation have a booth for the citizens to use?" Salena seemed surprised by this.

"Yes, for accidents and such," Grier said.

"They have to keep up appearances," Jaxx added.

"Aren't you worried they'll report how the beating happened?" Salena's arm brushed his as she walked unconsciously closer. She instantly righted her course to put distance between them.

"That they were out in the woods past the city borders hunting their shifter neighbors? No, I don't think they'll admit to being outside city limits. It's against the rules." Grier placed a hand on her shoulder. "You did what you had to. They made their choice. They attacked us."

"I know." She nodded. "I don't regret hitting him, but that doesn't mean I want his death on my list of sins."

"You keep a list of your sins?" Payton asked. Grier heard the playful tone in her voice, but she always sounded like that. He sometimes wondered if she took anything seriously, or if life was just one bored joke after another for her.

"It is something my father used to say. At the end, we're all judged by our list of sins whether they were intentional or not." Salena rubbed the back of her neck, looking up as she rolled her head to the side.

"I like that," Jaxx said. "Nice and simple."

"You wouldn't think that if everyone was constantly listing their sins to you," Salena mumbled.

"Yeah, I suppose I wouldn't." Jaxx nodded but didn't turn around to look at her. "That must be a heavy burden and one I do not envy."

Grier detected there was more to what Jaxx was saying and wondered what his cousin meant by that. When no one elaborated, he asked, "You mean when you interrogate people? Yes, I can see how that would be difficult."

"What else would she mean?" Jaxx turned around but kept walking in the same direction. He took back-ward steps, not watching where he was going. He gave Salena a thoughtful look. "Has anything ever surprised you?"

"When it first happened. I can say I was surprised

when the village elder told me he'd rather marry his wife's mother." Salena wrinkled her nose.

"That doesn't sound so bad," Jaxx said. "I mean, it's bad, but it's hardly the worst you could have heard him confess."

"I was seven years old, and he went into graphic detail as to why. That is how I learned about conception." Salena's tone was matter-of-fact, but he saw how her muscles tensed as if ready to ward off what might come her way. He wondered if she fought a memory.

Anger rolled through him as the full meaning of her words sank in—not anger at her, but anger for the childhood she had lived. He grabbed her arm gently and turned her to look at him. Every time he saw her eyes gazing at him, it became harder to pull away from her. He felt the pulsing crystal in his pocket, sending wave after wave of longing into him. Its energy was growing stronger, or perhaps it was all in his mind. Either way, the effects were real.

"What?" Her gaze darted to the side though she didn't turn her head to look. "Are we being watched? Do you hear someone? Do we need to run?"

"I do not wish to speak ill of your parents," he stated. The wind appeared to pick up, rustling the leaves. It pushed her scent against him. Everything about her was pure torture.

She arched a brow, confused. "Then...*don't?*"

"But it must be said. Why would they send a seven-year-old girl to interrogate an adult male with obviously questionable morals? Wives and children are to be protected and cherished. I would never let my daughter be alone with a man we wished to interrogate."

"Wow. That's freaky. You sound exactly like my father," Payton stated dryly. "Now tell her she needs to dress like a lady."

Grier realized the other three had stopped to watch them.

"It's not like they asked me to do it. I just...did it." Salena shrugged.

Grier loosened his hold on her arms. "You wanted to know about the elders', um...? I don't understand."

"Sure you do, Grier. Stop being insensitive." Jaxx frowned at him and lifted his hands as if to silently ask what he was doing. "It's not like she can help it."

"Help what?" Grier glanced between Salena and Jaxx.

Salena opened her mouth to speak but appeared confused, and in the end said nothing.

"What am I not seeing?" he demanded.

"The obvious," Payton drawled.

"Gods' bones, Grier, you do realize she can't help it, don't you?" Jaxx asked. "It's not something to turn on and off like a switch. Certainly you noticed that you have been unable to hold anything back when she is around. If she asks you something directly, you *have* to answer, no matter how mean or blunt that response may be. If someone else asks you something in her presence, it's a little easier to resist, but you still feel compelled to tell the truth, and you definitely can't lie."

Grier chuckled. "Nice try."

"Sacred cats, you're a daft one, Grier," Payton muttered with a small laugh. "Try telling her a lie."

"Why would I want to lie to her?" Grier answered the Var princess as he studied Salena's serious expression. "I have no reason to keep secrets from her. I am meant to be with her."

"Let's give them a moment." Jaxx pulled Roderic and Payton with him down the path only to stop several feet away.

"I'm sorry," she whispered. "I don't want to cause discord between all of you."

"You can't shut off your ability?" Grier asked. "Is that true? Olena said you could pull the truth from people, but I didn't realize it wasn't voluntary."

"I wish I could shut it off." Her eyes kept moving over his face as if searching for answers. "You really didn't notice that you had to tell me the truth? People normally realize that within three minutes of talking to me."

"It never occurred to me to try to lie to you." Grier hadn't noticed. He found no reason to keep secrets from her. If the gods used the glowing crystal to tell him he could trust her, then he would do so. They would not lead him astray.

"I don't think anyone has ever said that to me," Salena said. "Everyone tries to hide something."

"I'll tell you anything you want to know." He smiled. "Ask anything. For you, my life is an open book. There are no secrets."

Her eyes dipped down to his pocket where the crystal was hidden. His breath caught. He was sure she was going to say something about it.

"Federation, drunk farmers, angry citizens." Salena glanced around at the trees. "Are there any other threats out here?"

Grier heard the sound of voices in the distance. Roderic, Jaxx, and Payton must have heard it too, because they stopped walking and tilted their head in the same direction.

"Yes," Grier, Roderic, and Jaxx said at the same time.

"Probably." Payton gestured away from the voices. "We should go this way."

"What is it?" Salena reached for him. He looked

down in surprise and squeezed her fingers lightly to keep her from pulling away.

"Men talking," Grier said. "We're going around to avoid them."

Payton glanced over her shoulder. Seeing their linked hands, she grinned and nodded.

They walked in silence. Grier kept his attention on the muffled sound of talking until it faded. It had been just far enough away that he had not been able to make out any of the words. Whoever was in the forest, he didn't want to meet up with them.

14

Salena stared up at the sky. The light had softened, but it was still there. She didn't think she'd ever get used to constant daylight. She missed the safety of darkness. Right now, camping in the woods left them exposed to anyone who might happen by. She'd much rather be hidden.

"Are you sure I can't fly you somewhere more comfortable?" Grier sat next to her. They'd found a shaded spot where the plant life padded the ground. "We can return to look for the roaring sound you heard in the morning."

As nice as a bed sounded, it meant she would have to fly two more times.

"The ground is perfect," she said. It wasn't a lie. By comparison, it was better than flying.

Payton handed her a thin blanket out of the pack before dropping the bag on the ground by Salena. "This might help."

Salena nodded in thanks as she took the blanket.

"It's been a long time since we've all been camping." Roderic smiled, as if caught in his memories. He laughed and rubbed the back of his neck. "Long time."

Salena could have forced him to elaborate, but she didn't ask. Roderic pulled his shirt over his head and tossed it next to the bag, followed by his boots.

"Until the morning," he said as he walked behind a tree. His pants came flying toward her a few moments later, and she knew he was going to spend the night shifted. Salena automatically reached for his clothes and began folding them into a stack.

"You don't have to do that," Grier said. "We don't expect you to pick up after us."

"I don't mind. Small tasks give me the feeling of normality." She glanced up at Payton. "Do you sleep shifted as well?"

"Much more comfortable that way." Payton tugged at her boots. "People hesitate before messing with a giant sleeping cat, more so than they do a human."

"Don't let her scare you," Jaxx said. He also began to undress. "This forest should be safe and we'll all be around to listen for danger. If you need us, yell, and we'll fly—"

"Run," Payton inserted.

"Fly back," Jaxx finished.

Salena nodded. When they were alone, she said to Grier, "It's nice that both kingdoms live in peace together since you're neighbors."

"It wasn't always that way." He laid his forearm across a bended knee and let his hand suspend between them. He seemed unapologetic in the way he stared at her. The intensity of his eyes caused her to shiver. There was something about this man, a virile, raw power that had tried to consume her from the moment she first saw him by the tents. If life had been different, if *she* were different, there would have been so many possibilities with Grier. As it was, helping him to find the location of the Federation drop-off was the only thing she could do to earn her passage off the planet. Then she would not be in their debt and the jewels would be returned to Olena.

"I almost forgot." Salena dug into the pocket of her skirt and pulled out the pouch. "Would you give these to Princess Olena for me? I don't want to forget and take them. I prefer to earn my passage by helping you." She gave a small laugh. "And I admit, it will be nice to land a few blows to the Federation's plans."

"If she gave them to you, she'll want you to have them." Grier didn't try to take the jewels.

Salena placed them in the bag. "I insist. Already the kindness I have been shown is too much. I cannot in good conscience ask for more."

"How can kindness be too much?" Grier glanced at the bag before turning to her once more. He didn't appear to care about the jewels. His fingers moved lazily where they hung in the air as if touching something she couldn't see.

"I suppose when you're not used to it, you notice it more and do not wish to take advantage of those giving it." Salena gave a small shrug. "Ignore that. When I said it, I could hear how self-indulgent I sounded."

"Has kindness been so rare in your life?" His eyes held concern, but not pity. For that she was grateful.

"My parents were kind, but strict. My sisters were wonderful. We were very close." She smiled to remember them and would give almost anything to have just a moment back in the clay pits, digging in the ground beside them. "My mother made the most beautiful pottery. She had delicate fingers. My father helped her refine the clay and fire them in the kiln. Then he'd take us to town so we could help him sell the wares to incoming travelers. She was famous for her work, in our little area of the galaxy anyway. After our abilities started emerging, we didn't go to town as much."

"Abilities? Your sisters are like you?" he asked.

"Yes, they are—*were*? I'm honestly not sure what happened to them. I tried to find out but every story I heard did not have a good ending. I fear they are lost forever." Salena hadn't talked about her family in a long time, not like this. "Piera can read people by looking at them. She said it was like seeing colors emanating from their body when their emotions or intent was heightened. One look across a crowded room and she could tell you who was nice, mean, mad, evil, happy, scared, anything. There is more to her abilities than that. She sees things, ghost images almost, like shadows showing her things."

"And your other sister?"

"Fiora is my opposite. I get the truth from people, and she gives the truth to people. She'll divine things, events, stuff that has yet to happen or has happened, and feels compelled to speak about it. However, we devised a game where instead of just telling whatever it was she knew, she'd say it in riddles, so everyone who tried using her to predict things was always confused and irritated by the end of her telling. When we are by each other, the abilities become more sensitive and are amplified."

"How do they work?" he asked.

Salena pressed her lips together and shook her head with a small shrug. "I don't know. Pheromones? Brainwaves? Magic? That's one of the things the Federation would like to find out. When I'm not interrogating for them, they want to poke around my head to see if my ability can be replicated." Her hands trembled, and she felt moisture gathering in her eyes. She closed them, willing tears not to fall. "I can't live like that. I don't want to hurt people. I don't want to be hurt. Anything is better than being used like that."

"I assume you can lie to people, even if they can't lie to you?" he asked.

Salena nodded. "But I'm not lying."

"I know," he said, even though there was no way he could know for sure that she spoke the truth. "I want to thank you for telling me when you did not have to. I will guard your secrets and cherish your trust in leaving them with me."

Were these dragon-men for real? For a moment, she wondered if this was a hallucination and she was really on the Federation's operating table being poked and prodded.

Feeling a pebble digging uncomfortably into her ass, she determined things were a little too real to be drug induced. At least she hoped so.

"Are you going to shift and sleep like the others?" she wondered.

"No. I would rather stay close to you if you will allow it." His hand dropped from his knee to rest on the ground beside him.

Salena looked at his strong fingers and inched her hand closer. "I'd like that."

Their fingers touched but it might as well have been her entire body. She felt him against her, as if somehow their souls had escaped to be near each other. It was a fanciful notion, but that didn't make the sensation any less real.

"What happened to your sisters? How were you separated?"

I'm sure that we should run, Fiora's voice whispered through her memories.

I can see that we should stay, Piera's answered.

"I hesitated. That's what happened. I hesitated, and they found us."

"Who found you?" His hand slipped on top of hers, causing her to shiver under the warmth of his touch.

"Local thugs working for politicians. We were playing and ran into a rally in the woods. It wasn't on purpose. We knew better than to go around townsfolk. Suddenly the politicians started confessing a bunch of random sins in front of everyone. The villagers became angry, and the politicians blamed us. It was the final straw. When our parents refused to allow them to take us away to what they called a private school facility—which they ended up confessing was just whichever trade ship would take us first—they came back and killed them. We were sleeping in our room under the house. When we heard my father's boots pounding above, we knew we had to run, so we hid in the forest. And then I hesitated. We were caught and separated. I never saw them again."

"It's not your fault." His hand slid up her forearm and back down in a comforting gesture.

"It's sweet that you believe that, but I was there. I know what happened. I was the one who wanted to run in the forest. We were sixteen, foolish, and thought the woods were our domain. I should have known better. Later, I was the one who hesitated. If I had done anything other than freeze, we would have been safe."

"You were a girl," he countered.

"Hardly," she said. "It's not like I'll live to be five hundred years old. By Noire customs I was already a woman."

"You might if you stayed here with me. I'd share my lifespan with you." His eyes dipped down to her mouth. "I want you to stay with me."

"I can't." She wanted to, but it would be cruel to tell

him as much when she couldn't stay. But there was something she *could* do, something she could remember later.

Salena pulled her hand from under his and touched his bearded cheek. Hopefully this time the others wouldn't interrupt them. She pushed up on her knees and moved closer.

Salena brushed his hair out of his face. He was beautiful to look at, strong and proud, but he had kind eyes and a raw, primitive energy. She traced his lip, feeling the firm texture of it against the pad of her fingertip. His warm breath moved over her hands.

"I want you," he whispered. "Every time you touch me, I want you more."

With him, she definitely did not mind the flow of honesty when he spoke. "I want you too."

She kissed him, drawing her mouth against his in a gentle caress. His beard tickled, and she smiled.

A strong hand moved along her hip as he rolled her onto her back. The soft natural bed cushioned her as his weight pressed down. It was enough that she could feel him, but not so much that it hurt. She felt safe, unafraid of the light or the woods. She knew he would protect her with his life.

Even though he didn't say that, she knew. It was an overwhelming feeling.

Air hit her leg as he pulled at her skirt. Her body

ached, and she didn't want to wait. Every moment since they'd met had felt like foreplay, and she couldn't take much more. She gasped, arching into him. His arousal pressed into her, letting her feel how much he desired this. She reached for his hip, desperate to feel flesh. Her hand found what it was looking for, and she massaged her fingers along his naked ass. His lips moved to her neck.

His weight dropped down, crushing her. At first, she didn't mind, but when he didn't ease up, she tapped his hip. "Grier."

His lips stopped.

Was he...*sleeping?*

"Grier?" She ran her fingers into his hair and lifted his head to look at his face. His eyes were dazed, and he blinked heavily. "Grier, what's wrong?"

Salena wiggled until his weight slid to the side but his body pinned her clothes to the ground, still trapping her. She took a deep breath. A metallic dart poked from his shoulder.

Fear propelled her into action. She yanked the dart from him and moved with renewed purpose. She struggled to get her tangled skirts free so that she could protect Grier from whatever was happening.

She managed to turn onto her side and begin pulling at her skirt as she crawled free. Feet came from above and landed in front of her. She gasped, lifting her arms to the side to shield Grier.

"Get back," she ordered.

Her answer came in the form of a sharp sting in her chest. She blinked in surprise, her head instantly dizzy as she looked down. A dart stuck out from beneath her collarbone. The sight pulled forth a painful memory, and the drugs confused her thoughts. She wanted to pull it out, but her hands did not obey her brain as her arms dropped, lifeless.

A man snorted. "I told you it was..."

Salena's mind fell into darkness.

15

"WE HAVE TO RUN NOW," FIORA WHISPERED.

Salena didn't want to run as she clutched her sisters' hands. They were safe in the dark where the monsters couldn't see. She didn't want to run. She didn't want to be here.

The small pit where they had dug clay smelled familiar and safe. She wanted the firm ground beneath her bare feet to pull her in. This was home. She knew nothing else.

They knew nothing else.

"No. They'll find us if we run." Piera tugged her hand from Salena's and rubbed her eyes as if that gesture could erase all that she had seen. "We have to stay here."

"I'm sure that we should run," Fiora argued under her breath. Blood dried on her forehead but was still moist enough in places that it reflected hints of light when she moved.

"I can see that we should stay." Piera had mud caked along her arm from where she'd fallen.

"Salena?" they both whispered in unison, staring at her as they forced her to be the deciding vote.

Her unsettling dreams turned to blurred daylight as Salena was jerked awake. The lingering feel of her sisters' hands caused her palms to tingle until she realized she had balled her hands into tight fists. The ground moved beneath her body so quickly that she bounced. Her feet were elevated over her head as she lay on her back. It took a moment to find her bearings as she struggled to move.

She'd been tied to a travois with her wrists, ankles, and waist bound with rope to keep her in position. A cloth had been tied around her mouth, pulled so tight that it was between her teeth and against her tongue. It absorbed the moisture from her mouth and replaced it with the taste of dirt.

A man's large hands enveloped the poles by her feet as he dragged her behind him. He jogged through the forest, keeping a fast pace. His clothing was a bastardized version of what she'd seen the cat-shifters wear. It hung on his frame with small tears along the seams. The cross-laces had been frayed to the point they'd been torn apart and retied in a few places. They held his tunic together but were loose at the bottom where they swung against his hips with each step.

Her heartbeat quickened, and she blinked as tears rolled down her temples into her hair. Hard bits of debris and rocks ran along her back as she was pulled over them. Fear made her desperate to escape, but it also made it hard to rationalize how. This wasn't the Federation. If it had been, she'd know what they wanted from her.

Cysgodian? Marsh farmer? Var recluse? A new threat she hadn't thought of? It didn't really matter. In the end, she was under someone else's control.

We have to run now, Fiora's voice whispered through her mind, brought forth from her nightmares. *Salena, run.*

Being at a downward angle caused uncomfortable pressure in her head. She tried to kick, but the straps kept her foot locked into place and all she did was rock to the side. The man didn't even turn around to check. That's how little of a threat he thought her.

All her life, she'd been feared for what she might reveal but dismissed as a threat otherwise. Her would-be controllers were wrong to dismiss her. Salena wasn't going to wait around for Grier to save her. She might lack the natural physical strength of a man, but she was smart.

She might not be able to knock a guy out with her fist, but she could swing a club.

With that in mind, she began tugging at her wrists, testing to see if she could force a hand to slip free. She used the rhythm of her captor's gait to pull, keeping her eyes on him lest he became annoyed with her rocking and turned around. He didn't.

Pain shot up her wrists as she pressed her thumb toward her pinkie. The friction hurt, but better scraped wrists than whatever lies at the end of this journey.

"*Aah!*" A larger rock slammed into her back right beneath her shoulder blade, sending her off the ground only to crash-land seconds later. She cried out again. The blow was enough to help yank a hand free. However, her cry caught the attention of her captor.

Actually, *captors*.

The man dragging her glanced back and grunted to see her free hand. She pulled at the cloth tied around her mouth, but it wouldn't budge.

"Watch the cargo." A second man appeared within her eyesight as he dropped back to run behind her. He gave her a creepy little smile as he passed, and his eyes flashed with the glint of a shifter.

Until that moment, she hadn't realized there was anyone else there. She tried to lean up to look and glimpsed a third man leading the way. By their clothes, she could safely assume they were cat-shifters. Perhaps that is how none of the others had detected their being near the campsite.

Salena felt the rocks at her back and reached her hand to the side without stretching out her arm. A stone hit her palm. She tried to grab it but missed. She attempted a few more times before finally getting one. She turned her hand toward her skirt to hide it and waited to see if the man behind her would say something and was surprised that he hadn't noticed her grab it.

Salena craned her neck to look behind her. Seeing the shifter studying the nearby trees, she launched the rock as hard as she could over her head. He was close enough that she was able to smack him in the face and send him into a dazed stumble.

This time she wasn't subtle as she rummaged for another rock. Her transporter slowed. Finding a second stone, she lifted her arm so she'd be ready to hit the transporter in the face the moment he turned.

"You bloody *gwobr*!" The injured shifter seized her wrist from behind at the same time her transporter dropped his poles. Her feet crashed to the ground, and the momentum allowed her to wrench her sore wrist free from his grasp while still holding the second rock.

It didn't matter that three of her limbs were immobile. Salena had one arm, and she was going to use it.

Holding the rock like a weapon, she swung it back. She heard a thud as it made contact. She struck blindly, unable to land another blow. Seeing her transporter coming for her, she screamed against the gag and threw the rock at him. He tried to dodge, and it hit him on the neck.

"Sacred cats, what the hell are you two infants doing?" The shifter leading the pack took one look at her, and then his two comrades, before striding toward her. She flinched and covered her face with her free hand, only to detect a shadow pass by.

"Curtis, are we stop—?"

She looked in time to see the leader uppercut the smaller man, cutting off his surprised words. He flew backward out of her view, and she did not hear him get up.

"Beat up by a human. Valter's no use to us. Leave him." Curtis' eyes flashed gold as he let her see his anger. He grabbed her sore wrist and forced it back into position. He wrapped the rope around her. The pressure stung her wound. When he had finished, he lifted his fist and shook it in the air a few times in front of her face. It was a warning. "Pick up your load, Fergal. The sooner we deliver, the sooner we're paid. And make sure she doesn't get that mouthpiece loose. Her words are poisonous. We don't want her talking to us."

Fergal grabbed the poles and lifted her feet once more. Curtis turned his back on her, as if she were no more than a cart of dirt they were hauling through the woods. Her attempt at an escape might have backfired, but at least she had slightly better odds now, thanks to Curtis' temper.

16

"It was a mistake to bring her out here. I should have sent her with the pirates off this planet the second I knew the Federation wanted her." Grier rubbed his shoulder. It throbbed where he'd been hit. The only sign they had of Salena were drag marks where someone had pulled her across the ground away from him before disappearing into the woods. He stood at the end of those tracks, looking around for a clue as to where they had gone. There was no sign of her, and there was no clear idea of how long she'd been missing. By the sunlight, he could guess it had been several hours.

"Salena," he yelled. "Call out if you can hear me!"

She did not answer.

What if she is hurt?

What if she is dead?

What are they doing to her?

Why can't I detect her?

Why take her and not me?

"I've never seen these." Roderic turned the metal dart in his fingers. "They're too sophisticated for marsh farmers."

All four shifters had been hit with the darts. Whoever had done it either knew the forest well enough to slip around undetected or was some kind of elite super soldier.

Federation?

Cysgodians?

Aliens?

Var?

Farmers?

"Is it possible the farmers have a nef trade deal with the Federation?" Payton asked. "They are the only ones who would know the forest well enough to slip around undetected. Otherwise, I don't know how someone could get past four shifters."

"Or mask Salena's scent from me," Grier added. His heart beat faster, the fear filling him.

"They dislike royals, so it's possible they are trying to create their own agreements with off-worlders," Roderic answered, only to mumble under his breath, "those drunken idiots."

"Drunken *skilled* idiots," Payton corrected.

"The Federation won't harm her," Jaxx said. "They want her alive. That's good news for us. I think we head toward the city. It's our best bet."

She has to be alive.

She needs me.

I need her.

I must find her

Find her.

Salena!

Find Salena.

Grier tried to focus on what needed to be done, but it was difficult with panic tightening his chest. His flesh tingled, and he felt his skin hardening. He had promised Salena that he would protect her on this journey, and instead he'd let his emotions overrule his purpose. He'd been kissing her when he should have been guarding her.

It is no wonder the gods don't think me fit to have a wife.

Don't hurt her. Please, don't hurt her.

"We have to get her back." Grier's voice was gruff and came out a half growl. He tightened his fists. This was the same feeling of desperation he'd felt outside the marriage tents. The urge to shift built within him. The dragon wanted free.

The dragon wanted to kill.

"And we will." Payton touched his arm, and he jolted at the contact, almost swinging at her. She backed away with her hands raised before her to show she meant no harm.

"Cousin, look at me." Jaxx stood in front of him and lowered his jaw to stare intently at Grier. The man's eyes filled with gold, warning that he could shift at any time. "We all know you carry the unbroken crystal in your pocket. We know what that means, but you need to focus and keep control. You're beginning to act a little wild."

Grier breathed deeply, barely hearing him. His heart beat faster and faster. He would shift and tear the forest apart to find her. He would burn the entire area to the ground. He would—

"Well, I tried." Jaxx drew back his fist and slammed it hard into Grier's face.

The blow sent him flying onto his back. Grier skidded across the dirt. When he stopped, he looked up in surprise, blinking hard as his vision began to clear.

"Feel better?" Jaxx placed his hands on his hips but looked ready to do it again if he had to.

"Ow." Grier rubbed his jaw. "Yeah, thanks."

"Anytime." Jaxx reached out a hand to lift him from the ground.

"Did you have to hit me so hard?" Grier opened his mouth wide to stretch his sore jaw.

"Don't whine," Jaxx dismissed.

"Don't worry. I'll be sure to return the favor." Grier patted his cousin on the shoulder, hard. "But for now, let's track my woman."

"Are you sure you can't detect her?" Payton asked.

"They must have traveled a distance. Even if they masked it, I should be able to pick up her scent, but I can't." The thought caused Grier to panic. Should he take to the sky to try to see her through the thick trees? Or run along the ground where he had a better chance of detecting her?

"When did our planet become such a dangerous place?" Roderic grumbled as he searched the area. They all knew the answer to that pointless question, but Grier understood the man's frustrations.

"It was always dangerous," Payton said. "Only now, shifters are fighting together, not against each other."

"You three take the ground, I'll take the sky. Grier, you need to stay calm. Shifting won't help." Jaxx was already halfway out of his clothes as he said the words. Seconds later, his cousin was flapping his wings to surge upward.

"You two follow the tracks." Payton pulled off her shirt. "I'll run the forest and try to pick up a scent."

She ran down the path, leaping to shift. The crossties

of her pants stretched open to make room for her new body before falling away, along with her boots.

They left the bag on the ground. There was nothing in it they had to keep.

Grier moved in the direction the drag marks had been going, leaping over fallen logs and pushing through the brush. He searched right as Roderic went left.

"Anything?" Grier yelled.

"Nothing." Roderic jogged back to meet him. "This might be a longshot, but what about your crystal?"

"What about it?" Grier automatically felt his pocket where the stone was hidden.

"It seems to light in your pocket a little more when you're near Salena. It's faint, and she doesn't seem to notice it, but we can pick it up. Maybe we can use that to track her? If it glows brighter when she is—"

"It's never been done that I know of, but..." Grier dug in his pocket. The stone's glow had faded to a barely discernable light. His eyes shifted so he could detect any subtle change in its luminosity. He held it in his palm walking left, then right, then in a circle until it brightened by the smallest of degrees. "You're a genius. This way!"

Grier hurried through the woods, pausing whenever the light changed to reassess their direction. It was slower going than he would have liked, but at least it was progress.

"There." Roderic pointed at marks on the ground. The farther they went, the less the kidnappers had covered their tracks, and they became easier to follow.

As they came out of the trees to a path, he saw two distinct markings on the ground.

"Here," Roderic said. "They moved her by travois. It's most likely marsh farmers. They cart supplies like that. Wheels get stuck in the marshes, so they drag."

Both men followed the grooves in the ground. Now that he had an easier trail, Grier let the dragon take partial control. The animal gave power to his legs, allowing him to run faster. Roderic kept pace behind him. When Grier glanced at his crystal, he saw it becoming steadily brighter. They were getting closer.

Someone laid on the path ahead, arms strewn to the side and head partially hidden from view by a shrub. He couldn't see a face.

"Salena?" Grier shouted, his voice hoarse in his current state. He pushed himself harder.

Thank the gods it wasn't her.

A fallen marsh farmer was sprawled on the ground. Grier accessed the cat-shifter briefly as he ran past. He wasn't sure if it was drinking or fighting that had laid him out, for he reeked of liquor and had a bruised face. Perhaps both. Those he was with had left him behind.

The tracks continued, rutted in the ground. He ran between them, feeling with each beat of his boots against the path that he was getting closer to his heart.

Salena.

Salena.

Be safe.

I'm coming.

His thoughts were anxious, broken fragments of desperation and hope. They flowed through him, moving his lips as he mouthed his scattered prayer.

Be safe.

Salena.

He dodged tree branches and blindly took the curves in the path. She had to be close.

I'm coming.

The trail wound back and forth. The sound of the feet behind him changed as two became four. Roderic had sensed it too and shifted form.

Salena.

He swiped at a branch that hung in his way—and suddenly she was there.

She'd been strapped to a travois. Two men were turning to face him. The shifter carting Salena dropped her feet when he saw Grier approaching.

Grier leapt over her head and slammed into the cat-shifter who'd been dragging her. He didn't give the man time to shift as he threw an elbow into his neck. The blow did little to affect the farmer, and he stayed on his feet. He threw Grier to the ground.

Roderic roared, leaping forward even as Grier fell toward the ground. The cougar-shifter dodged the brute coming at Grier and took on the second man.

He wanted to look at Salena but knew he could not take his eyes off his opponent. He stayed in his half shift. This farmer was strong. If the scars marking his skin were any indication, he was also used to brawling.

"She's mine," Grier growled, trying to push up from the ground.

The brute's lips curled in a small smile. It wasn't a pleasant expression. A beefy fist came from above. Grier dropped his weight and rolled to the side before springing to his feet. The man punched the ground hard and his knuckles cracked but he made no noise as if he didn't feel pain.

The brute didn't miss a beat. He came at Grier, slashing hands that were now sharp with claws. The shift entered his eyes and by the time the cat reached him, he had mostly transformed into a lion. Grier's dragon skin stopped the claws from cutting too deep. He gripped a handful of the lion's mane and tugged hard.

The cat was all muscle and did not go down easily. They rolled over the ground. Their momentum was stopped when they hit underbrush. Teeth bore down on his forearm. Grier swung his arm as hard as he could. The lion-shifter hit the tree and his bite loosened. Grier pulled his arm free and slammed a fist into his head. Between his blow and the tree, it was enough to knock the lion out.

Grier didn't hesitate as he crawled toward Salena. Blood dripped down his arm. The wound throbbed, but he didn't care.

Salena was tied. Her wrists looked as if she'd been struggling to get free. The small scrapes on her face seemed to be superficial and would heal. Relieved eyes met his. She jerked her hands and moaned.

"Here." Roderic threw a knife as he hurried past. The blade embedded in the ground. He held a hand over his manhood as he strode to gather his clothes.

The shift seemed to melt off his skin as Grier grabbed the knife. He sliced her hands free and then her legs before helping her to sit. Salena pulled at her gag.

Grier cut the material around her mouth. She gasped and coughed, throwing the gag away from her as if it were alive.

"Thank you," she croaked, her voice hoarse.

"Forgive me." He hung his head a little. "I failed to protect you."

She rubbed her cheeks and worked her jaw. Her right hand looked worse than the left. He reached for it but stopped, not wanting to hurt her more.

"What did they do to you?" Grier wanted nothing more than to pull her into his arms and hold her.

Salena coughed again. She looked at the bite on his arm. "You're hurt."

"It's nothing." Seeing a water pouch near where her feet had been tied, he cut it from the pole and handed it to her. "Drink."

She took it and downed the whole contents. When she was finished, she gasped for breath. "If I weren't so sore, I'd hit that *gw-er* with a club, too."

"Are you trying to say *gwiddon*?"

"No, that," she pointed toward the unconscious lion, "*gwobr*."

Grier couldn't help the small laugh at her insult.

"What? They called me that first." Salena used his shoulder for support to push herself to her feet. She swayed right, to lift her ankle and roll it a few times, before leaning left to do the same with the other.

"*Gwobr* is an old insult that loosely means battle prize," Grier said.

"Well, that battle prize is lucky I don't have a stick right now," she blustered. "And that he's unconscious."

The sound of paws announced Payton in white tiger form before she showed herself. She skidded to a stop on all fours, looked at the fallen men, then Roderic and Grier. She gave a small snort of irritation and turned, walking back the way she came.

"I think she's pouting because she missed the fight," Roderic said as he began rummaging through the two farmers' pockets. "Again."

Jaxx circled overhead. Grier gestured to him that all was well and motioned that he should circle back and meet them by their supplies. Jaxx flew away.

"It's not your fault." Salena touched his arm to take his attention from the sky. "Those darts would have taken anyone out. You didn't stand a chance. They're not exactly sanctioned in most places, but that hardly stops black-market traders."

"The question, which I'm guessing will be easy enough to answer, is where did Curtis and his two brothers get them from?" Roderic moved to search the other man's pockets.

"You know them?" Grier asked.

"This is Curtis." Roderic patted the smaller of the two men before pointing at the larger brute. "That's Fergal. Sleeping beauty on the path back there is Valter."

"Curtis hit Valter because I almost escaped." Salena lifted her hand to show where the skin had been rubbed raw. "I nailed Valter with a rock before they tied me back up. It was highly satisfying and worth it."

"We've had a few run-ins with them during the nef deliveries." Roderic pulled a folded paper from Curtis' pocket. He glanced at it before shoving it in his own pocket. "They're skilled farmers. They can read the shadowed marshes like nature spelled out its secrets for all to see. But they're also about as feral as cats can get. Too many generations of drunkenness and wild living."

"Did they hurt you?" Grier lightly touched her cheek.

"Yes, but I'm fine now. You came for me. I knew you would. As far as I'm concerned, you didn't fail me. You saved me." She smiled at him, and he felt as if his heart would explode.

Salena pulled his hand from her face and held it.

"You should get her out of here. Have Payton escort you to the Var palace. She knows how to get you in without all the fanfare of visiting royalty. We have a medical booth there. I'll take care of these," Roderic grinned at Salena, "*battle prizes* and meet you at the palace."

"But we didn't find the drop-off point yet," Salena protested. "I'm all right. I can go on."

"It's not worth the risk," Grier stated. "These woods have become too dangerous, much more dangerous than we could have anticipated. We need to get you medical attention and regroup."

"And you," she said.

"Me what?"

"You need medical attention." Salena gestured at his arm. "You're bleeding."

"It's only a cut. It looks worse than it is," he dismissed.

"It looks more like punctures to me, so we should get it looked at."

"Did they say what they planned?" Grier asked.

"They wanted to deliver me somewhere so they could get paid. They also knew to keep me gagged so I couldn't ask them questions." Salena again stretched her jaw. The skin where the gag had been was slightly discolored. "I assume the Federation has spread the word they're looking for me. By the way they were in such a hurry to drop me off, it must be a decent bounty."

"I would say that's a safe assumption." Roderic pulled the cross-laces from the clothing Fergal had discarded during his shift. He tested their strength before moving to bind Fergal's hands and feet. "You should take a different route in case Valter wakes up and comes looking for his brothers. I'll meet you at the palace when I'm done here."

Grier nodded his thanks and escorted Salena away from the travois. He noticed she limped a little when she put weight on her left ankle, and he frowned. She didn't complain.

"Allow me." Without giving her a choice, he swept her into his arms and carried her.

She made a small noise of surprise but wrapped her arms around his neck and lay her head against him. The weight put pressure on his wound, but he didn't care. He'd much rather hold her, and this was the perfect excuse.

"It's a small journey to the palace, but I don't want to make you fly it," he said.

"As much as I want to enjoy flying, I'm afraid this is the highest I want to go for some time. I'm not sure I could hold on if we were to take to the air."

"Then I'll carry you."

"I'd protest, but my ankle is throbbing. I think it landed on a rock when Fergal dropped my legs."

Grier took her through the woods as gently and quickly as he could manage. She sighed softly. Her breath hit his neck. The intimate feeling stirred many emotions inside of him, and he never wanted to let her go.

"You're holding me too tight," she said, not lifting her head.

Grier realized he'd started hugging her and loosened his grip. "I won't let down my guard again."

"It's not your fault. We both let down our guard."

Salena made a tiny movement in his arms, cuddling next to his chest. He wanted nothing more than to lay her on the grass and make love to her, but now was not the time.

Apparently, there was never a good time for it. Every time something started to happen, they were interrupted. The gods had a terrible sense of humor.

IF THE DRAIG PALACE DISAPPEARED INTO THE landscape to remain hidden, with only its contours and the tops of its walls discernable from a distance, the Var castle sprung from the planet's surface to be seen from far and wide to dominate the surrounding forest.

The stark contrast amused Grier. He'd always thought of it as a reflection of their shifter personalities. Their differences were also the reasons why (most of the time) they coexisted peacefully.

But it was evident that their chosen architecture was an extension of their cultures. Dragons were contained, holding their power inside and subduing the urge to conquer all before them.

On the other hand, for as stealthy as they were, cats were also wild and bold.

Regardless of their contrasting attitudes, both fought fiercely for what they loved.

There was something to be said for both ways.

The village near the dragon palace had been laid on a grid of streets, orderly and symmetrical, a place where no one could get lost. In contrast, the cat-shifter village looked to be decided on a whim, spilling out of the palace's front gate with curved roads created a maze around the homes.

Despite this seemingly haphazard planning, the palace and homes were built with exceptional craftsmanship.

Grier set Salena down as they waited, staying near her so she could use him for support.

The gray brick of the rectangular two-story homes perfectly contrasted the red dirt on which they stood. The flat roofs were turned into spectacular living spaces colored and beautified by gardens that furnished the walls and helped purify the air. The Var had mastered outdoor living by artfully repurposing the roofs of their homes.

Grier watched Salena more than he looked at the palace. Her eyes moved as if tracing the square turrets that dominated the blue-green sky. The dark blue flag with the head of a panther flapped over each one, the symbol of King Kirill. The Var king was much loved, but also much hated. Aside from the marsh farmers, who seemed to hate everyone, there was a faction of Myrddians, named after a shifter purist and sadist, Lord Myrddin, who they had built into some kind of twisted spiritual leader.

Grier knew the dangers of his world, but there was something different about them now. Before, Myrddians and marsh farmers, Federation and Cysgodians, all of them had been a duty he must face.

And now that he had a woman to protect, they had become a much more fearsome prospect. Already three of those groups had come for Salena. He would make sure Myrddians did not try the same. He had no reason to think they would, but that didn't matter.

Grier stepped unconsciously closer to Salena and placed a hand on her shoulder.

"I'd try kissing you again, but Payton would suddenly appear," she said with a tiny laugh. "Our lips meeting seem to summon the nearest person, or the nearest danger."

At that, he smiled. "I am quickly losing my humor about it."

"Me too," she admitted. "But the view is beautiful."

"This palace has stood since before my father's birth," Grier said, liking the quiet moment together they were afforded. He inched closer to her, and she leaned her shoulder into him. "I'm told one of the king's brothers once programmed the central mainframe to be a pouty woman, so whenever she was insulted she reacted poorly, zapping people with electricity in their backsides. The brother then took off into space with his friends to sail the high skies and left the others to deal with the computer's temper."

Salena laughed. "Is that true?"

Grier shrugged. "I'm told it is. Her name was Siren. I also hear she had a crush on one of the princes."

"Had? So, the programming error has been fixed?" Salena laughed harder.

"I would hope so." He loved the sound of that laugh, and the fact she could still find pleasure despite all that had happened to her.

"I've never been to a place quite like your planet," she said. "It truly is amazing."

"All right. I'm ready. How do I look?" Payton came up from behind them.

Grier turned to see the Var princess in a gown. The dress was pretty, but her hair was a tangled mess, as if she'd struggled to put it on. She held a small circlet in her hand. Unable to help himself, he started laughing.

"Stow it," she grumbled.

"I think you look pretty," Salena said.

"You stow it too," Payton grumbled. "I look like a princess."

"You are a princess," Grier pointed out. "What's the occasion?"

"Skipped out on a banquet and didn't tell anyone where I was off to. Going to be in trouble. I find my father's temper is softened if I don't look like one of his soldiers." Payton shrugged. "He thinks he's tough, but he's all roar and no bite."

"Your father is a general?" Salena asked.

"Prince Falke of the Var, commander of the armies," Payton answered, rounding her eyes as if that was supposed to scare people but didn't.

"Huh." Salena slowly nodded her head. "That explains a lot."

Grier didn't bother to suppress his amusement. "Doesn't it, though?"

"What about your mother?" Salena asked.

"Captain Sam, space pirate and troublemaker," Payton said with pride before shrugging. "Or she used to be. Now she's," the princess threw her voice into a delicate whisper, "Princess Samantha of the Var, former troublemaker."

"I like your mother," Grier defended. "She's fun."

"I know. Me too. She's amazing. I'm just in a grumpy mood." Payton held out the circlet to Salena. "Can you figure this out and do something girly to my hair, please? I want to get the next three hours of lecturing over with."

"You might want to rub the dirt off your cheek," Grier said.

Payton grimaced and rubbed her face.

"Don't listen to him. There is barely any. Grier, stop being a boy," Salena scolded him. "Payton, you're *beautiful.*"

"Thanks, Salena." Payton arched a brow at him and smirked as if he were a kid who'd just gotten in trouble.

Grier watched as Salena combed her fingers through Payton's hair, straightening it before lifting a portion to loop over the circlet. The metal ring lay across Payton's forehead and was held in place by the layer of hair.

Salena smiled, giving Payton's locks a few more adjustments. "There. Perfect."

When Salena looked at him expectantly, Grier found himself saying, "You look very pretty, Payton."

"And I know it's true because you can't lie around my new friend," Payton said, hugging Salena's shoulders as both women faced him.

Salena's expression fell at the woman's words. It was a subtle shift of her features, but he saw it. Payton didn't seem to notice. He wondered if she was missing her sisters.

"What else do you like about me, Grier?" Payton asked, batting her lashes.

"You're a loyal friend and a good fighter," he said.

"I'll take it!" She gave Salena a little squeeze. "You look exhausted, new friend. Let's sneak you two into the palace, where you can sleep without the threat of someone darting you in the ass. No one will bother you once you're in a guest suite."

"So, Siren's not up and running?" Salena teased. "I heard she liked to zap people."

Payton laughed and led the way toward a back entrance to the palace, keeping parallel to the Var city. "Grier told you about that? Yeah, my uncle Jarek is hilarious. He has the best stories from his time in space. It's too bad you won't be here long enough to meet his old crew. Actually, it's some of his crew and some of my mother's old crew. Anyway, they visit every few years. Those are some wild parties. Since I was a little girl, I have secretly wished to stow away on their ship and go with them to space."

"From what I've seen of space, it sounds a lot more glamorous than it is." Salena limped a little as she stepped, and Grier slipped his arm under her elbow for support to take the weight off her ankle. She nodded her thanks. "Most of the time it's endless and boring, with a few stops along the way at questionable fueling docks that look like they're about to be rusted out of the sky. When you do land on a planet, the locals tend to look at you like you're a carrier of the yellow plague come to wipe them out. Which is how many of them secretly think, and they have no problem telling me, thanks to my *ever-so-wonderful* gift. The only place that didn't seem to care was Torgan, well at least until my nearness started interfering in some of their dealings."

"I've heard about that. The black-market planet," Payton said, sounding jealous of Salena's adventures more than deterred. "My mother kidnapped my father when he was shifted into his tiger form and tried to sell him on Torgan."

"Yeah," Salena drawled. "Not such a great place when criminals, pirates, and traders start confessing secrets. I barely made it off the planet alive."

"I can see how that wouldn't be fun," Payton admitted.

"Why were you there?" Grier asked.

Salena sighed. "I was looking for my sisters. I heard a rumor they'd been brought there to be traded. It was a dead end. No one knew anything about them and, believe me, I asked. It's like they disappeared. I think that is where the Federation first discovered who I am. I wasn't very subtle."

Grier wished it was within his power to find Piera

and Fiora for her. He would do anything to make her happy. If there were a way, he would make it happen. Between both kingdoms, they had a lot of space contacts. One of the old-timers, Lochlann, had been part of Prince Jarek's crew in his younger days and would still have intergalactic connections. Though he didn't remember the details, there was some story about how Lochlann found one of his cousins' sisters...or something. It was worth asking about.

The sound of cat-shifters in exercise grew increasingly louder the closer they walked. Salena stiffened at a roar.

"It's just the palace guard in training," Payton said. "Nothing to be afraid of. We're going to walk close to the field to use the side entrance. There should only be a couple of guards around there. Just walk like you belong with me and they probably won't bother you."

Salena nodded at Payton's back and glanced around. Her hand lifted to where he held her arm and she grabbed hold of him. He felt her jump ever so slightly each time the practice became loud and aggressive.

"See." Payton pointed to a courtyard where a variety of big cats had lined up in rows. The guards had stripped out of their clothing and rows of boots stood beside piles of discarded tunics and pants to border the practice area.

Salena stopped to watch.

At first it was a rumble that shook the ground and raised the hairs on the back of her neck. And then the rumble seemed to recede, only for a roar to blast her in the face, pulling her hair back and stretching her skin. She was stunned momentarily, and when she'd managed to shake it off, she saw the clowder of big cats coming toward her like a troupe of feline acrobats moving swiftly in unison, creating a stunning cascading pattern of leaps and rolls until the field was a living surface of agility and strength.

"It's beautiful," Salena whispered.

"They'll be at it for hours," Payton said. "Shifter formations help build muscle memory for battles. My father says repetition is key."

"Do you have many battles?" Salena asked.

Payton glanced at Grier.

"It's always wise to be prepared. Both dragons and cats have been ramping up their training programs since the Federation's arrival," Grier answered.

Salena nodded. "Smart."

"Come on," Payton urged. "If they see his dragon highness entering the palace, this will turn into a dignitary function faster than you can say *get me the hell out of here.*"

"Your home is..." Salena looked up the side of the castle toward the sky. "The detail is..."

"Queen Lyssa called the tile work and archway patterns *Morrican? Montycam? Moroccan* style? Something like that. I can't remember for sure. It reminded her of Old Earth somehow. My ancestors were obsessed with inlaid tiles and symmetrical patterns. They're everywhere. They even hid the computer consuls behind them. It's looked like this for such a long time that I think everyone is afraid of suggesting renovations for fear of disrespecting our cultural history."

"I think it's lovely," Salena said.

"I suppose," Payton dismissed. She walked a little faster. "Greetings, palace protectors, fine day, isn't it?"

Two stoic men merely glanced at her.

Payton patted both of their arms as she passed by. "Nice chatting with you, as always."

The palace door was open to let in a breeze. Payton led them through the archway into the hall. The tile work she'd mentioned lined both sides of the hallway in exquisite patterns of blue, red, orange, green and gold. Each doorway they passed had been hand-carved along the frame, perfect down to the last millimeter of design.

"Oh, I should warn you," Payton said as she kept walking. "You saw the streets outside? How they're all haphazard and make no sense?"

"Yes," Salena said.

"It's like that inside the palace too, only worse. If you

don't know where you're going, you'll get lost fast. The mainframe computer has been programmed into each room and inner courtyard, but if I enter you into the database to find your way around, the elders will be alerted, and they'll make a fuss over visitors." Payton chuckled. "Just another thing from the old days they don't want to renovate."

"The dragon palace is the same in that regard," Grier said.

"That it is," Payton agreed.

"They made half the hallways go to dead ends, with doors along the way that don't all open," Grier told Salena.

"It probably deters people from storming the palaces," Salena reasoned. "Makes sense."

"This way." Payton turned a corner and stopped at a door. She pressed her ear to it and lifted her hand for quiet. After a few moments, she opened it and ushered them inside. A medical booth had been set up in the small chamber, along with a couple of chairs. She grabbed a short gown off the hook on the wall. "Put this on and climb in. Let's do something about that ankle."

Salena looked at Grier and he nodded that she should. He turned his back to give her privacy as she changed into the medical gown. Payton took a handheld from a hook on the wall and went to heal the punctures Grier received during the fight.

"Will it hurt?" Salena asked.

"Have you never been in a medical booth before?" Grier turned as she slid into the narrow opening between two large panels. The light material clung to her. It was more seductive than if she'd been naked. She glanced at him and shook her head in denial. Her body couldn't rotate now that she was between the panels, and he had a full view of her curves.

"You're going to feel something clamp your ankle and the bed is going to recline. Just lie still and relax," Payton instructed as she went to the control panel. "Let the lasers do the rest."

"At worse, you'll feel an injection for medicine," Grier said. "The lasers will feel warm."

Payton nodded, tensing as the unit began to recline. It stopped when she lay at an angle and started its preliminary scans.

Grier moved closer to the panel and whispered, "Do a full scan, would you?"

Payton nodded. "Already on it."

"On what?" Salena asked. "I can't hear."

"Body scan," Payton said.

"Oh." Salena had her eyes closed when he leaned to look at her face. Lasers ran along her body, concentrating on areas where they found something of medical concern.

"You should feel heat on your ankle now as it heals," Payton said.

"Okay," Salena answered, a little loudly. She held her body rigid and kept her eyes closed.

Payton lifted her hand and motioned him back to the console. She pointed at the image the unit had made of Salena's form. It was only a 3D outline, but it still caused his stomach to tighten with a reminder of how his body had been denied the one thing it craved.

Payton elbowed him to get his attention off Salena's form and pointed at the readings next to the picture. Grier frowned and leaned forward to read. He pushed a button to highlight the notations on her image. Her body showed signs of long-term malnourishment, healed fractures, and a foreign object lodged in her upper thigh.

He shared a look with Payton and nodded. The woman ordered the machine to repair the old fractures better than they'd mended on their own, and to analyze the object in Salena's thigh.

Grier went to check on her. "Salena, how are you?"

"It tickles—*oh, ow!*" Salena's eyes widened, and she stiffened.

"Payton." Grier lifted his arm to command Payton to stop.

"Relax," Payton dismissed. "It's an injection to balance her levels."

"In my backside," Salena grumbled. "A little warning next time would be nice."

"Incoming, second hemisphere," Payton announced.

Salena tensed, holding her breath until the shot was over. "Does it normally take this long to fix an ankle?"

"No," Grier and Payton answered at the same time.

"My ankle feels better. Can I get out now?" Salena questioned. Her hand reached from inside the booth and waved in the air.

"No," Grier and Payton repeated in unison.

"What are you doing?" Salena drew her arm back in and the panel vibrated as if she'd pushed on it.

"We're trying to see what's embedded in your leg," Payton answered. "It doesn't appear to be a tracker."

"My leg?" Salena repeated, clearly confused. "What's wrong with my—*wait, you can see that?*"

"You know what it is?" Grier joined her, not wanting her to be scared, but when he looked at her, she seemed more amused than anything.

"Pottery," she said.

"Why do you have pottery in your leg?" Payton asked.

"My sisters and I were playing around by the kilns and they accidentally bumped me into a stack of pots."

Salena leaned her head back. "There were shards everywhere. My leg took a long time to heal. I always thought I felt something in there, but my father said it was scar tissue."

Payton leaned on his arm to look at Salena. "You want it?"

"You can get it out?" she asked.

"Sure. Standby." Payton pushed away from him and went back to the console. "Switching to surgery function."

"Do you know what you're doing?" Grier asked.

"It's pushing buttons. Besides, I've always wanted to try this." Payton lifted her finger and said. "Three. Two. One." She tapped the button. "And commence numbing."

Grier knelt, watching to make sure nothing went wrong. The position gave him an all-too-perfect view of her upper thighs. If he weren't worried about her, he wouldn't have been able to look away. A needle gave Salena a series of injections before a laser created a small cut. He balled his hand into fists. He'd seen bloody wounds in battle, but this was different. This was Salena.

She held her leg still, lifting her head once to peek down. Seeing a retractor coming toward her, she closed her eyes and turned her head away. Blood ran down her leg and a decontaminating laser began cleaning it as the surgery progressed.

"Retrieving pottery." Payton came around to watch over his head. "That is astounding."

The retractors pulled a dark shard from Salena's leg and disappeared into the side panel.

"Salena?" he asked.

"I'm fine. Is it almost done?" she answered.

"Oh, yeah, hold on." Payton hurried back to the console. "Closing the incision."

Salena's thigh lit up as the booth worked to heal the wound.

"It's warm," she said.

"Almost done," Payton answered.

When it was over, it appeared like nothing had happened.

"And done," Payton announced. "My first surgery was a success."

Salena reached down the best she could in the enclosed space to feel her leg. "I can't feel the bump that was there."

"That's because I'm an amazing surgeon," Payton announced. She went behind the panel. "There should be a tray-drawer-something around here somewhere."

As Payton searched behind the panel, Grier stood and reached his hand inside the unit to touch her cheek.

Tears had entered her eyes, and he brushed his thumb beneath one to keep it from falling.

"Where do you hurt?" he asked. It was over, and she shouldn't be feeling any pain.

"In my heart," she whispered. "I miss my family."

He nodded, knowing there was nothing he could say to make that ache go away. He could not envisage losing all his family, but he imagined it was much like the idea of losing Salena. The ache he felt with that thought flowed through him as he gazed into her eyes. He wanted to take away every reason she had to leave. He wanted to be the reason she stayed.

"I love you," he whispered.

At that her eyes closed, and she took a deep breath. "I'm sorry."

"I'm not." He let her cheek go and stepped back. "Payton, are you finished?"

"Got it!" Payton appeared from behind the booth holding her prize. The broken shard was blue with a black glaze.

"Let me out." Salena held out her hand for the pottery piece. Payton handed it over and went back to the controls. Salena turned the shard in her fingers as she waited to be set free.

Grier turned his back, politely giving her privacy to change. Though, if he were honest, it was more for him than for her. He could not take much more of his bubbling desires. He was afraid the animal inside him would pounce if allowed to take over. That could never be permitted to happen. He would never harm Salena or do anything that wasn't her will.

"Grier," Payton whispered to get his attention. When he looked up at her, she gestured that he should turn around.

Salena had gone to her knees on the floor, still wearing the medical gown. She stared at the pottery in her shaking hands.

"Payton, could you help her with the gown?" Grier asked.

"Of course." Payton was uncharacteristically gentle when she picked up the gown and knelt beside Salena. She took one of Salena's hands and eased the sleeve on, before doing the same with the other. Then, she lifted the dress over Salena's head and pulled it down over the medical gown. "There. Come on. You need rest."

Payton helped her stand.

"I miss them," Salena whispered.

"I know." Payton gave him a meaningful look and nodded that he should take over. "I think it might have given her a sedative because she needed to rest."

Grier didn't hesitate. He lifted Salena into his arms to carry her. Payton led them back into the hall, taking them quickly toward a guest room. She opened the wide door to let them in. "It's not the biggest suite, but I have a feeling she won't care."

"Thank you," Grier said. "This is perfect."

The guest suite consisted of a bedroom with a small seating area, and a bathing area partially hidden by curtains hanging from the ceiling. Woven rugs matched the tile patterns on the walls. A banner with the silhouette of a cat standing on two legs graced the wall next to a small fireplace. Rings of light created a cylindrical light fixture.

"There is a food simulator left of the fireplace, but I'll have servants bring you some real food in a few hours when I'm done being scolded." Payton took a steadying breath and shut the door.

"You know she acts like she doesn't care as a front to hide her insecurities, right?" Salena mumbled sleepily when they were alone. "I don't even think she knows she's doing it."

"Did she say something to you?" Grier carried her to the large bed. There was a step to get onto the platform it was placed on.

"No, but I know people well enough after a lifetime of hearing their secrets. I won't ask her about it and embarrass her," Salena answered.

He lay her on top of the coverlet before pulling up

the end to wrap her in it. Her eyes were closed, and she was breathing softly. The pottery piece was still clutched in her hand. He pulled it gently from her fingers before walking around the bed to sit next to her.

Grier studied the shard. It was difficult to tell what the pot would have looked like from the tiny piece but the black glaze on the blue stone was a stunning contrast. "I would have liked to see these."

"It's difficult to find the blue clay deposits. A blue pot brings good luck." Salena's eyes did not open, and she sighed, half-asleep.

Grier watched her chest rise and fall in steady breaths. He leaned over the side of the bed and placed the shard on the platform, close to the wall for safekeeping, then pulled the bracelet with the crystal from his pocket for the same reason. Settling next to her on the bed, he kept the coverlet between them as he curled around her back and draped his arm over her waist. It didn't matter what tomorrow would bring. For now, he had her next to him, and he would protect her from all her troubles.

18

Salena anticipated the voice of her sister telling her to wake up. When Fiora didn't speak, she waited for the warmth of her surroundings to fade. She had no idea how long she lingered in that limbo between wake and sleep before her eyes cracked open. The safety of darkness surrounded her, compounded by a weight over her side and the heat of her blanket.

A soft light came in the form of a vertical line near her feet. She couldn't be sure but thought she discerned a shift in the darkness, like material rippling all around her. She reached her hand forward and felt the soft plush of curtains around her bed. At her touch, the vertical line expanded and contracted ever so slightly.

She drew her hand back to feel the protective weight

draped over her side. Before her fingers found skin, her tired mind registered what was happening. They were in the Var palace, in a guest room. Grier lay behind her, curled around her to hold her while they slept. It was much different from the wedding tent when they laid on their backs, fingers touching.

Her hand tingled at the memory. So much had happened in that brief time as if the universe was trying to give them a lifetime of memories in the short while they had together before Salena must leave. The attraction she'd felt from the first moment had been tinged by fear. That fear was now gone, replaced by a gentler counterpart—hope.

Perhaps it was foolish to be hopeful with all she faced, but life did not feel as daunting at the moment. She had rested. Her body felt better than it had in a long time, every ache and pain gone. The uncertainty of tomorrow could not invade this cocoon they were in. The politics of his world, ones that kept her from staying for the real threat of starting a war with the Federation, and the reality of who she was and what she searched for did not matter. This moment was theirs. She wanted it. She'd hold on to it for as long and as hard as she could, knowing that it would slip away as all things in her life did.

But not now.

Now it was here.

Now she was his, and he was hers.

This time was theirs and no one else could have it.

With these thoughts churning in her waking mind, she wiggled beneath the blanket to adjust herself under his arm until she was on her back. His leg was pressed tightly against hers, separated by a blanket that kept her from touching him fully.

He hadn't moved but his eyes were open, his gaze clear, as if he'd been watching over her for some time. There was no denying the force between them, the tightening of the thread that held them together. He loved her. He'd said it. For that, she was sorry. Her leaving would only hurt him more.

But then, it would be agony for her as well...for she loved him too.

Salena refused to say it, knowing that it could only make things worse for him when the time came. As much as the idea of him moving on hurt, she hoped that he was wrong about the gods and that he would find a way. She'd put his happiness above her own heart. That is what love was sometimes. It was a sacrifice of one's self, of one's needs, of one's heart for the sake of another's.

They lay for a long time, gazing into each other's

eyes, both feeling the connection. Salena was almost afraid to kiss him as if doing so would somehow summon a new threat to attack them and keep them from finishing what they both wanted. It was foolish to think that, of course, but still...

The risk was worth it.

Salena leaned forward, pressing her lips to his. The gentle pressure as he returned the affection caused her to shiver. One hand was trapped beneath the covers, but she was still able to hold his head with her other hand. Her fingers tangled in his hair. His beard tickled her chin.

As if thinking the same thing, they both parted and looked toward the strip of light at the end of the bed, holding still as they listened beyond their immediate world. Grier's eyes flashed with gold and narrowed as if he listened past all barriers.

"Is the universe imploding?" she whispered.

He grinned. "If it is, we better hurry."

Salena laughed as he rolled her on top of him. The covers pressed between them, padding the feel of his body, yet somehow seductive by the teasing way she was forced to move against him to determine his shape. She kissed him, deeper than before. Her arm freed, she ran both hands along his arms, drawing them away from her and pinning them down. His fingers clasped around hers, trapping her hands to his.

The kiss deepened. He refused to release her fingers, and she ended up squirming over his length, trying unsuccessfully to rid them of their covers. The skirt of her gown blocked her movements. She pulled her mouth from his, gasping for breath. The desire she felt didn't need much prodding as it flamed to the surface. She drew her lips down his neck to the hot flesh she found there. His pulse beat against her mouth and she smiled, knowing that she affected him as much as he affected her.

Her legs parted, straddling him, but her body was still blocked by the covers. She yanked a hand free and moved it between them, tugging the blankets down the best she could as she shifted her weight to the side. It was hard going, but she managed to push it down to their feet. Next, she reached between them again to lift his tunic shirt. The warmth of his skin caused her to moan in appreciation.

Finally, flesh.

With his shirt lifted to reveal his stomach, she drew her hand down to his waist. The skirt of her gown was annoying in its limitations, but that didn't stop her hand from discovering the perfect shape of his hip. He released her captured hand. Salena sat astride him. She rocked back and forth, working the skirt from beneath her knees. When she could pull the gown over her head, she tossed it aside. She was surprised to find the sheer medical booth gown was underneath.

He touched her sides, and his heat soaked easily through the thin material. It clung to her skin, caressing her breasts. The clear intent of his arousal was unmistakable as she lowered against it. He drew her hips forward so her naked sex pressed to his stomach.

The intimate contact sent a jolt straight through her system. She lay the flat of her palms to his chest to steady herself as her breath caught. Grier reached behind her and pushed his pants from his hips, using his feet to pull them off and kick them aside.

When he looked up at her, their eyes met and held. There was so much longing in his expression that it pulled at her heart and she couldn't look away.

Grier took her by the hips and slid her back. This time, no barriers kept them apart. He lifted her, angling her body to accept him.

Salena gave a small nod, encouraging him.

The head of his shaft pressed along her folds, parting her to accept him. The moment was more than the driving need of two bodies. It was the ache of two souls needing to join.

He entered her slowly as if every second mattered.

Her eyes closed, unable to remain open at the pleasure filling her. She couldn't believe it was finally happening. All the teasing kisses, the lingering touches, the accidental brushes...had led to this.

Grier's hands felt like they were everywhere at once as they roamed over her. She rocked her body, testing the tight feel of him inside her. He cupped her breasts, rubbing the nipples through the thin material. His head pressed back as he held her hips and lifted his own to go deeper.

The feelings were too much. They'd waited for too long.

Their lovemaking became a frenzy of movements, seeking and giving pleasure. He rolled her onto her back, driving into her. Soft moans filled each breath. She grabbed his tunic, balling it in her fists as she held on.

The passion built with each thrust of their bodies, surging forth until it couldn't be contained. Her release hit her hard, tensing each muscle as she gasped. A series of tremors beset her, as wave after wave of pleasure washed over her. He worked his hips, giving her every sweet moment before taking his own release. He stiffened over her, moaning in pleasure as he came.

They stayed joined long after the trembling subsided.

Salena smiled lazily. Grier pulled out of her and lay beside her on the bed. He gathered her into his arms.

"I was right," she whispered, suppressing a yawn. "The universe is imploding. I felt it."

Grier laughed and kissed her forehead. "I think you may be right. We should stay here, just to be safe."

19

"Food! Are you awake? Grier? Salena? I have food."

Salena opened her eyes at Payton's call. The sound of a door closing reverberated from outside the bed curtains.

"Give us a moment," Grier answered. He still held her.

"Mm, I thought we'd do that again," Salena whispered with a small pout.

Grier grinned.

"Grier, you might want to explain shifter hearing," Payton called.

Salena stiffened. Grier kissed the tip of her nose and winked.

Grier reached for her gown at the end of the bed and handed it to her. He then tugged on his pants.

Salena pulled the medical gown off before dressing. Grier's eyes were on her when the gown came over her head. Gold swirled in their depths and she knew he wanted more. She did too.

He reached for the curtains and pulled them aside. Light poured into the dim enclosure.

Salena rubbed her eyes as they adjusted.

"How did things go with your father?" Grier stood and held his hand out to guide Salena from the bed. She put her hand in his and stepped down a platform step.

Payton placed a tray of food on the small table by a chair. She'd changed her clothes and now wore tight black pants and a looser tunic shirt beneath a tight vest with cross-laces. Sighing, she fell more than sat in the chair. "He lectured me about responsibility and royal duty, and how a princess should not leave the palace without telling someone where she is going because of dangers in the world. I told him Roderic knew I was going to Draig territory to visit my friends, but apparently that's not good enough, since Roderic was with me on my foolish adventures and he didn't tell anyone either."

"It sounds like he worries about you," Salena said. "I

wish my father was still around to worry about me like that."

Payton scrunched up her face. "Way to drain all the enjoyment out of my righteous indignation by being reasonable."

"You're welcome." Salena gave her a small smile and crossed over to the tray of food. She didn't recognize any of it. Small balls were piled in a bowl next to a platter of meat and spread.

"Roderic's here. He's talking to his mother but will join us as soon as he's finished," Payton said. "He took care of the marsh nuisances. Threatened the full force of the palace guard if they came after Salena or a royal again. Their father was none too pleased. Apparently, he started slapping them upside the head and gave them extra chores. I know they took you, and Roderic would have done more, but we don't need to stir up the marsh farmers."

"I understand," Salena said. "You have enough to deal with."

"Try the tantren fruit." Payton took a small piece of pink fruit and tossed it into the air before catching it with her mouth. "It's a new hybrid. If you inject Qurilixian rum into them they're amazing. They also make good missiles if you're bored at a banquet and want to annoy the guards."

Grier took a handful of the fruit and threw one at Payton. She laughed when it hit her.

"I never understood why you and Grace never became best friends," he said.

"Who's Grace?" Salena asked.

"Grier's cousin." Payton picked up the fruit he'd thrown at her and rolled it in her fingers thoughtfully.

"She has the same adventurous spirit as Princess Payton." Grier handed Salena one of his fruit to try before placing one in his mouth. "And her father is the dragon commander."

Salena sniffed the tantren. It had a muted, pleasant aroma.

"The answer to that question is simple," Payton said. "She thinks she's too good for us cat-shifters."

Grier frowned, pausing as he drew another piece of fruit to his mouth. He lowered it without eating. "Is that how you really feel? I never knew that."

"And I never would have told you that if not for your truth-serum lady there," Payton admitted. "But now that it is out, you know it's true."

"I know no such thing," Grier said.

"I'm sorry I asked," Salena said. Clearly, this was a sensitive subject, not one she'd intended to stir into an honest conversation with her simple query. "We don't have to talk about this."

"Really?" Payton gave an unamused laugh, ignoring Salena as she focused on Grier. "Every time we came around, she'd run the other way. We visit the palace, and she is conveniently gone. We show up for camping or hunting, and she would have to leave with some lame excuse as to why she could not stay. It's been obvious since childhood. She hates cat-shifters."

"No, she..." Grier turned his gaze to the door, but no one came to justify his attention or save him from having to answer.

Payton gave a wry smile and sat back in the chair. "If not that, then what? And you have to answer honestly. This truth-purveyor thing works both ways."

"She doesn't want to marry Korbin," Grier said.

"Like my cousin wants to marry her." Payton laughed.

Salena frowned at both of them. "Then why would that even be an issue if Korbin and Grace don't wish to marry?"

"Politics," Grier and Payton said in unison.

"Oh." Salena determined she would not ask any more questions and tried to change the subject. She put the fruit into her mouth. It had an almost grainy texture and tasted overly sweet. "These are...interesting."

"I don't think either side thought the people would put so much stock into that stupid peace treaty. Queen

Lyssa is not pleased," Payton paused to explain to Salena, "That's Korbin's mother," before continuing to Grier, "You should see her face every time it is mentioned. I think it's the only thing she and the king fight over."

"Princess Pia, Grace's mother, isn't either," Grier admitted.

"Why?" Salena grimaced at herself. So much for her determination to change the subject.

"The elders have never said, but I think when they agreed to it, neither side thought the dragons would have female children and it would be a non-issue. Female children are rare. The blue radiation that gives us our long life makes having shifter females difficult. It is why we do things like the breeding festival. It is one of the few ways that marriage is possible for the dragon men. Grace is a rarity, the only female born of our generation."

"Did you have to call it the breeding festival?" Payton giggled. "That is so crass, and there is no *breeding* going on that night from what I hear."

"My ancestors were peculiar," Grier admitted. "Half the time I think the whole thing was for someone's amusement—loincloths, not having sex on the wedding night as a form of ultimate torture, the grooms not being able to speak their truths to convince the women to remove the mask, the woman not being able to see the groom's face until she agrees to marry him, the hiring

Galaxy Brides, whose attention to detail has been histori-
cally questionable. And you should have seen the dresses
brides used to wear."

"What? Walking around saying, *come, come,* isn't
speaking your truth?" Payton laughed. "My brothers and
I used to watch the bridal banquet and take a drink each
time one of the grooms said it."

"What?" Salena asked.

"The grooms are allowed one word, *come.* When
dragons are wearing the mask it the only word we're
allowed to say. It is to communicate that the brides are to
follow to the tents, to avoid confusion and having to
resort to picking them up and carrying them," Grier
explained.

"The bridal gowns I saw were not that bad," Salena
said. "They were pretty."

Payton held up her hands, leaning forward to interrupt again as she laughed. "Sacred cats, they were
hideous." She gestured to her upper body. "They fit right
all through here to about mid-thigh. The skirts were
hanging strips of material, and they had this belt thing..."
Payton stood and held her arms straight, a few inches
from her hips. "Instead of fastening in the front, each
side tied to a wrist to limit movement."

"We're trying to call it a mating ceremony now, but
the name isn't holding," Grier said.

"I have a question." Against her better judgment, Salena ate another tantren. It was as sickeningly sweet as the first. She tried not to let her distaste show. She swallowed with some difficulty.

"You don't have to eat those," Payton said. Salena's attempts to hide her feelings were clearly unsuccessful.

"What's the question?" Grier prompted.

"Princess Olena had that drink, Maiden something," Salena answered. "But she wouldn't let me have it. What was in it?"

"Maiden's Last Breath." Grier shook his head slightly as if the very concept annoyed him. "It's this traditional drink they serve the night of the ceremony. It was used in religious ceremonies many generations back and was believed to open a person's soul to accepting what they truly wanted, to make decision-making easier and to block out negative voices or insecurities. Galaxy Brides Corporation was supposed to be telling the brides about it in full detail before they landed, but when it became clear the uploads they were giving the brides about our planet were sorely lacking, we began limiting Maiden's Last Breath's use."

"What did it do to the women?" Salena asked, eyeing the meat and wondering if she should taste it.

"For dragons, it does what it is supposed to, and we understand its purpose." Grier picked up a piece of the meat, dipped it in the spread and handed it to Salena to try. "For certain aliens, including humans, it does work, but it also seems to have a subtle euphoric effect, which was not its intention. Since no woman has ever, or will ever, be taken against their will by a dragon, we will not serve it unless a woman asks for it with full knowledge of what it is. Everything about our ceremony is designed to make sure the woman chooses her future. We wear the mask because all men are equal when it comes to finding mates. We wear little clothing to show we will not hide anything from our wives. We do not have sex, but we do try to convince our mate of our worth with our actions. We're not allowed to speak until they remove the mask as a sign of acceptance, because no bride should be pressured by words."

Salena hesitated before placing the food in her mouth. The savory flavor was much more acceptable, and she nodded in approval. She reached for another piece.

Payton and Grier both smiled at that.

She thought of what Grier said of the marriage ceremony. He'd wanted her to take off his mask, but when the large man in the crowd threatened her, he'd taken it off himself and spoke to protect her. Even then, in that first moment, he'd put her above himself. He broke tradition in front of everyone for her. At the time she hadn't known, but since, she'd come to understand the full impact of what that meant to a man in Grier's position.

"So, what's our next move? Back out to look for where the ships are landing?" Payton's eyes lit as she contemplated continuing the adventure.

Salena knew what she'd choose. She wanted to remain in this room, hiding from the world and responsibility, but Payton's question brought the outside back in, and now that it had invaded her and Grier's world, it was impossible to ignore. The weight of it settled on her shoulders and she felt her body become heavy.

"I think I need an audience with your uncle Quinn. Is he still in charge of ship dockings?" Grier dropped the remaining fruit in his hand back into the bowl.

"Yes, but you can't be serious. If you talk to him, then they will all want to greet you, and then my father will ask questions, and it will become this big thing." Payton shook her head. "Let's not do that."

Grier turned to study Salena, his expression strangely controlled. He took a deep breath as if he didn't want to speak. Around her, that wouldn't be an option.

"You kept up your end of the bargain," Grier stated.

"What bargain?" Payton asked.

Salena glanced at the woman but didn't answer. She knew what was coming. An ache filled her. Tears welled in her eyes, threatening to spill. She shook her head in denial. It was too soon for this. She wasn't ready. They hadn't been given enough time.

"Salena helped me narrow down where the Federation has been secretly landing ships, and in return, I'm going to secure her passage off this planet that is not Olena's space pirate friends." Even though Grier answered Payton, his eyes stayed steadily on Salena.

"Oh, yeah, you don't want to travel with those aliens unless you like sleeping with the cargo," Payton agreed. "I don't think the pirates would hurt you, but Captain MoPa would not make the trip pleasant."

"I didn't help you find the landing site yet. We have to go back out." Salena didn't want to leave. She needed an excuse to stay. She glanced at the bed, desperately wishing to start this day over.

"The deal was you'd help me narrow it down," he countered. "You've upheld your end."

"I can do more." Salena watched his expression for any sign that he wanted her with him. His eyes did not give away his secrets. She could have bluntly asked him but was too afraid to hear the answer. What if he'd decided he didn't want her? She again glanced at the bed. Being with him was the happiest she'd been in a long time. She felt whole with him, connected to something beyond herself.

"It's too dangerous," he dismissed. "Our trip to the woods should be enough evidence of that."

He was right, of course. She didn't need him listing out the many groups that appeared to want her captured.

"I promised to protect you and to send you somewhere safe and nice. It is too dangerous for you here," Grier said. Salena began to shake her head again, but he placed his hand on her shoulder. The wall over his feelings crumbled away, and she saw the torment in his eyes. The look pained her even as it brushed aside her momentary insecurity. He did want her, as badly as she wanted him. "This isn't just about us, or how I feel about you. It's about the shifter people. That hasn't changed. The Federation has clearly spread the word you're wanted. If it's discovered we're hiding you, they'll claim it as an act of war if we don't turn you over. The best we can hope for is that the Cysgodians will hunt you, and probably the marsh farmers. The Federation will send others."

"It will be the excuse they need to overrun the planet." Payton closed her eyes and nodded. "I understand now." When she opened her eyes, she looked at them with pity. "I'm so sorry."

Salena thought about begging Grier to come with her, but ultimately kept her mouth shut. That would not be fair to him. This was his home, and he did not need the pain of temptation making the situation more difficult.

"Of course, we'll talk to Quinn. He'll know of a ship that will give you safe passage. Roderic is most likely with his father now." Payton pushed up from the chair and walked toward the fireplace. She picked up a bundle from the floor. "I brought you a change of adventuring clothes. I thought you might like something that is better suited to what we were doing. You can keep them. I think space travel is probably better if you're not in a dress."

Salena nodded her thanks. A tear managed to slip down her cheek, even as she tried not to cry.

"I wish it was different. I like having you around." Payton gave her a nod and put the clothes on the chair. "I'll wait in the hall. You two should talk privately."

When the door closed behind her, Salena shook her head. "What if I'm not ready to leave?"

Grier cupped her face in his hands and leaned his forehead to hers. He wiped her tear with his thumb. "I'll never be ready for you to leave, but it's not safe for you here. I promised to protect you and getting you off this planet to somewhere safe is the best way I know how to do that." He took a deep breath and closed his eyes, not letting her go. "I could have lost you in the forest."

"You didn't. You came for me." She put her hands

over his, prying them gently away to force him to look at her. "You protected me."

"I dropped my guard and lost you."

"You saved me."

"I was lucky. What if I hadn't found you?"

"You *saved* me."

"I was the reason you were in danger in the first place. I should have helped you leave after the festival night. I was selfish."

"You." Salena gave him a brief kiss. "Saved." She kissed him again. "Me."

He looked forlorn.

"Say it," she ordered firmly.

"I saved you."

"See, it's true. You can't lie around me." She smiled, but she didn't completely feel the emotion. She felt sadness, and the threat of loneliness that stood along the edges of her future just waiting for her to come back to it.

He kissed her, the pressure of his mouth instantly deepening as if he considered doing more. She would not have stopped him. He moaned as if in pain and pulled away. "You should dress. We'll meet with Prince Quinn and then hopefully we can sneak back here to be alone."

"Is there any way you would change your mind about this?" she asked. "Can nothing be done?"

"Not now, but in the future when it is safe I can

contact you and maybe you'll want to come back to me," he said.

Salena nodded, knowing she would. She couldn't imagine being with anyone else. Not after Grier.

"My mother always said, no one promised life would be fair. She was right. This isn't fair." Salena wiped at her eyes to stop crying.

"We'll hold on to the hope that I can get the Federation off this world. I'll get rid of the threat. I promise," he said. "I can't lie to you, so you know it will happen."

What he sincerely believed to be true and what the future would hold were two very different things. She knew the danger of hope. She had hoped to find her sisters. She had hoped to wake up safe at home and not on some horrible fueling dock. She hoped that they'd find a way she could stay.

Hope was for fools because it led to this feeling forming inside her. She wanted to cry, to shout, to curl into a ball and give up.

The worst part was, there was nothing she could do about any of it.

"Yeah." She managed a nod. "Someday I'll come back. When they're gone."

She didn't believe it. Life was not some magical tale that ended well for all.

He smiled, but it didn't reach his eyes.

Salena pulled away to change her clothes. The outfit was much like Payton's—tight pants with boots and a looser shirt. She debated whether she should pull on the vest but thought it rude not to. It molded to her body, tightening with cross-laces. It cupped beneath her breasts, supporting them.

"You're beautiful," Grier said.

"You're handsome." She gave him a small smile.

"You're everything." He came to her, kissing her deeply. When he held her, she instantly forgot all but the moment.

20

"WE CAN SECURE YOU A RIDE ON THE ESC SHIP scheduled for takeoff this evening." Prince Quinn had the kind of face that gave no hint to his age. At times he looked old and wise, at others he appeared boyish and carefree. His bright blue eyes reminded her of Roderic as did his steady character. "My wife led a team to the shadowed marshes to do their ten-year soil sampling as they monitor the long-term effects of the bioweaponry King Attor tried to engineer. This team makes several stops. You'll have your choice of safe places to disembark."

Tonight?

Never had the future come so fast as it did when talking to Prince Quinn. After explaining their situation, and Payton begging him not to tell her father, the royal ambassador took pity on Salena and offered his assistance.

That. Very. Night.

Salena didn't speak as she stood in the palace office next to Payton and Grier. Roderic had yet to join them. Her eyes focused on the beautiful tile work on the walls, which surrounded a fireplace with no fire. Long banners and a woven rug decorated a seating area.

"Salena?" Payton whispered. "Is that all right with you?"

Salena blinked, turning her attention back to the stone desk where the prince sat looking at the ship schedule. Not having heard what was asked of her, she glanced at Grier.

"Yes, thank you," Grier said. "We do not want the Federation tracking her."

Quinn frowned and nodded slowly as if struggling to keep his opinions of the Federation to himself.

"She can travel under my star papers," Payton offered. "It's not like the Var elders will ever let me go anywhere. I don't care if there are two Princess Paytons of the Var roaming around the universes."

"That won't be necessary. I'm sure we can arrange some ESC travel credentials and a new identity," Quinn said. "I'll issue her Var paperwork. We don't track our population like other planets. They will have a hard time proving travel papers issued by a royal family are fake. If anyone asks, tell them you were born without shifting abilities and decided to leave."

Salena wasn't sure anyone would believe she was part of the Exploratory Science Commission. She knew little about galactic sciences. "My science is not strong."

Please, not tonight.

"No one will be asking you to solve any problems. I'll arrange a couple of basic uploads for you when you're onboard to pass basic examinations should any agencies stop you. Perhaps you will like the ESC ship and sign on as a lab technician," Quinn said as he made notations on the encrypted holographic file spread over his desk.

Salena wanted to protest. Her mouth opened, but no sound came out. They were so efficient, and the solution was about as perfect as she could ask for.

"Thank you," Grier answered for her. "For the safe passage and your discretion. And could you set her up with a space credit account under the new identification? I'll transfer funds to fill it."

Stop it. Not tonight. It's too soon.

"I respect what you are sacrificing for your people, Grier," Quinn said. "It's too bad they will never know all that you gave up to ensure their safety."

Grier nodded.

"Do Queen Rigan and King Ualan know about this?" Quinn asked.

"No. And this burden will not fall on them, or the rest of my family. No one else needs to know. They would try to intervene, and make this harder," Grier said. "I appreciate your discretion. I'm in your debt for this."

"No, Prince Grier, you're not." Quinn closed his clipboard. "Everything will be waiting for you on the ship, Lady Salena. I would like to acknowledge what you must also be giving up. On behalf of the Var, I thank you. Our road with the Federation has not been an easy one."

Salena nodded. If she spoke, she'd scream, and she wouldn't stop.

"May I assume you don't want to dine at the banquet tonight?" Quinn walked toward the office door.

"No, thank you. We'd rather go back to the guest room," Grier said.

Salena nodded in agreement.

"I'll walk with you," Payton said under her breath. "Wouldn't want you getting lost."

"Safe travels, my lady," Quinn told her as they left. All she could do was keep nodding.

They walked back to the guest suite. The halls were empty.

"This is wrong," Payton said. "I vote you stay. Curse

the Federation. Let's take them all on. War is coming either way, what better reason to fight than for love?"

"I won't give them an excuse to hurt anyone," Salena whispered. "The will of two is nothing compared to the lives of many."

And, oh, how she hated saying it.

"Fine. Grier, go with her," Payton said. "Let one of your brothers take the crown. Altair...all right, not him. But Creed? There are enough men in the royal family. Someone can take your place. King Ualan can choose a new successor."

Salena stopped walking, feeling as if she'd been punched. And that was why hope was horrible. With that one revelation, it became clear just how far away a future with him was. Small pieces began falling into place. He had so much honor in him.

Grier and Payton paused and looked at each other before turning back.

"You're the future king of the dragons?" Salena asked.

"Didn't you know?" Payton looked at Grier. "Didn't you tell her? How could you not tell her that?"

"I..." He gestured helplessly. "I didn't think to. I just assumed..."

"No. No you didn't tell me that. I would have remembered if you'd told me something like that."

Salena felt dizzy and leaned against one of the walls. She ran her hands into her hair.

"This changes nothing between us," Grier said. "I am the same man."

"You can never leave. And the crazy idea I had that maybe I could come back and hide away with you...that can't happen if you're the king." The cinched vest held her too tight. Salena tugged at it, taking deep breaths. Her back slid down the wall.

Instantly, Grier was there, lifting her into his arms. "My love for you does not change with my title."

She barely noticed the trip back to the guest suite.

Grier carried her to the chair and sat her down. "Help me with this."

Payton and Grier loosened the vest, and he pulled it over her head.

Salena gasped for air, and with it, tears trailed down her face. The pain in her chest was too much.

"Salena—" Grier began but Payton put her hand on his shoulder.

"Let her breathe a moment," Payton said. "She just needs to breathe."

No one spoke as Salena regained control of her panic.

"What can I get for you?" Payton asked.

"Old Earth whiskey?" she answered, trying to make a

joke.

Payton went to the wall by the fireplace and pressed a tile. A compartment opened to show a food simulator. "Do you know the code for it?"

"I was joking. I've never had it." Salena tried to smile. She rubbed her eyes. "I'm better now. I don't need anything."

A knock sounded before the door open.

"Are you in here?" Roderic called.

"Yes," Grier answered.

"I stopped by my father's office. He said you're leaving tonight, Salena?" Roderic asked. "I'm sorry to hear that."

"Me too," Salena answered.

"It's for the best." Grier knelt beside her chair and placed his head on her lap.

Salena touched the back of his hair, stroking him.

"We'll be back when it's time to meet the ship," Payton said. "Come on, Roderic."

Salena pulled off her boots and then slid off the chair to join Grier on the floor. She lifted his head to kiss him softly. When she pulled away, she whispered, "Make love to me again, Grier."

Grier swept her into his arms and carried her to the bed. He stood her at the end where the curtains were parted. She took off her shirt and tossed it on the floor before pushing her pants from her hips. Naked, she inched back onto the bed. Grier followed her lead, disrobing before he joined her.

Salena lay on her back, watching as he crawled over her. The light from the room haloed his body. Every muscle, every movement, was a seduction.

He made love to her slowly, taking his time. He explored every facet of her body, touching and kissing her from head to toe. His tongue trailed from her knee to her inner thigh. By the time his lips met her sex in the most intimate of kisses, she was beyond reason. The pleasure was unlike anything she'd ever felt.

Grier brought her to release with his mouth, seeming to enjoy the trembling he caused. When she could take no more, she pulled on his hair to get him to come over her. He entered her slowly, tenderly.

His gold-tinted eyes held hers. Each thrust, each soft breath, was in unison. Time had no meaning in these moments. It was a second. It was forever. It was infinity.

It was hers.

Salena's thighs tightened on his waist as the climax built once more. As her body clenched his, he also found release. His body stiffened, and his mouth opened in a light moan of ecstasy.

They stayed frozen in the abyss of release for a long time. Every bone in her body felt as if it had turned to liquid and she wished the bed would soak her into it, so that she could stay forever in this room, in this very spot.

"Whatever comes, this is our moment," he whispered, as if reading her soul. "This is the moment I will hold until I find a way to bring you back to be my queen."

She wanted to believe. She wanted to hope. She wanted *him*.

Salena nodded. "If you don't—"

"I will," he put forth.

"But if something happens and I do not return, I will understand if you find..." She couldn't finish it. How could she tell him to move on? To find another woman? She knew what he believed about the gods, but the idea of his never having a family pained her.

"I already told you. The gods will only bless me once, and they have with you. A lifetime, a second, I will take all that they will give me, and I will spend the other seconds remembering each moment we were together. This is our moment, Salena. Yours and mine. None of our enemies can take this from us."

She nodded. It was a nice thought and she would not ruin his words. He said them, so he believed them to be true. Maybe that is what he needed to move forward, and to keep going.

He pulled out of her, lying next to her on the bed.

She knew they wouldn't dare sleep.

"Where do you think you will go?" he asked.

"I'm not sure," she answered, snuggling next to him. "Wherever I think I can find a clue as to my sisters' whereabouts. I've been looking for them so long. I'm not sure what else I can do. Maybe staying with the ESC is the best bet. I can stop at each place and inquire. But I don't want to think about any of that now."

Grier ran his hand over her leg. "I put that shard we pulled from your leg on the floor over there, so it wouldn't get lost." He gestured behind him.

Salena pushed up from the bed and climbed over him. He smiled as she maneuvered over his waist. She leaned over, blindly feeling around on the floor.

"Can you find it?"

"I think..." Her fingers bumped something, and she heard a faint tinkling noise. She felt lightheaded for a moment and assumed it was because her head was angled down off the side of the bed. "I think I dropped it."

She swung her legs around to sit up into a better position and pushed at the curtains until she found where they parted. She pushed them open and stepped down to search the floor.

Grier's bracelet lay on the floor. Tiny shards surrounded it.

"Oh blast," she swore.

"What happened?" Grier appeared next to her.

"I'm so sorry. I didn't mean to." She stepped off the platform and grabbed his bracelet. He turned it over to find the crystal was shattered, and no longer glowed. "I broke your stone."

Grier smiled. "You only finished what could not be undone. In my heart, you were already my mate. Now it is official. You broke my crystal."

"Did I just accidentally marry you?" she asked.

"According to dragon custom, you're my wife," he affirmed.

She found she did not mind.

"Now I *have* to find a way to make sure you're safe, so that you can come home to me. Perhaps when you find your sisters, you three will all come back here." He rolled onto his back and held up his arm, signaling that she should rejoin him on the bed. "All of you will have a home here, and family."

Seeing the pottery shard, she picked it up and brought it to him. "Well, then, husband, I want you to keep this." She gave a small smile. "It's literally a piece of me, and the blue clay will bring you luck."

"It will never leave me," he promised.

Salena sat on the bed, gazing at him as he lay on his back in naked perfection. She felt complete.

21

GRIER PRESSED THE POTTERY SHARD AGAINST HIS palm so tightly that it cut into his skin.

Payton hugged his wife, whispering something just beyond his hearing. The blue-green sunlight had dimmed with the evening. They stood on an extension of the Var palace where visiting spaceships docked. The wide platform was near the roof, towered over by stone turrets and accessible only through a reinforced steel door.

The ESC ship was impressive as far as ships went. Prince Quinn had done well with his arrangements. The few scientists loading supplies appeared friendly but efficient.

"Have you seen to the funds?" he asked when Quinn came down the loading dock of the ship.

"It's arranged. She'll be well taken care of," Quinn assured him. "I also have their communication bank coordinates, so that you may send her messages. It might be months before she receives them depending on where they are docked, but she will receive them as long as she is with the ship."

Grier watched Salena. Roderic hugged her and handed her a piece of paper. Salena nodded at him.

The ship began to make a whirring noise as the engines engaged.

Grier hurried toward his wife and pulled her against him. He held her tight. "I'll be able to send you messages through ESC. Stay with them. The second it is safe, I'll send for you."

She nodded. "Don't worry. Space travel does not frighten me. I know what I'm doing."

He held her as long as they would let him. The sound of the steel doors opening behind him reverberated over the area.

"Grier, we have to get behind the doors," Payton said. "The ship needs to take off."

"I love you," he said.

Salena pressed her face to his neck and whispered, "I love you, too, Grier."

It was the first time she'd said the words, and they were a bittersweet sound. He held her tighter.

"Grier," Roderic said. "We have to go."

His friends pulled him away from Salena. She watched as he was urged to the steel doors. She lifted the paper Roderic had given in her fist and waved. She kept her eyes on him.

The door closed, blocking out the light. The metallic thud might as well have been against his chest. His heart felt tight, and he pressed his fist over it as if that could stop the pain. He kept his eyes on the door even though he could not see. His eyes shifted as he stared at the smooth texture of metal. His ears strained for each indication of takeoff. He heard the docking plank close. He heard the engines engage. He heard her leaving his planet.

"I'm truly sorry," Roderic said. "I can't imagine what you are feeling, but I do know what you gave up for your people."

He wanted to slam his body into the metal doors until they either dented under his weight or he was knocked unconscious. At this point he didn't care which.

Roderic grabbed his arm, his eyes glowing with the threat of a shift. "Whatever you're thinking, don't. You need to let her go. Use what you're feeling to do what you must."

"I'll get her back," he swore. "The Federation has ruined enough lives."

"You are not alone in this quest," Payton said. "We will all help to get her back. I promise, Grier."

He nodded his thanks. It didn't help end the ache building inside him. The loneliness would fill every crevice and there was only one way to rid himself of it. He needed his wife.

"What did you give her?" Grier asked Roderic. "What was that paper?"

"The marsh farmers were carrying a likeness of her with the reward bounty notice. I thought she might like the souvenir," Roderic said. "Come, let's get you drunk."

"I don't want to go." He stared at the door, even though he could no longer hear the ESC ship.

"How about I make sure everything with their takeoff went well, and then I will come to find you?" Payton asked. "Go with Roderic. I'll join you with news soon."

Grier nodded. "Perhaps one drink."

"Perhaps a dozen," Roderic said. "Tonight we will commiserate for tomorrow we tear down our enemy once and for all."

Grier didn't want to leave the door as if it would open and time would rewind.

Roderic hooked his arm and pulled him down the corridor. Grier couldn't speak. The pain inside him was too strong, building with each step. He knew it would hurt, but he didn't imagine it would feel like this.

The dragon wanted out.

Grier had no desire to stop it.

He ripped his arm away from Roderic and ran. A stairwell connected to the corridor and would take him to the top of the turret. He felt the dragon clawing to be free, but he couldn't shift inside an enclosed space.

"Grier," Roderic yelled. "Stop!"

The dragon did not listen to reason. His jaw popped out of place, filling with sharp teeth. Grier's body began to shift, his skin hardening. He skipped steps as he ran, imagining he was running after the ESC ship.

As he burst through the door leading to the open walkway that would take him across to another turret lookout, he leapt over the side. Grier barreled toward the ground, his body spinning.

The dragon needed to fly. The pressure brought on a shift. His clothes tore as his body expanded. The dragon inside was desperate to be free. It felt like all his bones fractured at once. The cracking sound in his mind was as loud as his thumping heart, and as wild as the urge to set fire to everything he gazed upon. But not nearly as strong as his need for Salena.

As his wings flapped, he knew what the animal wanted to do. It expressed that innate part of him that did not listen to reason and duty. It was pure emotion, and right now his feelings were on fire with rage and heartbreak.

Fire erupted from his chest, and his stomach contracted, not giving him a choice as he spouted a long flame into the sky. The fire was carried by his agonizing roar. His wings flapped harder, and he shot upward like a missile after the ship. He had found his mate, and it had taken everything in the man to let her leave. The dragon was not having it.

His taloned hands clenched, and he wanted to rip the spaceship from the sky. He saw its lights as it broke through the safest layer of the atmosphere for a dragon. The air became thin, and it was difficult to breathe. He pushed his body harder. He tried to roar, but the sound was choked. His lungs burned.

He remembered thinking that in all the long moments of his life, the one outside his wedding tent would be the worst. That was before he saw her. That was before he knew just how painful true heartache could be.

Grier followed the ship with a stubborn determination, forgetting about his safety. And with each inch of Qurilixen atmosphere he passed through, he came perilously close to the mesosphere where he could not return from.

The awareness of where he was and what would happen to him came crashing down on his tortured soul at once. If it were not for the fact that he was fully shifted and in dragon form, his humanoid form would not have sustained his broken heart.

Grier followed the ship for as long as he could until the air did not give him oxygen and his wings were so fatigued they could not beat. And just as quickly as he'd gone into the heavens, he was sent back to the planet's surface. The dragon was instantly repelled from the border of the mesosphere, sending Grier hurtling back toward the planet. Shifting as he fell, his body spun as he plummeted headfirst.

The ship powered through to space as ships do, taking his heart with it. Blackness threatened him, and he fought for consciousness, knowing this was not a battle he would win.

22

I'M SURE THAT WE SHOULD RUN, FIORA'S VOICE whispered.

I can see that we should stay, Piera's countered, in one of the rare contradictions of their abilities.

Salena? both voices demanded at the same time.

Salena pressed her back to the wall and kept her eyes closed as the ship moved through Qurilixen airspace. Her heart beat hard, each thump painful.

"Piera's right. We should have stayed in the pit," Salena said to herself. That was the true moment all of this started. "I shouldn't have hesitated. I should have made a decision and stayed with it."

Salena clutched the paper Roderic had given her. It felt like it had a life of its own and had become a living, breathing thing she had to hold on to. She felt it pulsing against her hand, keeping time with her rapid heartbeat.

Logically, she knew it was her hand that pulsed and not an inanimate force, but still she kept her fingers balled as if the paper could connect her to something beyond.

"We have to run now," Salena said, repeating her sister's words, invoking the memory as she kept her eyes closed. She didn't want to look beyond her thoughts.

She held the paper tight, the pulsing in her hand reminding her of the moment she'd clutched Fiora and Piera. She had held on to them so determinedly, thinking they could never be torn apart.

We have to run now. Fiora's whisper followed hers as it surfaced from within.

Like now, Salena hadn't wanted to run. She hadn't wanted to leave.

The darkness was safe. The monsters couldn't find them in the dark. Salena let herself slip into that moment, remembering each instance of fear and pain.

The clay pit had been a favorite playground where they could draw pictures in the dirt and pretend they were somewhere else—miners on Bravon pulling ash from the tunnels, before the planet had burned itself up, or scientists on Sintaz excavating alien ships. Their father had told them a great many fantastic stories.

Salena curled her toes in her boots, recalling how she had been barefoot that night. The sound of the villagers' attack had awakened them from sleep.

We have to wake up now, Fiora said. *Salena, we have to wake up.*

"We have to wake up now." Fiora's insistent shake woke Salena from her dreams.

The sound of footsteps overhead was nothing new. Her father moved over them, which meant it was still early enough in the night that they didn't need to be up. The sound of his feet was comforting in its familiarity. It meant their parents were close, watching over them. Next to her, Piera sighed in her sleep. The room smelled of wet clay, some from the walls, some from the storage of processed wedges of clay ready to be made into pots.

"Salena, we have to wake up," Fiora insisted. The bed they shared shook. "Piera."

"What is it?" Piera mumbled.

"Something is coming," Fiora whispered. Tiny streams of light from the room above came through the narrow openings in the floor slats. "I can feel it."

"It's only nightmares," Salena dismissed. "I should never have told you the men from the forest wanted us gone. Their not appreciating the truth and their doing something about it are two very different things."

"I didn't like their colors when I looked at them," Piera said. "They are not good men."

"Their constituents probably tied them to a tree and left them for the animals after the sins they confessed," Salena tried to comfort her sisters. "It's like mother said. Monsters can't find us in the dark."

"It's not a nightmare," Fiora insisted. A glint of light reflected off a tear. She was terrified. "Something bad is coming. I can see fragments."

Fiora slid off the bed and reached beneath it for her boots. She tugged them on her bare feet. The thump of their father's pacing quickened. A knock sounded, and they all looked up to see what they could through the slats. The shadow of their father moved to the cottage door.

"Go away," their father ordered. "I told you, we're not interested in your proposal."

Piera's hand crept onto Salena's leg and tightened in fear. Out of all the sisters, she was the most delicate in temperament. They stared at the shadows coming through the floor to their bedroom ceiling.

A muffled response answered her father.

"Put these on." Fiora dropped their boots on the bed,

getting dried clay on the pretty quilt their mother had sewn for them. They ignored her.

Wood reverberated, as if their father had unlocked the door but blocked it from opening with his foot. Salena always thought him a large, imposing man, so strong that he was able to carry one of his young daughters under each arm like a load of sticks and the third on his shoulders without strain.

"There is nothing to talk about. Now go. We want no trouble with the village," he said. The door reverberated again as if he'd tried to close it but was stopped by someone.

"Those are bad colors," Piera whispered.

"Emil, reconsider our offer. It is best for everyone if your girls leave." It was the voice of one of the politicians, Garegin. "Think of the education they will get at a private school facility, the opportunities they will have that you—a potter's husband—can't give them. Do you really want them growing up covered in clay?"

"How I raise my children is of no concern to you. It is like I told you before. I am not sending them away. Thank you for the offer, but I must insist you go now. It is late, and this is a family that must work with the dawn." Her father again tried to shut the door, but a loud crash threw the shadow of his body back into the room.

More shadows spilled into the room above, outnumbering their father greatly. Salena was sure she'd never seen so many people in her home at one time.

Fiora climbed up on the bed.

Piera whimpered.

Salena's sisters hugged her from both sides, as they all continued to watch.

"I am sorry to hear that, but you don't have a choice. If you do not do it willingly, we will have to force your hand for the good of the village." The shadow she guessed to be Garegin stepped back. His next words were a low crack of sound. "Destroy it all."

The upstairs became a chaos of movement. They saw her father fighting, throwing men against the walls, crashing them into tables. For a brief instant, Salena wholeheartedly believed that he would win against such odds, for he was so strong, so brave, their proud father.

But there were too many, and even the best fighter could not win against such odds, and he was thrown to the floor.

Their mother's footsteps came from the loft where her parents shared a bed. She began shouting at them to get out of her house. Pottery crashed. Assailants moaned and swore. The chaos continued.

"We have to run." Fiora tugged at her arm.

"We should help them," Salena countered, not taking

her eyes from the ceiling. "Get me a knife. I'll stab them in the feet."

"We don't have a knife," Piera answered.

"You can't, they'll find us," Fiora said.

Their mother screamed, and the sisters clutched each other tighter. A body thudded to the floor. Something dripped from above, the warm liquid hitting Salena's arm.

"Avelina!" Their father's anguish rang over them. "What have you done?"

Their father ran to the fallen body. When it was lifted, the light revealed their mother's dead eyes staring down at them through the slats. Blood dripped from her mouth through the floor. Salena looked at her arm, her eyes wide as she realized what had dripped onto her.

"Look upstairs," Garegin ordered. "Find the girls."

Footsteps thundered like a storm above them. Salena slipped off the bed, ignoring the boots. There was no time left for that or changing out of their nightclothes. She pulled at her sisters' arms to force them off the bed.

"We have to go," Salena said, finally agreeing with Fiora.

She crossed the room to the airflow vent in the ceiling that would lead to the yard. They had a small trunk they kept beneath it. Salena climbed on top and stretched her arms up as far as she could. She pushed up on the vent, hard. She dislodged it, but it remained over her.

"Piera, leave it," Fiora ordered.

Salena glanced to see Piera holding the pot their mother had given her. Fiora ripped it from her arms and tossed in on the bed before pushing her toward the vent.

"Fiora, you first." Salena clasped her hands, ready to launch her up as they did when they wanted to climb out of the clay pits.

"Piera, don't move," Fiora ordered her before climbing onto the trunk. She placed her foot in Salena's hands, lifted her arms so she could grab the vent, and then nodded.

Fiora gave a small hop as Salena pushed her sister's foot upward with her joined hands. In one motion, Fiora tried to push the vent while scrambling to get out. Her head smacked the vent's edge, and she managed to slide it onto the yard above. Her weight came back down to the trunk.

Fiora touched her bleeding head and looked at her hand. "I'm fine. Do it again."

Loud thumps sounded from above and the light brightened. An orange glow filled their room, and she smelled smoke.

Salena pushed up as her sister jumped, launching out of her hands. Fiora went over the side and then reappeared with her hands reaching into the hole from above.

"Piera, get up here," Salena ordered.

Piera obeyed, not speaking as she placed her foot in Salena's hands. Fiora grabbed Piera from above to help. Salena launched the second sister as Fiora pulled. Piera managed to hook her stomach on the ground above. Her feet dangled as Fiora pulled her onto the yard.

Moments later, both sisters had their hands down the hole. Each grabbed hold of one of Salena's forearms. Salena jumped as high as she could. Her sisters pulled. Salena's toes slipped against the hard clay wall for leverage as they pulled her from inside. Her body slid along the grass as she was tugged onto the yard.

Voices coming from the front of the house caused Fiora to grab hold of Piera, forcing her to follow when she would have looked at the flames that were devouring the house. Salena glanced back before following her sisters toward the clay pits. They traveled the ravine that took them to the pits every day and could run the path blind. Only the sound of their feet hitting the dirt marked their passing. Salena placed her hand on the small of Piera's back, forcing her to run faster.

Fiora led them to one of the smaller pits and climbed inside, urging Piera and Salena to do the same. It was shallow enough they could stand and see over the edge.

Breathing hard, all three sisters sat on the ground, hidden. Salena grabbed her sisters' hands as they sat on either side of her.

"I don't understand." Tears rolled down Piera's cheeks, but she didn't cry out. "Why would they hurt them?"

"Because that's what evil does," Fiora answered.

"Where will we go?" Piera insisted. "They burnt down our house."

"That doesn't matter right now," Salena said. For now, they were safe in the dark where the monsters couldn't see them. Darkness had protected them at the house, and it would protect them now. It had to. The familiar smell of clay was home. It was supposed to be safe at home. "We can't go back there. We have to figure out what to do. What would father tell us to do?"

"We have to run now," Fiora whispered.

Salena clutched her sisters' hands so tight that she felt as if their pulsebeat became part of her through her throbbing fingers. She wanted the firm ground beneath her bare feet to pull them in and hold them. This was home. She knew nothing else.

They knew nothing else.

"No. They'll find us if we run." Piera pulled her hand away and rubbed her eyes with the backs of her hands as if that gesture could erase all that she had seen. "We have to stay here."

Fiora touched her bloody forehead where she'd hit the vent. Blood had started to dry but was still moist along the wound. The light reflected off its shiny edges when she moved.

"I'm sure that we should run," Fiora argued in a hushed voice.

"I can see that we should stay." Piera had mud caked along her arm from where she'd fallen. She tried to reach a dirty hand toward Fiora's head in concern. Salena grabbed Piera's hand and held it once more in hers. She needed to feel her sisters with her.

"Salena?" They both stared at her as they forced her to be the deciding vote.

Run or stay?

She didn't know.

Stay or run?

What would their father say to do?

Protect your sisters. They weren't his words, but the thought came in his voice.

"Salena?" Piera asked.

She shook her head, not knowing what to decide. Fiora touched her arm. She was always so much sturdier than their delicate Piera.

"Run?" Salena asked more than commanded.

No one questioned the decision. The majority vote would always win when it came to the sisters and there was no time for debate.

Piera looked terrified as Salena stood. At the look, she hesitated.

Fiora climbed from the pit. "Hurry. We have to run now before it's too late."

"I..." Salena wondered if she'd made the right decision. She glanced toward the house, seeing an orange light in the night sky. The loss filled her with uncertainty. Maybe they should stay and hide. Each of the sisters' abilities was known to be reliable. How did she know which one to choose?

"Salena," Fiora insisted.

"Come, Piera." Salena forced Piera to her feet and half-lifted, half-shoved her from the shallow pit.

"There!"

That one word rang like a death knell through the forest.

"Run," Fiora screamed. Salena pushed up from the pit as Fiora and Piera ran ahead of her, but her slight hesitance had wasted precious seconds that cost them dearly. She felt rope hitting the backs of her legs as a bola wrapped around her ankles, tripping her. The two weights at the end of the cord propelled it to tangle her calves as she fell forward with a scream.

Two more thuds and two more screams followed hers. Salena tried to free herself. Pulling the weighted balls to unwrap her ankles. By the time she finally managed, two men stood above her. She recognized them as Garegin's thugs. They'd been in the forest with him when the sisters had come across their political rally quite by accident. It was the incident that had put this night into motion, but not the only incident the villagers hated them for.

"Leave us alone," Salena ordered.

"No, please," Piera cried. "Stop! Leave us alone."

"I see your future—and you do not end well," Fiora warned, her tone harder than Piera's.

"Let's kill them and throw their bodies in the pits," a skinny man who looked to be more bones than muscles said. He had stringy blond hair and watery, leering eyes. "Let's see how much trouble they can make when they're dead."

The slightly larger man next to him grunted a response. Salena couldn't tell if that meant he agreed with his friend or not.

"No." Garegin appeared behind his thugs. "We have traders waiting to take them, and they'll pay well for the privilege. Tie them up and make sure they can't speak."

The sisters fought but in the end they were bound and carted to the shipping docks. The spaceships always emitted a distinct smell, especially the older ones. After they were herded into an open crate like animals, three men stood guard to make sure they didn't run. Two faced outward to the docking area. The third faced toward them, staring with cold eyes.

Salena drew her bound hands to Fiora's head to check the wound now that they had more light to see. The cut was deep and triangular, like the tooth of a tree saw.

"We'll be fine as long as we stay together," Salena said. She hooked her bound arms over Piera's head to hold her the best she could. Fiora pressed to her side. "I promise. We need to stick together."

"Got them," the skeletal thug said, coming to the cargo's open door. He smiled as he looked at them and raised a pistol. "Good night, ladies."

A dart hit Piera. She slumped, and Salena tried to hold on as her sister fell to the floor.

"No," Fiora cried.

The whiz of another dart sounded, lodging in Salena's chest. She tried to grab it, but her arms were too heavy. Fiora's words became a mumble of indecipherable tones. Salena didn't feel the metal floor as she struck it.

23

WE'LL BE FINE AS LONG AS WE STAY TOGETHER.

Salena loosened her grip on the paper and took a steadying breath. That moment in the cargo hold was the last time she'd seen her sisters. In one night, she'd lost so much, and she'd almost made that same mistake again.

Being with the ESC was probably the best opportunity she would ever have. She was lucky to get it, to get the backing of a Var prince, to get papers hiding who she was. It was a decision for her future. A smart decision.

It was a decision she was not going to make.

"We'll be fine as long as we stay together, Grier," she whispered.

Salena opened her eyes and looked up at the sky from her place huddled next to the palace wall. The ESC ship was a mere blip of light. Her feet had stopped moving even before stepping onto the docking plank to leave. She hadn't been able to board. The scientists hadn't cared. They had a schedule to keep and wished her well on her journeys.

But now what?

Grier would only find her another ship in the name of keeping her safe, and she couldn't leave.

She looked at the paper in her hand. Now more than ever.

The steel doors opened along the same wall Salena leaned against. Payton ran out onto the platform looking upward. She shaded her eyes.

Salena pushed herself to her feet and looked to make sure the princess was not followed. She whispered, "Payton, over here."

Payton turned and dropped her hand. "Salena?" She glanced upward and then back. "What happened?"

Salena's hand shook as she held the paper balled in her fist toward Payton. "I can't leave."

"What is that?" Payton reached to take it. Salena had a hard time letting go. The princess pulled it from her fingers and began to uncrumple it. She looked at the image and frowned. "The Federation made a poster for the bounty hunters, so what?"

"So..." Salena snatched the paper back and held the

picture up so Payton was forced to look at the image. "This isn't me!"

"It looks like you," Payton said doubtfully. She pushed her hair out of her face as the breeze changed directions and became colder. "I mean, a drawing is no holographic likeness, but—"

"No, you don't understand." Salena shook the paper, trying to get the words out over the emotions whirling frantically inside her. "This isn't me."

Salena turned the drawing around and flattened it against her palm, keeping it from flying away as she held it in front of Payton. "Do you see the scar on the forehead?" She pushed her hair back. "I don't have a scar there."

"It's a misprint," Payton said. "Happens all the time with parchment. It's why no one hardly ever uses it for important documents anymore. But it is highly transportable and isn't going to set off any security systems."

"I don't have a scar, but my sister does." Salena shook the paper, desperate. "This isn't me. This is Fiora. I feared she was dead. I have been all over the universes looking for her, following every lead. Why would the Federation have a picture of Fiora unless she is here on Qurilixen? And if she is here, maybe Piera is too. Maybe Fiora has escaped them and they're out looking for her."

Payton took a deep breath and glanced at the steel

doors. "What will you do?"

"I have to get back to Shelter City. Someone there must know something." Salena shook so badly she had a hard time coming up with a plan. Her mind rushed with the knowledge that her sister might have been closer than she realized. What if Roderic had never given her the picture? She might be in space right now letting her breaking heart take over her spirit. "All I know is I can't leave. I know Grier wants me to go for my own safety, and it's best for the shifters if the Federation doesn't know you all helped me, but I'm not—"

"Blast the Federation," Payton broke in. "I believe you saw this picture for a reason. The gods clearly do not want you to leave. And I know Grier doesn't want you to go. He's torn between his duty and his need to protect you. It's clouding his judgment."

"Why didn't you say something before?" Salena asked.

"You didn't make me tell you, and it wasn't my place. You two made a decision and I must respect that." Payton looked around the windy docking platform. "It happens a lot with shifter royalty, I'm afraid. Duty and honor and tradition is drummed so deep inside us that we can't see past it. Well, they can't. I'm not like them. And, now that you've decided to stay, I'm going to help you."

"I can't ask that of you. I consider you a friend and do not wish to get you in trouble. There is too much political risk."

Payton laughed. "Stop that. Do you think I'd pass up such an adventure? What you can't do right now is tell Grier. He'll try to stop us. He'll also never forgive me later if I let you go alone. So we're going to Shelter City to find your sister. Together."

"How?"

Payton took a deep breath. "How are you at climbing?"

"I can if I have to," Salena said. She folded the picture and shoved it in the top of her boot for safe-keeping.

"Good." Payton took her arm and guided her to the short wall that acted like a railing around the platform and leaned over. She pointed down the great height. "Because this is how we're sneaking out of here undetected."

Salena gripped the wall and leaned over. The stone was textured but looked too smooth to climb. Her heart began to pound at the idea of scaling down the wall for the full height of a castle, for they were near the top. There were no exterior stairs leading down from the platform. The only safe way off was to go back into the palace between the metal doors.

Payton took Salena by the jaw and turned her head to direct her attention to narrow stairs below them leading to a palace door on the level below them. "We climb down there. If we go inside, someone will see us."

"Oh, thank the stars," Salena swore. "For a moment I thought you meant for me to jump off the roof."

"Even I am not that adventurous. Cats prefer their feet on the ground." Payton led Salena along the wall to the corner of the roof. "Watch me. Use the footholds and when you're close enough to land without hurting yourself, jump down."

Payton hopped onto the ledge and held on as she lowered her feet over the side. Salena leaned over to watch where the woman put her foot. The rocks jutted out like narrow steps. Payton maneuvered herself down a couple of feet before pushing off the wall and dropping down to the landing. She looked up and waved for Salena to follow.

Salena made the mistake of looking at the trees below. Her stomach knotted, and she had to concentrate on trying not to shake. She grabbed the ledge. Something about the fear made her think of that night, to her sisters climbing out of the vent. The thought of them gave her courage, and she didn't let herself contemplate the danger as she moved her feet over the side.

"Left," Payton instructed.

Salena swung her foot to the left and found a toehold. From there it was easy to climb to the landing.

"The adventure begins." Payton led the way down the stairs. "I know a place we can go for supplies."

Salena looked up at the castle. She felt Grier as if there was an invisible cord linking them together. She wanted to be with him.

"Salena, he won't want you to go into danger," Payton said. "He'll want to protect you. He's a dragon. It's what they do. I told you, it's ingrained in him."

"Promise me. If something happens to me, you'll tell him—"

"Nothing," Payton interrupted. "I'll tell him absolutely nothing. Because if something happens to you, it'll happen to me too. I won't abandon you, and I sure as fire will not go back to Grier without you. I'd be one roasted kitty."

"Fair enough." Salena couldn't help but smile.

Payton rushed down the stairs, leading the way along the wall. When they neared the bottom, the way to the forest was blocked. The only option was a door leading inside.

Payton climbed over the wall as if she'd done it many times. She sat on the wall and waited until Salena joined her. They jumped down together and ran into the forest.

24

"WHAT THE HELL HAPPENED TO YOU?" RODERIC asked as Grier limped into the palace.

"Do you have that drink you offered me?" Grier asked. Leaves stuck to his hair and beard, and dirt smudged his naked body. How he survived the fall, he'd never know. He woke up in his human form in thorny underbrush feeling as if he'd been run through with a sword a few hundred times.

Two guards tried to run up behind him, but Roderic held up his hand. "It's fine. Back to your post, please."

Grier kept walking, heading toward the guest room he'd shared with Salena. He wasn't the best at navigating that part of the palace, but he was sure he could figure it out.

If he put his face to the pillow, he might be able to smell her.

If he closed his eyes, he might be able to feel her.

If he begged the gods, he—

"Sacred cats, Grier, your back looks like you landed on a bed of spikes." Roderic strode next to him. "Let's get you into the medical booth."

"I need a drink," Grier said by way of denial.

"You need medical attention," Roderic argued. "What did you do?"

"I tried to stop the spaceship. I failed," he said.

"You let the dragon make the decisions?" Roderic's tone said what he thought of that choice. "I see that worked out well for you."

"I will punch you in the face," Grier grumbled, knowing he would never.

"After the medical booth," Roderic said. "Then you can drink and punch as much as you want. I won't stop you."

"Fine."

"You're going the wrong way," Roderic said. "Unless you wanted to make a naked appearance at the dining hall to say hello to the cat-shifter elders?"

Grier stopped his own wayward course through the palace hall maze and followed Roderic's lead by turning around.

"I know you dragons pride yourself on the whole living simply thing, but here at the Var palace we have these things called communication devices. With a few buttons we can hail spaceships that have left our airspace," Roderic said.

Grier grunted. "Slargnot."

"Call me all the names you like." Roderic led him to the medical booth door.

Grier paused and looked at the booth, remembering Salena inside it, her body covered in light, and the sheer gown she wore when he'd later made love to her. He looked at the wall where the gown would usually be hanging. It was missing. He wondered if it was still in the room they had shared, along with the pottery shard from her leg and his broken crystal.

Wait, no.

Grier had held onto the shard. He turned to leave. "I dropped something. I have to go."

How he was going to find a tiny piece of pottery outside the Var palace was beyond him, but she had said it was a piece of her and he couldn't lose it.

Roderic touched his arm gently. "I'd rather your anger have a direction than to sit inside you and boil. So yell at me, hate me, argue with me, punch me. I don't care. But first, get your ass in that booth."

"I dropped the shard Salena gave me," he said, as if that would explain why he had to leave.

"This?" Roderic reached into his pocket. The pottery shard was smeared with Grier's blood. "You dropped it before you flew off on your little death wish."

His hand shook as he reached for it. He studied the unglazed side of the blue clay. "Thank you."

"Thank me by getting in the booth," Roderic gave him a push, no longer gentle in his request.

"Salena was in there. She had so many old fractures," Grier said, more to himself than to his friend. "I shouldn't have let her go. I should have locked her in a tower and hidden her from the Federation."

"For the rest of her life?" Roderic reasoned. "Only the cruelest of husbands would wish such a fate on their mates. You know that. It's why you sent her somewhere safer. The ESC has the best security and ship facilities for their staff. You couldn't have put her on a better vessel than that."

Grier took a step toward the booth, wanting to be close to his mate in any way possible. Her body had touched the booth walls. Now his would. He climbed in and closed his eyes. He remembered every line of her form, every degree of her smile. The booth moved, laying him back at an angle, and the warmth of the lasers began their trip over his body to repair the damage from the fall.

"Don't fix the pain in my chest. It's all I have of her right now," Grier said.

"Now who is the *slargnot*?" Roderic answered. He appeared next to the booth as it worked to heal Grier's cuts. "She is still your mate. A billion galactic miles will not change that. Self-pity will do you no good. But if you must wallow, you have one drunken night to do so. Then this cat-shifter will claw your stupid ass if you talk like that ever again after tomorrow morning, dragon prince."

"Deal," Grier mumbled. He held the shard between two of his fingers. He knew his friend was right, but that didn't make what he was feeling easier. "But your supportive talks leave much to be desired, Var ambassador."

"So I'm told." Roderic chuckled. "You're lucky I'm not Payton."

"Payton would have skipped the booth and gotten me the liquor," Grier countered.

"True, but she'd also convince you to shift with her and attack Shelter City while you were both drunk. She likes Salena. I haven't seen her take to someone like that in a long time."

"I like that plan," Grier said. "Go get me Payton."

"No clue where she is. The last I saw her, she was supposed to be checking on the ship. All is well with the takeoff or my father would have informed me otherwise."

The console beeped, pulling Roderic away. "If I had to guess, I would say she ran into her father, or she's avoiding him. That tiger has been wild since the day she was born."

"Even so, would you mind having your communications check with the ship just to make sure Salena is settled?" Grier asked.

"Of course. I'll put a request in as soon as we are finished here." The sound of his friend pushing buttons on the console interrupted the conversation. "Three hundred fifty-two cuts. A broken rib. Sprained wrist. Dislocated ribs. Knotted muscles along your spine. The list goes on. Sacred cats, Grier, how far did you fall?"

"Not sure. I passed out before hitting the ground," he answered. "I barely remember the descent."

"And what were you going to do if you actually caught a spaceship? Hold on as you went into orbit to die without oxygen?" It was clear by this tone that Roderic thought he was a dumbass.

"The dragon didn't plan that far ahead."

"Evidently not," Roderic grumbled. "Fractured arm."

"That would explain the numbness in my hand."

"No, that would be the pinched nerve." The sound of Roderic pushing commands into the console again cut off the conversation. Finally, he said, "There. Now all you have to do is lay there while it fixes you."

"Just do the major things," Grier dismissed. "The rest will heal on its own."

"You stay right there and let it work, or I'll have this medical report sent to your parents," Roderic threatened.

"You really are a slargnot," Grier swore.

"You're welcome," Roderic said.

"Yeah, thank you," Grier grumbled. He closed his eyes. He didn't feel Salena by lying in the booth like he thought he would. All he felt was the hard shell of the panel holding him up. Salena was softer than that. But he could remember her body under the lights, her thigh during the surgery, the look in her eyes as she peered out at him. He held on to the feelings she evoked.

Grier barely felt the burn of the Old Earth whiskey as he swallowed the entire contents of the tall glass Roderic had handed him. It would take a lot more than that to get him drunk, but he was desperate to stop the agony.

There was an alien saying that time made things easier, lessened pain, something like that. Those aliens had probably never felt a tenth of what he did for his mate. If they had, they'd know that time would not ease his pain. If anything, it would only give it the chance to grow worse until it ate him from the inside out. There was only one thing that could stop the breaking of a dragon-shifter's heart, and that was his wife.

He now understood the hollowness he'd seen in dragons who had lost their mates. It was in their eyes, ghosting every conversation, every laugh, every action. Bachelors thought they knew the depths of what mating meant, but the truth was no one could know just how deeply the bond formed until they'd had their crystal broken. That moment had solidified what was between them.

Grier knew the moment the crystal shattered. It sent a vibration through him, as if calling to the gods to say, *it is done.*

Roderic didn't speak as he refilled the glass. Grier downed that one as well.

As he handed it back for yet another refill, his eyes turned to the bracelet on his wrist. He'd sewn the shard into the jewelry where the crystal had been. He would not drop a piece of her again.

Tomorrow he would fight. He would fly to Shelter City and camp out on that watchtower until he had the solution he needed to take down the Federation, save the Cysgodians from their rule, and get his wife back.

Tonight he would drink and figure out a way to breathe without his heart.

25

THE FOUL-SMELLING MUD NAUSEATED SALENA AS Payton smeared it across her brow, over her cheeks and the rest of her face. She forced herself to concentrate beyond the discomfort as she focused on the task at hand. And that was to find her sister.

A stolen scarf that smelled of old socks wrapped the lower part of her face, and a gown three sizes too big—and just as smelly as the scarf—hung on her frame. It completed Salena's disguise.

Payton instructed her to walk with a limp and keep her head down as she led the way through Shelter City.

Payton wore a jacket over her clothes, the length hitting her midcalf. Her hair was tucked into a hat that draped down on both sides to cover her ears. A coat of dust covered her face as if that could hide her beauty.

Salena had gotten a glimpse of Shelter City during her escape, but that was nothing compared to walking through the middle of it. Buildings were held together by rope, rusted bolts, and careless welds. It was as if the Federation had given its citizens scrap metal from ships. From where they walked, Salena couldn't see the pristine buildings towering over the city.

The sidewalks were nothing more than boards and rusted metal laid over the ground, most likely held into place by mud and nothing else. The chaotic sounds of Shelter City were so loud that it distorted most of what was being said—people shouted, children played, vendors advertised their wares and customers haggling for a bargain. Not to mention the ruckus that appeared to spring from substandard living conditions. She'd seen more than a few rumbles in the street as men hit each other with fists, and just about any other object they could find lying around. Salena tried not to stare. Everyone around them ignored the disturbances as if they were just another fight, another day.

Payton kept a determined pace without making it obvious they were in a hurry. Shouts followed them through the narrow market alleyways and wider streets.

"Meat. Nearly fresh," a woman offered, waving a fistful of questionable food hanging from strings. "We accept trade."

"Has anyone seen my boy? Anyone?" a father yelled, running through the streets. "Caspar?"

"Fight tonight. Test your mettle against our reigning champion. He's never been beat. Do you have what it takes to go up against the king of fists? There, you, you look like you want a good beating!"

"Fresh from the marshes, drink yourself numb. Only a half stone per pint!"

"Refurbished light sticks, short-range communicators, time keepers." The man in a bright yellow shirt was hard to miss. "Or if late-night company is your desire, I have the best part of a pleasure droid, yours for the wooing, men, for only two stones. She don't talk. She don't complain. She doesn't have a head. Who needs the whole robot when I have the only part you really want."

"Oh, gross," Payton muttered.

"And if it's servicing you ladies need, well, that's free. I got what you want right here." Yellow-shirt cupped his crotch. No one seemed too eager to take him up on the offer.

"I'd rather cut myself in half," Payton added under her breath.

A passing woman heard the comment and cackled. It clearly prompted her to turn and yell at yellow-shirt, "You'd have to pay fifty stones before any of us would climb up on that tiny, diseased rod."

Salena followed Payton's lead and limped faster past the metal establishment.

"The thief has struck again, raining terror on those who would suppress us." A woman stood on a crate to set herself above the others in the street. Her gown was torn and stained, but she looked as if she'd tried to style her red hair on top of her head, as it was pulled up into a neat bun. Her face and hands were clean. She gestured her arms wide as if beckoning the attention of all those who passed. "Why do we sit idly by when one faces the many on our behalf? We should join forces. Show our strength so that the tyranny of Shelter City—"

"Shut your black hole, Justina, before you bring the wrath of the Federation down on us!" The words were followed by a clump of mud smacking the woman in the chest to knock her over.

Justina stumbled under the blow, and it became clear where the other stains on her gown had come from.

"They should fear us," Justina argued. "We are many in number, if only we would join in the common cause. Life does not have to be like this!"

Justina's declaration was met with jeers and more mudballs.

Payton paused and whispered, "That woman is crazy. She's going to get herself killed if she keeps up that kind of talk about the Federation."

"I wish we could help her," Salena answered just as softly. "I wish we could help all of them."

"There is nothing we can do right now. We're here to find Fiora, that's all. If the Federation knew shifters were coming into their city..."

"I know," Salena answered, not needing the reminder. "War. Death. Destruction. The overthrow of all shifter government."

"What do we have hiding under here?" The smell of liquor filled the air as a man swayed close to Salena. She automatically recoiled when he tried to pull at her gown. Payton slapped his hand.

"Do it and lose more than a finger," Payton warned, throwing her voice a little so she sounded gruff. "She's got the unmentionable. Radiation won't cure it. One touch of that and you'll have parts falling off that you might miss."

The man recoiled from Salena. He fell on the ground before scrambling away.

"My contact is through here." Payton crossed the street before slipping into a narrow opening between two metal structures. They had to turn sideways to fit between them. "Yevgen knows everything that is happening in the city. He'll be able to point us in the right direction."

They turned a corner into another walkway just as

narrow. Metal sheeting had been placed over the top to cast it into darkness.

"Are you sure you know where we're going?" Salena asked.

"He's afraid of the blue radiation and stays out of the sunlight," Payton answered. "Watch your feet. There's a step."

Payton reached to hold on to Salena's arm as they turned another corner. The princess moved upward and Salena followed her up a step, lightly stubbing her toe on the edge as she blindly felt her way.

The princess pushed on a board, causing it to swing open. A blue glow came from within. The room appeared to be made from the exterior walls of the surrounding buildings. This caused it to be a collection of strange angles and colors.

"Take off the scarf," Payton instructed.

Salena pulled the scarf from around her neck. Monitors had been set up along one wall and were the source of the blue light. Though some of them were grainy to look at, they all appeared to show different angles of the city. The largest monitor focused on the Federation building's entrance. A low hum of the muted voices from outside sounded more like chaotic music than an actual conversation.

The sound of metal casters rolling across the ceiling

announced the entrance of a man sitting in a sling. His chair hung from the ceiling and moved over a series of tracks. His arms hung out the sides and his legs were missing. When he looked at them, it was not with the eyes of a man, but those of a cyborg. The mechanical irises focused on them like a camera. Salena glanced at the wall and found her face in all its muddy glory appearing on one of the screens.

"I don't know you," the man said to Salena, his voice surprisingly pleasant in its low tones.

"You know me, Yevgen," Payton said.

Payton's face replaced Salena's on the screen. A heart burst over Payton's picture and twinkled before disappearing. Yevgen smiled. "Welcome, Princess. It has been too long since we last met."

"I'm sorry. It has been harder to sneak into the city lately, but I sent my regards with your runners when they picked up the food supply," Payton answered. She touched Salena's arm and said, "I'd like you to memorize Salena. She's the future queen of the dragons."

Yevgen's eyes flashed, and the monitors blipped. The poster of Fiora appeared on the screen. "I know this face. She belongs to the Federation. Bringing her to the city is foolish. You should smuggle her off the planet at once. She is not safe here."

"I can't leave," Salena said.

"How is it a level-one prisoner of the Federation is to be the future queen of the dragons? I have heard nothing about this. Has an arrangement been made between the dragon-shifters and the Federation? What are the terms, for they cannot be for the good of Cysgodians." Yevgen's sling rolled him closer to Salena. "Why are you nervous? Never seen a cyborg before?"

"I have," Salena answered, not backing away from the man. "I'm nervous because I've been told you may be my only link to finding my sister." She pointed at the poster on the monitor. "This isn't me. It's my sister, Fiora. I believe the Federation has her, or *had* her, just as they had me held prisoner. I need to know where she is. I need to know if you know anything about her whereabouts. Is she still at the facility with them? Did she escape? Is she here in the city? Have you seen her? She looks like me but has a scar on her head, here."

Salena pointed at the forehead on the poster where the jagged scar had been drawn.

"You have many questions," Yevgen stated.

"Do you have answers?" Salena resisted the urge to grab the man by the sling and shake him.

"It depends on what you have to trade for them," Yevgen said. "Nothing in Shelter City is free."

"What do you want for them?" Salena looked helplessly at Payton.

"That is not how this works," Yevgen answered, his eyes narrowing and his tone hardening.

"I told you who she is." Payton took over the negotiations. "Is helping the future queen of the dragons not trade enough? Don't you want her to look favorably upon you and feel as if she is in your debt?"

Yevgen's expression instantly changed. He grinned and laughed as if he had been joking. "Of course, it is. Besides, Payton, you know that I'm in love with you and I will do anything for you."

"Careful, I think your programming is glitching again. You need to quit telling us girls that you love us. One day one of us will become jealous, and you do not want a jealous woman standing outside your door."

"Perhaps you are correct." Yevgen seemed pleased by the flattery. "Do not worry, future queen. I will not tell you I love you, for I do not wish to incur the jealous wrath of a dragon prince."

"Wise decision," Payton put forth.

"My sister?" Salena asked, eager to get the conversation on track.

"Forgive her, she has been looking for a long time," Payton interrupted. "How have you been, Yevgen?"

"Running long hours," he answered. "The streets have been busy. I have some recordings to show you."

Yevgen reached for the small console beside the

monitors. He brought up a series of recordings, the images paused.

"We saw this one," Payton said, pointing at Justina. She wore a different dress but stood in the same spot. "Sounds like you have a thief terrorizing the Federation on behalf of the city. One of yours?"

"I wish. No one knows anything, only rumors. I've been trying to catch the thief but whoever it is either is skilled at not getting caught or is simply a legend being built by an out-of-control game of misinterpretation." Yevgen seemed almost enamored with the mysterious bandit.

"Game of what?" Salena asked.

"When someone says one thing, then when the next person repeats it they change it a little, and then the next paraphrases, and by the end the rumor isn't even close to reality," Yevgen said.

The second image began talking. Yellow-shirt, though he was no longer wearing yellow, announced, "Food simulators, never starve again!"

"So that's who raided our stash," Payton grumbled. "We had to relocate our shipment."

"I have my people working on getting them back. They're watching to see where he hid them. So far, no one can afford his prices," Yevgen said.

"Who's this?" Payton pointed toward a man in a

black cloak. "He looks angry."

"He is full of rage." Yevgen turned on the recording. "He's a charlatan of the worst kind."

"...through what they call the blue radiation from their sun, but we know better," the man yelled. Though they couldn't see anything beyond his face, they heard people cheering as if a mob gathered. The image fluttered and distorted. "The key is not the blue sun. That is merely a distraction they hang in the sky to hide the truth. If anything, it's hurting us with its poison. We are dying, our lives shortened, our children's future corrupted and stolen by the greed of others."

"This isn't good," Payton whispered, crossing her arms over her chest.

"The Federation caused the virus and then pretended to save us as they took over our dead planet," the charlatan continued, each word tainted with rage. "They moved us here, into this valley of disrepair."

As voices cheered, Salena asked, "How big is his following?"

"Growing daily," Yevgen said. "Keep watching."

"Now, why is it our shifter neighbors live five times— no, *ten times* longer than a Cysgodian man? They breathe the same air, and they feel the same sun, yet they do not suffer the loss that we do. They eat while we starve. They fly free as we are trapped in this city of rust." The recording glitched and the sound disappeared even though the man's mouth kept moving.

"Who is he?" Payton asked.

"I don't know his given name, but they call him Doyen," Yevgen answered.

The sound returned. "...survival of our people depends upon action."

More cheering sounded.

"No one wants to go to war, but if we do not fight, we will die." Doyen lifted his arms. "They delivered us to this battle!"

Again, cheering.

Salena hugged her arms across her stomach, not taking her eyes from the monitor.

"If it's not the sun, if it's not the air, if it's not the dirt we all walk on, what is it? What is the key?" Doyen demanded.

"Blood," the crowd shouted.

"It's in the blood," Doyen yelled, throwing his head back.

"Blood, blood, blood," the crowd chanted as Doyen led them, pumping his fist into the air. "Blood, blood, blo—"

Yevgen stopped the recording.

"They're talking about shifter blood, aren't they?"

Salena whispered, horrified by the rage she just witnessed.

"Yes," Yevgen answered.

"In relation to the population of Shelter City, his following is small, but it grows by the week." Yevgen clicked a button, and the last saved recording played.

It was of a man walking, his face masked by the angle of his body. The words were distorted as if they'd been electronically enhanced. "Forest runs will cost you double."

The recording ended.

"You have your hands full," Payton remarked.

"I think we interrupted one of those forest runs," Salena said.

"Really? Did they say what they were doing?" Yevgen's eyes appeared to zoom in on her.

Salena wasn't sure how much she should say and wished she would have kept her observation to herself.

"No. They attacked Grier and Jaxx when they were escorting Salena in the woods in the borderlands," Payton said.

"What did they want?" Yevgen asked. The monitors behind him blipped as if controlled by his mind more than the console. "Who were they?"

"There were four of them. Raimon, Partha, Bharath, and another one seemed to be their leader. I don't remember a name, but he had two scars that crossed over his cheek to create an X." Salena frowned. "And I can't be certain, but I think they wanted the shifters to change form, so they could hunt them and eat them."

"Thank you for the information. I will add that to my database and watch the men you speak of," Yevgen said. One of the monitors began flashing as if searching the city for faces.

"Do you know anything about the girl in the poster?" Payton asked.

"Tell me about her," Yevgen said. "Is she like you?"

"Yes, she looks like me," Salena said. "I'm a triplet."

"Is she *like* you?" Yevgen repeated.

Salena didn't know how to answer. She wasn't sure she trusted this man. With cyborgs, it was difficult to tell how much was human and how much was a robot. They were all wired differently. Robots were logical and ran functions according to their programming. Men were, well...men.

"Does she have abilities?" Yevgen asked.

Salena nodded. "She does. But not exactly the same as mine."

"How did you know about that?" Payton asked.

"The man in me wants to speak only in truths. The machine understands this is not a logical compulsion. There is only one difference in my environment, so it can be deduced Salena is the cause of this change. She is not a machine, so it must be a natural ability." Yevgen turned to stare at Salena. "I have been scanning for that image. I have seen it before, but it was not a poster. It was an electronic transmission, an invitation to see the powers of a future-sayer who speaks only in truths."

"That would be Fiora," Salena said. "Where is she?"

Yevgen's sling carried him toward her. His cyborg eyes dilated as he looked at her face. "I am not sure the answer will bring you comfort."

Salena felt her chest tighten in fear. Her hands shook, and she held her breath as she waited for him to tell her that her biggest fear was being confirmed.

Please don't say she is dead.

"She is being held as a level-one prisoner of the Federation in their facility. She is their prize. They keep her in a cage, always watched and monitored, and only bring her out to speak her truths," Yevgen said.

"What are they asking her? Do you know?" Payton asked.

"They have her talking to generals and captains who need convincing of Shelter City's relevance." Yevgen continued to stare at Salena. "They have been escorting off-world dignitaries into the facility all day for another of their big gala events, but I have logged many who have visited the facility over the last several weeks. They land with planetary clearance for other reasons, but it is your sister they seem to reference the most in communications."

"How do you know the dignitaries for the gala are off-world?" Payton asked.

"Shifters generally are not blue in color," Yevgen answered.

"How would you get her out?" Payton asked.

"I would not." Yevgen shook his head, sounding matter-of-fact. "There is no way to free her from this fate. They will not let her go. If you are like her, Salena, they will not let *you* go."

Salena felt weak and stumbled back. She put her hand against a jagged wall for support and leaned over as she took several deep breaths.

"Salena?" Payton asked, coming to her side. She rubbed her hand over her lower back.

"She's alive," Salena whispered. "Fiora is alive."

"What about the other sister?" Payton asked. "Do they have her other sister?"

"Not that my database shows, but I will watch now that I have the information to add." Yevgen moved toward the console and began typing.

"We have to get her," Salena said. "She's here."

"We will," Payton assured her.

"The odds of being able to free her are not in your

favor," Yevgen argued, not turning back around. "Doing so will strain relations between shifters and the Federation."

"We will," Payton mouthed for Salena's benefit.

"Thank you for the information." Salena reached for the board that would swing open and let her out of the strange alcove.

"Yevgen." Payton walked to him and grabbed him by the face. She gave him a quick kiss on the corner of his mouth. "You are the best. Thank you."

"I knew you loved me," he said, smiling. "All the ladies do."

"Can I bring you anything next time?" Payton asked.

"Encryption codes for the Var communications tower," he suggested.

She laughed. "Nice try. Don't worry. I'll surprise you with something brilliant."

Salena pulled the board and left. She felt her way through the dark toward the lighted path that would take her out of the narrow walkway. Her heart beat fast and she felt as if it was hard to breathe.

Fiora was alive. She didn't care what the odds were. She needed to rescue her sister and not risk the shifters' standing with the Federation. Failure was not an option.

"Salena," Payton said behind her. "Wait."

Salena pushed out into the street and took a deep

breath. She looked up at the sky, pulling at her neckline. Tears rolled down her cheeks. So many fears, so much searching, and she finally had an answer. Fiora was here.

A sound between a cry and a laugh escaped her. All around her, the streets quieted. She hadn't meant to draw attention to herself but as she looked at the street, she saw that several people had stopped to stare.

"Salena." Payton appeared next to her, shoving a scarf at her. "You dropped something."

Payton looked around the street as whispers started.

"We need to go." Payton grabbed her arm and began walking her down a wooden sidewalk.

Salena gave up the earlier pretense of limping. They turned a corner. Payton held up her hand and listened. The building they leaned against provided cover but no escape. A fence blocked the alleyway so the only option was to head back to the street and continue straight.

"What is it?" Salena wrapped the scarf around her face to hide her mouth.

"I think you were recognized. They're coming." Payton looked around and pointed at the ground. "Grab that pole. We might have to fight."

Two men appeared before their hiding spot. They blocked the escape. There was nothing remarkable about them. They looked like a hundred other men roaming the city.

"I told you," the blond said to the man with black hair. They both stared at Salena.

Salena lunged to the side and took the pole. She held it in her hands.

Payton immediately took an offensive body stance, feet apart, one slightly in front of the other. Her hand brushed Salena's as if to say, "stay behind me." But Salena was already inching her way out of their hiding spot.

Less cautious probably because of arrogance, the taller male coming toward them lunged at Payton. The princess sidestepped the attack and neatly kicked him in the back of the knees. His body buckled in two and she added a swift sidekick to his backside, sending him flying into their hiding spot.

Salena watched, holding her weapon as she looked for a way to help. The thick folds of her baggy dress made it hard to move.

The first man's defeat seemed to spark the shorter one into action. He had a more aggressive approach as he ran full steam at Salena. She swung the pipe in warning. He shouted something as he dove at her, connecting to her stomach with his shoulder. She was launched backward, only to be stopped by a wall. She fell to her knees. The blow knocked the wind out of her, and she gasped violently to regain it. She wasn't sure if it was the blow or the smell coming off her attacker that made it harder to breathe.

The man's shoulder had not felt as if it was made of flesh, an observation proven when she noticed one of his electronic eyes zooming in on her. The man loomed over her but didn't readily attack as if he was scanning her face.

"Sweeper borgs," Payton called as she brushed her nose. "Dumb as fuck, durable as a dump ship, and stank as sweaty garbage."

Payton's attacker was back on his feet with no sign of what just happened.

"Don't let them cut you. They'll infect you with god knows what, and we don't have a handheld medic," Payton ordered as she circled her man.

Salena moaned from her place on the ground, still partially winded from the Sweeper driving her into a brick wall. She tried to push to her feet.

"Here!" Payton held a hand out for the pole still in Salena's grasp.

Salena flung it at the woman.

Payton caught the pole as her would-be assailant lumbered toward her. Twirling the rod in her fingers, she assumed a more confrontational pose, feet wide apart, butt out, ready for the Sweeper who clearly did not know he was up against a trained shifter. Salena recognized some of the moves from when she saw the Var soldiers on the practice field.

Payton made quick work of ending the Sweeper's programming when she lunged forward to stab the cyborg in the chest. Salena finally managed to push to her feet to face the remaining cyborg. She lifted her arms, ready to fight.

Turning on a heel, Payton swung around and grabbed the shorter one by the hair, stopping him mid-lunge as he tried to pounce on Salena. With a surgeon's precision, she put the metal pole through the Sweeper's neck.

"Salena?" The sound of Grier's voice filled the street before she saw him.

He almost ran past the alleyway, only to grab the edge of the building to stop his momentum as his head turned in her direction. He wore the pants and shirt of a local and was breathing heavily as if he'd run to get to her.

Seeing the Sweeper, Grier's eyes flashed with gold and he surged forward to defend the women.

The cyborg did not try to defend himself. He blinked and reached for his neck as if he didn't feel pain but was confused as to why his body was not responding to commands. The Sweeper fell onto the ground and made a strange buzzing sound seconds before Grier reached him.

Grier kicked the fallen cyborg out of his way and sent him skidding into the side of the building. He hurried toward Salena. "What is happening here?"

"Sweepers," Payton answered simply.

"What?" Grier stopped in front of Salena and searched her for signs of injury.

The fight had sent adrenaline surging through her veins. Now that it was over that sensation did not stop. Her husband was here. The sight of him caused her to shake. It had only been a short time, but she had missed him terribly. All the emotions she felt tried to bubble forth, unable to be contained.

"Sweeper borgs. They're rubbish collecting droids that the Federation reconditioned into cheap hitmen. They police the citizens of Shelter City, but for me they're only a nuisance." Payton sniffed at her hands and wrinkled her nose. "A smelly nuisance."

"I know what a Sweeper borg is," Grier retorted. "What are you doing fighting them?"

"They came after me," Salena defended her friend. Why wasn't he wrapping her in his arms? "Payton was protecting me."

"Come on." Payton tugged at Salena's forearm, taking her from Grier. "We have to go before more show up. I know of a private alcove if you insist on starting a fight with us, Grier."

Salena let Payton pull her behind her, but she glanced back to Grier to make sure he followed. His anger was barely contained as he again kicked the fallen cyborg as he passed. His lips moved, but whatever it was he was trying to say did not vocalize as he followed them away from the evidence of their skirmish.

"WHAT ARE YOU DOING HERE?" GRIER DEMANDED, as if still unable to believe what he was seeing.

"What are *you* doing here?" Salena repeated back to him.

Payton stood guard near the opening of a small inlet between buildings, so that they could talk in private, away from prying eyes. It would seem there were several confusing hidden nooks within the ill-planned city.

Grier's hand lifted and for a moment she thought he would touch her, but he balled it into a fist and held back. He didn't appear to trust himself at the moment. He took a deep breath as if having a conversation was taking all of his concentration and effort.

"My plan was to go to the watchtower and figure out a way to throw the Federation off the planet, so that I could get my wife back," he said. "Imagine my surprise when I discovered you never boarded the ESC ship. Then, imagine my further surprise when I track the two of you to Shelter City, where I find my wife sparring with ruffians."

"Sweeper borgs," Salena corrected softly.

He arched a brow at that and ignored her comment. "Why didn't you get on the spaceship like we planned?"

"I was going to." Salena wanted to remain calm, but seeing Grier stirred all the emotions she'd been trying to hold back since leaving him. It had been difficult to suppress her feelings for her husband while she had attempted to figure out what happened to her sister. "Fiora is alive."

"What?"

Salena leaned over and reached into her boot to pull out the paper she had shoved in there. She handed it to him. "Roderic gave me this right before I left. It's Fiora. She has that scar. Payton's contact had heard about a woman the Federation is using as a party trick for guests. They have Fiora telling the futures of generals, and I'm assuming dignitaries they need to impress, like some kind of trained pet. We think an event might be happening tonight. Yevgen said that it looked like off-world dignitaries were being escorted into the facility for a gala."

Grier looked at the picture and then at her, as if comparing them.

Salena pointed in the direction of the Federation facility. "She is up there. They have her held prisoner. I intend to free her."

"I will find a way to free her. Payton will take you back to the palace where it is safe." Grier suddenly pulled her close, holding her tight to his chest as if that would protect her from all the cruelties of the world. "You should have told me what you were doing. I'll take care of this for you."

"No, I shouldn't have." Salena pushed at his chest and made him release her. "You can't be here. I will not be the cause of a shifter war. People die in wars. You are the future king of the dragons. If I'm caught, they'll bring me back to the facility because I'm only an escaped prisoner to them. If you're caught—"

"I promised to protect you," he countered, as if that statement would negate anything she said.

Salena knew he was angry, saw it in the way he moved. She also knew he would never hurt her. His anger came from a loving place, but it wasn't needed right now.

"And, well, I promise to protect you, too, then," she said. "So there. I'm protecting you. Fly away."

"I can't very well fly out of this city. It's bad enough that we're even here," he said.

"Then walk out," she commanded. "I'll let you know when I'm done."

"Salena..." he warned.

"You can go now." She waved her hand in dismissal. "I said I'll contact you when I'm done."

"Salena." He put his hands on his hips.

She mimicked his stance and tone. "Grier."

He took a deep breath, his eyes narrowing in frustration. "What's your plan?"

"Still trying to come up with it." Salena bit her lip. He arched a brow in her direction. "What? I'm thinking. I've planned how to sneak away from the Federation's strongholds. I never thought about sneaking back in. Before I could even process that my sister was alive and here, those blasted Sweepers decided they wanted to capture me, so there hasn't been any time to formulate a plan."

Grier took a deep breath. She could tell she was trying his patience.

"What are you thinking?" she asked, unable to tell.

"That the pleasure I am feeling at having you near me is challenged by the fear of seeing you attacked in the city streets, which is furthered by my anger that you would dare to put yourself in this kind of danger," he answered. "I'm not sure if I want to kiss you or lock you in a tower."

Salena came closer to him, drawn to be near him. She was always drawn to be near him. The closer they were, the better she felt. She tried to calm his anger and reached for his hands, lifting them to kiss his knuckles. She stopped when she noticed the pottery shard he'd sewn in place of his crystal on the bracelet and smiled, touched by the gesture. When she looked up at him, she said, "I know which one I'd prefer."

His eyes dipped down, and he frowned as if he just now noticed the baggy dress. "What are you wearing?"

Salena pulled the dress over her head and dropped it on the ground. The pants and loose shirt had been underneath. It felt nice to get the weight off her shoulders. She eyed his disguise. "I could ask you the same thing."

The excitement of the fight still pumped in her veins, made tenfold by the nearness of her husband. She wanted, no, she *needed* to touch him. When she was by Grier, she felt whole. The idea of leaving him had been so painful she now clung to him. Her arms slipped around his neck and she pulled him to her kiss. When their lips met, it was as if all their fears and heartaches were poured into the frantic movements of their mouths.

They each fought for control. The sounds of the city

faded, a mere backdrop in their private alcove. He cupped a breast, squeezing it. His breath became hot as if the dragon inside him tried to push out.

Salena grabbed his ass, pressing him to her so she could feel how much he wanted her. The length of his thick arousal caused her sex to tighten and respond. She ground her hips forward, seeking release even if it was through their clothing.

Grier had other ideas in mind. He tugged hard at her pants to expose her hips. Salena stepped on the toe of her boot, freeing a single foot. He pulled away from her kiss, kneeling to remove the pants from her legs forcefully. All she needed was one free leg.

He had his pants around his hips before she had time to reach for them. His cock stood proud and ready. Her pants hung from a booted leg as he lifted her.

Salena's back practically slammed into the metal wall. It reverberated loudly as the press of his hips held her legs open. His hands gripped her ass to keep her in place.

He thrust into her fully. When he took her, it was hard and frantic. He poured all his frustration into his movements. Salena didn't care. She needed him just as badly. She held on to his shoulders.

Pure, raw need took over. His hips pumped hard as if

marking his claim. The sound of his breaths kept time with each wild plunge.

"There, there," she moaned, so close, eager for the release his sexy body promised. His hips slowed, and he rolled them in tiny circles as he gave small, hard thrusts into her.

The combination of danger, anger, and her incredibly talented husband were too much to resist. Salena cried out as she came. He didn't let up as he kept pumping, prying every last tremor from her sex. Only when she was gasping and weak, did he finish, meeting his own groaning climax inside her.

Grier held her against him, keeping her legs off the ground and his shaft buried deep. His swirling eyes met hers as if the primal dragon wished to tell her of his dominance over her. Only his eyes shifted, but man and beast stood before her now, and both knew he'd ridden her good.

"You're mine," he whispered, his voice hoarse.

Salena nodded and gave a weakened, "Yes."

"Hurry it up," Payton yelled. "Time to go."

"I protect what is mine," he said, lowering Salena's feet to the ground. "We'll free your sister together, as a team. No more sneaking away with Payton. And when we find Fiora, you're both coming to stay at the dragon palace. Then, we're going to find your other sister. I don't know how this is going to work, if we'll have to hide you away, or what, but we'll figure it out together. I can't lose you again."

Salena nodded in agreement and began to pull on her disguise. "All right. Together."

Grier fastened his pants and righted his shirt. The fire inside him had calmed, and he gave her an exasperated smile. "I love you, wife."

Salena grinned. Honestly, if this is how he planned on winning arguments, she predicted a lot more fighting in their future.

Out of all the plans to free her sister, Salena never would have thought walking in the front door of a secure facility would be one of them. And yet, here she was, wearing a ridiculously tight dress with a morphed face, compliments of the old morphing ring Payton retrieved from Queen Lyssa's private collection.

By retrieved, Salena inferred stolen.

Why the Var queen had outdated (and, if memory served, highly illegal) spy technology sounded like a long story that Salena knew better than to ask about.

Why that technology turned the wearer into what she could only describe as a genetically altered living pleasure droid, was also more than Salena wanted to know.

The moment she'd turned the ring on her finger, it

had changed her hair to a darker auburn, lengthened and narrowed her nose, and plumped her cheeks. Her form softened and rounded, stretching taller. Even the brown of her eyes was erased and replaced with green.

Salena could see why such deceiving technology would be made illegal.

"I love you," Salena said to Grier, causing him to cringe at the high whine of her new voice. They stood outside the facility, waiting for the signal that Payton and Jaxx were in place. When he'd gone to get a better view of the Federation facility from the sky, Grier had found Jaxx napping in the same cave Salena had hidden within.

"I, ah..." He nodded by way of acknowledgment. "All right."

Grier's disguise was less concealing. Payton had colored his face and hands with a muddy orange and adhered tufts of fur down the center of his forehead. The fur was suspiciously the same color as hers when she shifted.

While she'd glued the fur to Grier's face, Payton had said, "This almost makes up for my shaved ass."

Jaxx had laughed as if sharing a joke with her.

Grier tried pulling the fur from his face, but Payton had caught his hand and said, "You're doing this for Salena."

The shouts from the city below had settled, still there

but fewer in number and not as loud. Salena was able to deduce the general area they had been in. The exact street was not visible from her current angle near the facility.

A spout of fire showed from the watchtower. Jaxx was in his lookout position. Salena lifted her hand to wave in his direction. He breathed another blast of fire to signal he had seen her. Payton would be nearby as well, but they did not expect a signal from the cat-shifter princess.

"I still don't know how this is going to work." Salena tried to suppress the emotions running rampant through her, but it was difficult. They could not fail in this mission. It was that simple, and that complicated.

"We'll figure it out as we go," Grier said. She knew that he did not like the fact that she was coming along for this rescue. If he had his way, she would be locked up safely inside the dragon palace surrounded by guards. "There is no time to come up with a better plan, and this is our opening."

"And then what?" Salena slipped her hand into his and held tight.

"We will figure it out when the time comes." He sounded so certain that she wanted to believe him. "I'm not leaving here until I have you and your sister safely with me."

"All right." She nodded. "Let's go. Let's do this. Let's get it over with."

The sound of her own voice didn't help calm her nerves.

Grier walked in front of her toward the facility. The two Federation guards at the entryway wore the black uniforms of low-ranking soldiers. One with a nametag that read Rigger carried an electronic scanner and held it up at their approach as if the gesture was automatic. Grier lifted his hand, blocking the device.

Rigger lowered the scanner. His partner, Briggs, rested a hand on his belt where he carried a blaster pistol in warning. "Lower your hand. All guest must be scanned to ensure their presence on the guest list."

"Private delivery for General Sten," Grier said. He stepped to the side to let them get a better view of Salena behind him. "She's not to be put into the receiving logs."

Grier made her sound like a prostitute. Salena's eyes widened. She did her best to give Grier a meaningful look as she tried to figure out what he was up to. He ignored her.

She tried not to frown, reminding herself that she was not Salena right now. She was morphed bimbo droid.

Rigger smiled at her and made no effort to hide the fact he was looking her over.

"All guests must be scanned to ensure their presence on the guest list," Briggs repeated. He pulled his blaster and held it at his side.

"We had ship trouble and are running late. You will not find us on that list because this isn't exactly a delivery General Sten wants on record." Grier reached behind him and pulled Salena to his side. "I'm sure you can see why."

"All guests must be scanned to ensure—" Briggs tried to say again.

"Right," Grier drawled. "I'm obviously trying to break into a facility on this nothing planet to disrupt whatever guest list you're busy scanning by walking in the front door with an early model retro pleasure droid for General Sten. I left my comfortable megaplex to travel through the stars for...? What? Do you know how far the X quadrant is from actual civilization? Trust me. There is nothing here that anyone wants to take."

"All guests must be scanned—" Briggs held his blaster higher, aiming it at Grier's feet.

"Hold," Rigger ordered, lifting his hand to stop Briggs from drawing the weapon any higher. "Does she speak?"

"Speak, droid," Grier ordered. If she didn't know better, it appeared as if he was enjoying himself.

"Hello," Salena answered in her whiny voice. "You will take us inside now."

"Eager thing, isn't she," Grier said. "I'll wait as you go get General Sten and bring him out here to confirm, but you're not taking our pictures. Either way, I get paid for this hand-delivery, and there will be a return fee if I have to take this unit back with me."

Grier moved as if to stand beside the door.

Walking up to the door and asking to see the most powerful man in the base? This had to be the worst plan in the history of rescue plans.

The soldiers hesitated.

"The general is—" Briggs began.

"I'll take you someplace where you can wait for him," Rigger interrupted. "He is entertaining guests tonight."

"Thank you," Grier acknowledged.

Rigger thrust the scanner at his partner. "Wait here. I'm not going to be the one to get in the way of the general and his pleasure droid. Maybe if he's got this thing he'll ease up a little. I'll stick them in the holding room closest to his office, report it, and be back. Do not abandon this post."

Rigger placed his hand on the wall scanner to open the door to the facility. Inside, the halls were pristine white with no welcoming décor. The doors along a corridor looked to be evenly spaced down to the tiniest measurement. Federation buildings were not meant to be beautiful. They were functional. They were predesigned to precise specifications and used wherever the Federation quickly set up a base.

"I do not know what the order requirements were for this unit, but you might want to reconsider her programming," Rigger said. "The general does not strike me as the type of man to want a..."

"Yes?" Grier prompted.

"An eager partner," Rigger finished. "I'm not sure why I'm saying this, but I think it might help when the time comes for the droid to cool the general's desires."

"Hmm," Grier answered. She walked behind the two men and saw Grier's fist tighten slightly. It was the only indication that he was not enjoying this conversation. His voice was tight as he ordered, "Droid, when you meet General Sten, activate fear mode."

Salena pressed her lips tightly together and was unable to think of a proper answer. She hated her ability. That was one statement she did not need to hear, and an image she did not want in her head.

Rigger paused and looked back when she didn't answer.

Grier did not turn to look at her. "Droid, did you hear me?"

"Yes. Fear mode," Salena said.

Rigger again looked her over. "Does she bleed?"

Before she realized what was happening, Grier had pulled his arm back and punched Rigger on the side of the head. The soldier slammed into the wall and slid to the floor.

"Disgusting," Grier muttered.

Salena looked up and down the corridor. "What are you doing? What if someone saw you?"

"He asked if you'd bleed," Grier said by way of defense. He lifted the man over his shoulder and began carrying him. He paused by a door. "I don't hear anyone in here." He opened the door and carried Rigger inside a supply closet. "Find something to tie him with."

Salena tried not to think of the danger and did as he asked. The shelves were arranged neatly with an array of items. Most of it appeared to be medical supplies for field kits. The only thing she could find to tie someone with were the cords from a couple of handheld medical units. They were connected to a portable power source. She pulled the handhelds free and brought them to Grier.

"This is all I could find." Salena handed them over.

"This will do." Grier made quick work of binding Rigger's hands.

Salena took one of the handhelds and activated it. She injected Rigger with something that would make him sleep for a long time.

"Good thinking," Grier said. He took the unit from her and tied the man's ankles.

He paused to listen at the door. After a few seconds, he motioned that the coast was clear. He led her back into the hall.

"What now?" she asked.

"I'm going to listen for signs of an event and we'll try to slip in to join the festivities," he said. "From there, it should be easy to see if your sister is attending."

"How did you know that thing would work with the general?" Salena hurried to keep up with him as he strode through the halls.

"I have known men like General Sten for a long time. He is not the kind of man who would want the entire base knowing he had to pay for female company. I hoped his men would assume the same thing."

Grier held up his hand for silence and leaned against the wall. He placed his hand over her waist and pushed her next to him. They waited as the sound of footsteps moved around a turn in the corridor and faded.

He let loose a long breath. "I hate that you are in here."

"You don't have a choice," she answered. "I'm not leaving."

"It's too late for that anyway." He threaded his arm around hers and escorted her through a series of turns.

The sound of voices became more pronounced as they walked. Music played, a soft undercurrent to discussions.

Salena felt a shock move over her and she gasped, holding her chest. "I feel her."

"What?" Grier pushed her back around a corner in concern.

"I feel my sister. She is close." Salena pressed her hand to her chest. Tears welled in her eyes. "I forgot what it felt like to be near them. She's really here, Grier."

Grier held her tight to his chest. "We will. Try to breathe."

She took a deep breath and nodded. Grier swiped his thumbs over her cheeks to wipe away the tears. "I'll be fine. The feeling took me by surprise, is all."

He studied her as if to ask, *are you sure?*

"I'll be fine," she insisted.

"Once we join the party, you cannot react like that. If we see her, don't stare. Smile and pretend you belong." His hand shook slightly as he lifted hers and placed it on his arm. "Whatever you do, don't let go of me."

The large hall was as white and sterile as the rest of the building. Men in black uniforms acted the part of servants carrying trays of various liquors and foods around to the guests. All of those in attendance appeared to be from off-world. They carried themselves with importance.

There was an unexpected mix of at least six dozen aliens, and ones she would not have expected to be in the same room with each other. Salena knew the Dokka traders by their green skin and oval-shaped heads. She had never heard of a pleasant run-in with that particular alien. They spoke with a G'am gentleman.

This was her first time actually seeing a G'am, and she couldn't help but stare. He—*she assumed it was a he*—was a willowy creature, his thin, white-tinted body nearly transparent. G'am did not wear clothing, and the light shone through him to accentuate tiny, pulsing organs and the seemingly random pattern of vessels beneath his skin. Though he walked upright with humanoid legs, he had long, thin, wiggling tentacles instead of hands at the end of four cylindrical arms.

Many of the humanoid creatures looked like humans but with varying differences, like protrusions along the cheeks, disproportioned features, or an extra eye in the middle of a forehead.

"What are they doing here?" Grier frowned.

A Fajerkin nobleman, the rank evident by the two feathers hanging from his hat, stood with his arms crossed in displeasure.

"What?" Salena asked.

"The Fajerkin people own several fueling docks and have deals with us for several hundred-thousand space credits worth of fuel orders a year," Grier whispered. "I find it curious that they are here to speak with the Federation. They would have no business here, except to arrange a deal for *galaxa-promethium*."

"That's the fuel ore the dragons mine, right?" Salena questioned, remembering Jaxx had said something about it.

Grier nodded.

"Do you want me to ask him?" she offered. "I can make him tell us."

"No. We're here for your sister. Let's keep looking. I'll deal with the Fajerkin later." He guided her through the throng, acting as though he was above speaking to the others even though they received curious glances. Since Grier's alien disguise was wholly made up, there was no way for them to know what manner of creature he was. This caused them to stay back. It did not, however, cause them to stop staring openly at Salena.

She searched the crowd, desperate for a sign of her sister. She still felt her but began to wonder if it was wishful thinking.

Seeing General Sten, Grier changed direction to avoid him. They moved across the party. He grabbed a glass of liquor off a passing tray and sniffed it. He made a slight face of displeasure and did not drink. Musicians played in a corner, not making eye contact with any of the guests.

Suddenly, Grier stiffened.

Salena gripped his arm tighter and looked to see what happened.

"She sounds like you," Grier whispered.

Salena inhaled sharply. All she could manage was a weak, "Where?"

Grier nodded as he led her through the crowd. The gathering became dense and harder to maneuver through. That didn't stop her husband as he pushed his way to see what everyone was watching.

Salena gripped Grier's arm for support as she finally found Fiora. Gazing at her sister was like seeing a piece of her childhood come to life. Their time apart had been so long, so filled with fears and regrets, and now here they were.

Salena started to move toward her, but Grier pulled her back and gave a small shake of his head. She glanced around, seeing all eyes on her sister.

Fiora wore a white tunic and pants as sterile as the facility that held her prisoner. Her hair was pulled up and covered with a white cap. Her eyes were closed as if she concentrated. She sat in a large chair, unchained but watched over by two guards. When she opened her eyes, the gaze appeared lifeless.

"After the moon sets for the last time, you will journey to a tree and there you will find the key to your victory," Fiora told a Slit'therne. He was a snake-like alien whose kind favored remote, swampy locations. The upper half of his body was humanoid, except with green-yellow scales in place of flesh, and his hands were webbed. When it looked like he'd protest, a guard stepped forward in warning and the Slit'therne propelled himself backward on a large tail that replaced what would have been legs.

"Next," the guard ordered.

Fiora sat up straighter and looked around the crowd. Her eyes scanned in Salena's direction but did not stop on the disguise.

"Next," the guard repeated.

A Lykan stepped forward, his fur brushed flat and sprayed into place. His voice was gruff as he said, "What of my wife?"

Fiora closed her eyes only to open them quickly. She frowned. "You don't have a wife."

A tiny growl sounded in his throat. She held up her hands and closed her eyes. "I see a bride in your future. Two space years."

He grunted and nodded, stepping back as if pleased by this news.

Salena frowned. They treated Fiora like the main attraction in a traveling carnival ship.

Grier moved her to the side.

When a human woman made a move to step forward for a turn, Grier touched the lady's arm, let his eyes swirl and shook his head. She made a weak noise and stepped aside. He pushed Salena forward. No one tried to stop him.

Salena approached Fiora. Her hands shook as she reached out.

"Don't touch," a guard warned.

Fiora lifted a hand to stop him from moving forward. "No, it's all right. She won't hurt me."

The guard did not seem pleased but nodded that Salena could approach.

Salena took her sister's hand, unable to believe it was true. Fiora stared for a moment before her grip tightened as if realizing what was happening. Her breath caught.

"You poor thing," Salena said in her high-pitched whine. "I have seen fortune-tellers before. You look as if you need a break."

"That's enough," the guard said. "Step back."

Fiora sighed. "I think she's right. The images become clearer when I am rested. I need a small break. There are many futures in this room."

Salena began to pull back into the crowd.

"Don't you want your prediction?" Fiora asked.

Salena nodded.

"You will find what you are looking for," Fiora said.

Salena smiled. "Thank you."

Fiora stood and swayed on her feet. "I must excuse myself for a moment."

Grier escorted Salena through the crowd while keeping an eye on Fiora. The guards followed her as she left the festivities.

"She's leaving. Now what?" Grier asked.

"Get me to her. I have a plan," Salena said.

Grier led Salena in a random pattern through the party before slipping her out the door the soldiers had walked through. They saw them stationed near another door.

When they approached, the surly man from before stepped in their way. "Turn around. This area is closed."

Salena wasn't sure what came over her. She started to give a sweet smile, but decided seduction probably wasn't her strongest con—so instead, she hiked her tight skirt and kicked the man in the balls.

He doubled over in pain.

Instantly, Grier punched the other soldier before he could sound an alarm. Then he backtracked and kneed the first man's face as he was still doubled over.

"I normally won't kick a man while he's down," Grier

said, "but in this case, I think rendering him unconscious is actually a kindness."

Salena pushed inside the door. Fiora was there, pacing the length of the room.

"Who are you?" Fiora demanded.

Salena turned the ring on her finger before ripping it off. Her body changed back, and she ignored the discomfort of the transformation. She practically slapped the morphing ring against Grier's chest before running to her sister. She wrapped her arms around Fiora and held tight.

"Salena?" Fiora whispered, shaking. "I didn't know if I could believe it. How?"

"There will be time for questions later," Grier said. "We have to figure out a way to get you out of here."

Fiora looked at him, eyeing the strange markings on his face.

"It's all right. This is—" Salena started to explain.

"No. Don't tell me. You shouldn't have come," Fiora said. "I can't leave here. If I don't show back up soon, they will send people after me. They will find me. And, if they ask me who you are, I'll have to tell them because I cannot lie. So don't tell me anything more. Just put that face back on and get out of here."

Fiora tried to push her from the room.

Salena resisted and instead motioned at the door.

"Grier, hide those men. We don't want to draw suspicions if anyone looks this way."

Grier nodded and left to do as she asked.

When they were alone, Salena said, "Take your clothes off. I have a plan."

Fiora frowned and made no move to do so. "Salena?"

"You can't lie, but I can. We're going to change places. I'm going to tell fortunes and you're going to walk out of here dressed as a pleasure droid bimbo."

"What about you? That means you'll be stuck here. I can't do that. I can't leave you here. You don't know what it's like to be locked in a cage by the Federation. I'm a toy to them." Fiora shook her head even as Salena began stripping.

"I do know what it's like. I'm here because the Federation brought me. They came for both of us. I was lucky enough to escape. And that man with me is my husband. He's a prince on this planet. If anyone can protect us, it is him and his family." Salena stood naked and tried to give her sister the dress. "I'm here to rescue you. You're coming with us. My lies will create a distraction in there. And once started, you know they will not be able to resist telling each other the truth. I have a feeling that crowd has a lot of secrets they do not want told. I also assume they have strong opinions about some of their fellow partygoers that they will be only too willing to share. You can't have that many alien races in one room without someone holding a grudge or feeling superior."

"You haven't changed," Fiora said.

"Yes, I have. I will not hesitate again." Salena shook the dress. "Now hurry."

"Is Piera with you?" Fiora asked, pulling her shirt over her head.

"No. I hoped you knew something about her." Salena took the shirt and tugged it on.

Fiora slipped out of the pants and began wiggling into the dress. "What do you mean, you won't hesitate again?"

"That night they killed our parents. I hesitated, and we were captured." Salena took a deep breath and pulled on the pants. "I'm so sorry. I will not hesitate again."

"You can't honestly blame yourself for that night." Fiora pulled the hat off her head and the string holding up her long hair. "We were children."

"Not according to Noire law." Salena looked at the hat and string.

"We were children," Fiora repeated, not leaving room for argument. "Kneel."

Salena knelt on the floor as her sister tugged at her hair to get it off her face. The door opened, and both women instantly turned to look.

Grier stood with his hands over his eyes. "I heard your plan from outside. Are you dressed?"

"Yes, you can look," Salena said. "Do you have the ring?"

"Here," he answered, holding it up.

"Show Fiora how to use it. You're going to escort her back to the party. I'll be out shortly." Salena paused only long enough to kiss him.

Fiora placed the cap on Salena's head. "Don't forget to speak in riddles. I never tell them their futures plainly."

"I remember." Salena had helped Fiora come up with a way to hide the predictions. Fiora might not be able to lie, but she didn't have to speak in plain truths. People thought they aspired to know the future but in reality they sought to be told only what they wanted to hear.

When Salena stood, Fiora grabbed her hands. "I still cannot see my own destiny, so if this goes poorly, I love you and thank you."

"Nothing is going to happen to you," Salena said. "Stay by Grier. You can trust him with your life."

GRIER DID NOT LIKE THIS PLAN, FOR IT TOOK HIS wife from his side. However, since he did not have a better one to offer in its place, he went along with it.

Seeing Salena next to her sister had been surreal. Aside from Fiora's hair being longer, and the scar on her forehead, they were identical. His dragon-shifter eyes could barely tell the two of them apart by just looking. Yet, when he used his feelings, he knew who his wife was.

He felt Fiora take his arm. Her fingers worked nervously. They both watched the door, waiting for Salena to enter. It felt like an eternity before she did.

The sound of tapping feet acknowledged her entrance. Fiora's breathing became shallow, and she didn't speak.

Salena took the chair and looked over the crowd. "Who is next?"

The Lykan man returned to stand before her.

"They are not supposed to do that," Fiora said. "Everyone gets one turn, one question."

Grier took a step closer to his wife, watching for any sign of trouble.

"What about my children?" the Lykan demanded.

Salena shut her eyes and swayed in her seat. "I see many children if…"

"If?" the Lykan demanded.

Salena stood and moved forward to whisper something to the man. She looked to the side before continuing to speak. The Lykan turned to follow her gaze to where the Slit'therne stood. Just as demurely, she returned to her seat.

"I hope my sister knows what she's doing," Fiora said.

"I trust her," Grier answered.

"You do more than trust her," Fiora smiled, and the look somehow managed to appear sweet even with the morphed face. "I can feel it between you two. You're connected. You have the kind of love for her that I have rarely seen in my life."

Grier couldn't help his small laugh. "You are blunt like your sister. I take this to be a family trait."

"I know what you're going to ask me. But first you

must tell me what you're thinking right now," Salena said, "for I believe I may have a more important message for you."

"That I do not believe I had to wait to go after a smelly Lykan," a Dokka trader answered. His confession caused a round of laughter.

The Lykan had been sneaking up on the Slit'therne and turned at the Dokka's comment.

"And you with the lustful eyes? What are you thinking?" Salena demanded.

"That I would like to bend over the Klennup's wife," another Dokka answered.

More laughter erupted.

"And you?" Salena demanded, eliciting several more unsavory confessions. "And you?"

"What is going on here?" a yell came from across the room.

Grier focused his hearing, moving closer to get his wife out of the mounting chaos.

"If you do not stop your dealings with the general you will be cheated, and you will lose everything," Salena told the Fajerkin. "Stay with your current ore supplier at any cost. The dragons already know that you are trying to stab them in the back. You must appease them. It is the only way to secure your fortune. If you continue on this current course with the Federation, you will lose everything you hold dear, including your life."

"Dammit, Salena," Grier muttered, even as he could see the humor in what she was doing. The Fajerkin seemed to take her premonition seriously.

Fighting broke out. It started as shouts but quickly devolved into the throwing of fists. The Lykan grappled with the Slit'therne. The Dokka missed his target and hit the Fajerkin dandy. Bodies collided, escalating the brawl.

Grier took Fiora by the arm and escorted her as he rushed through the crowd. He angled his body to keep her safe as he pushed people out of the way. When he reached his wife, he pulled her with him.

Soldiers filed into the room to get the chaos under control. Grier turned toward the crowd and thrust Salena behind his back so no one would see him smuggling the fortune teller out of the party. He inched away slowly.

A soldier began to approach and Fiora let loose a loud pitched scream. She pointed across the large room. "They're killing the general."

The soldier and several others automatically stopped what they were doing and rushed into the crowd.

Grier used the distraction to get the women out of the main hall. He held them by their upper arms, guiding them as they entered the long corridor that would take them outside. He began to run and did not let them go.

"Grier," Salena protested.

He skidded to a stop by the door that would take them outside. His heart pounded. He didn't hesitate as he burst through the doors to catch Briggs off-guard. Without warning, he threw his elbow into the man's face and sent him flying.

"Close your eyes," Grier ordered. He grabbed them both by the wrist and pulled them to the edge of the cliff overlooking the city. Fiora screamed as he jumped off.

His body ripped apart and his hands turned to talons, holding the women as he beat his wings. He was sorry for the fright they must be feeling. Grier flew hard and fast along the edge of the city, looping around so he could land near the tower.

When he put distance between them and the facility, he lowered them as gently as he could across the valley on the cliff beside the watchtower. Jaxx landed next to him, shifting as he ran toward them naked.

Fiora took two wobbly steps and fainted. Jaxx caught her. Salena covered her mouth as if she were nauseous but appeared sturdier than her sister.

"I can't believe we did it," Salena said, jumping a little before moaning as she grabbed her stomach. She fell to her knees.

"Wait, Salena?" Jaxx looked at the unconscious woman in his arms.

"I'd like you to meet my sister." Salena reached for the ring on Fiora's finger and turned it off. She morphed into her regular form, still completely out.

"Jaxx, help me get them back to the dragon palace before Fiora regains consciousness," Grier said. "I'm afraid I gave her a terrifying ride."

Jaxx nodded and lowered Fiora to the ground. He let his dragon form take over before grabbing her by the shoulders and taking to the sky.

"We should go too," Grier said. "Can you ride?"

Salena covered her mouth and shook her head in denial, even as she said, "If I have to."

29

"Babies have the cutest feet, especially dragon babies, and..." Queen Rigan's joy couldn't have come at a worse moment. Grier's mother hopped up and down in excitement, embracing her new daughter as she continued to ramble strange confessions about wall colors, baby features, and hating floral patterns on gowns.

Salena was motion sick from the flight and had to press her lips tightly together to hold back her nausea. She wanted to beg the woman to stop shaking her, but this was her mother-by-marriage and already she felt like she was making a bad impression on the queen.

They stood in front of the double doors that opened into a large dining area. The vague impression of banners over the hall was about all Salena registered of the room's decor. Servants carried trays, and they definitely appeared to notice the sorry state of the dragon prince and his wife.

Salena's hair felt like a tangled, windblown mess. The white fortune teller outfit she wore was stained with dirt along the knees. The king and queen pretended not to notice. Neither did they comment on the muddy clay color covering their son's face. He had swiped off the fur, but the strange color still marred his features.

"Mother, let me take Salena home." Grier pried his mother's arms from around Salena. "It's been a long night."

"Of course, I'll bring by a tray for breakfast and—" the queen started to offer.

"I promise we'll talk later. Right now we need sleep," Grier broke in firmly. "We'll see you after we have rested."

Thankfully, the dragon king was a little more reserved in his affections. He held her shoulders briefly and nodded, "Welcome to the family, Lady Salena."

She nodded, hoping her smile was convincing.

To his son, the king said, "Grier, I expect a full report as soon as she's settled."

"Of course," Grier answered.

Salena still felt the impression of the queen's shaky hug as Grier escorted her away from his parents.

"Let me know if there is anything I can bring you," the queen called behind them enthusiastically.

Salena hung her head forward.

"Thank you, mother," Grier answered loudly, only to add in a quieter tone, "I apologize. She's excited."

"She's nice," Salena managed to answer. All she wanted was to lay down and never move again. Her head felt like she was still in the air while her wobbly legs were trying to navigate the ground. "What did your father mean about a report? Could he know what happened?"

"Probably not exactly what happened, but our state has to raise questions," Grier said. "As does the fact we did not appear after our night in the marriage tent to announce our union as is customary. I'm sure I'm in for a lecture about how I did not leave word, but we won't worry about any of that now. That conversation can wait."

Grier led her through the dragon palace. The fortress was hidden behind the face of a cliff and did not have windows. Essentially, it was a giant cave, the rooms carved from the stone. The idea that so much rock protected them was oddly comforting. As much as she wanted to appreciate the beauty of the sculptures and paintings adorning the red halls, she found it difficult when her vision kept blurring.

Jaxx had managed to slip Fiora by the king and

queen undetected while they were busy greeting Salena. They waited near a statue of a small dragon wearing a crown. Fiora looked worse than Salena felt. Her features were drained of color and she only mustered up enough of an expression to scowl at Jaxx when he tried to grab her arm to hold her upright.

Salena recognized the dragon statue to be her husband's shifted form, which considering the two hellish flights she'd just endured wasn't exactly a pleasant sight. She grabbed hold of the dragon's stone shoulder and leaned over. Nausea filled her, and it was all she could do not to heave on the pedestal.

"Salena?" Grier urged her to look at him.

"Move me and I'm throwing up on one of you, Grier," Salena warned. "I need the world to stop spinning first."

Fiora did more than threaten.

The sound of her sister's heaving brought Salena's head up. Fiora held a hand over her mouth, looking horrified at the fact she'd thrown up on Jaxx's crotch.

Fiora's dismay was nothing compared to Jaxx's. He stood frozen with his hands to his side as if he had no idea how to handle what had happened.

Fiora moved her hand as if to speak only to moan and shake her head. She pressed her fingers against her mouth once more. She swayed ominously on her feet.

"Let's get you ladies some place where you can rest." Grier gently guided the sisters away from the statue, sidestepping the mess. Fiora walked beside Salena, staying close. To his cousin, the prince said, "Jaxx, Kane should be home. You can bathe there. He'll have something you can wear. And call a servant to send a cleaning droid to help with this, please."

When Salena glanced back Jaxx was staring after them, not looking too happy.

"Sorry," she mouthed. Fiora grabbed her arm, leaning into her.

"I promise you'll be safe here," Grier told Fiora. "No one can get to you while you are in the palace."

"They'll come," Fiora whispered. "It won't take them long to figure out who took us. Two beasts in the sky will not go unnoticed."

"They're called dragons," Salena said, able to concentrate better when she had her sister to think about.

"You have many fights ahead," Fiora's shaky prediction of doom continued. Her eyes were brimmed with red and she knew this was more than a reaction to flying. The Federation had been pushing her sister too hard for premonitions and she was beyond exhausted. "I see red and violet—"

"Shh, you don't have to speak now." Salena patted

her back. "You don't have to look at the future. We're safe now."

Grier walked ahead of them to open a thick wood door. He stepped aside and waited for them to enter.

"Two is stronger," Fiora insisted. She stopped before stepping through the door and grabbed Salena's hand. "Together we might be able to find our missing piece."

Salena hoped that was true. The overwhelming joy she felt at finding one sister was lessened by her fear of still missing the second.

"Do you know anything?" Fiora insisted, her voice as frail as she looked.

"No, and I've searched many places." Salena guided her sister's elbow to walk her into Grier's home.

The living space was the size she would have expected for the future dragon king, but it had a modesty to the decoration which seemed fitting to her husband. Like the corridor, the walls were made of red stone but here they were covered by blue and gold tapestries. Each tapestry depicted a scene—dragons in flight, half-shifted dragons in battle against upright cats, strange swirling lights in what appeared to be dark caves.

A domed window capped the high-vaulted ceilings. Curtains were partly drawn, showing the cliff jutting upward from the home against the green-blue of the sky. It provided the interior light.

"You should lie down," Grier said. "I'll show you to..."

Fiora stumbled, going toward one of the blue circular couches in the middle of the room. The furniture surrounded a giant fire pit, but there was no fire burning behind the black grates. Her sister's body collapsed more than sat, and she fell over onto her side. A gray pillow, embroidered with the insignia of the dragons, was knocked onto the floor.

Salena followed her sister.

Fiora's eyes were barely open, and she stared into the distance not seeming to focus on anything in particular. Her feet were still on the floor and her arms remained where they had dropped next to her body.

Salena picked up the pillow from the floor. She glanced at Grier who nodded at her. He stayed back as Salena eased the pillow beneath her sister's head. She then pulled off her shoes and drew her feet up onto the couch. The tight pleasure droid disguise couldn't have been comfortable but Fiora didn't look like she wanted to move.

Grier appeared next to her with a blanket and gently laid it over Fiora's body. She hadn't heard him go to retrieve it.

"You have to sleep now, Fiora," Salena whispered as she brushed back her sister's hair.

I can see that we should stay, Piera's voice whispered through her mind.

Her sister's eyes closed. Salena gazed at her face, stroking her hair for a long time, almost afraid to turn away for fear Fiora would disappear into a dream. Time had stolen the innocence from their features, but even after all the years Fiora was like looking into a mirror to the past. The scar on her forehead had healed.

A tear slipped down Salena's cheek as she remembered all they had been through. Moments came at her in a rush—laughing and throwing clay at each other in the pits as children, the spinning sound of the wheel while their mother worked, the clop of her father's boots and the feel of his grip as he carried them under his arms through the forest.

She stopped petting her sister's hair and covered her mouth to keep from crying out. Tears spilled down her cheeks. Instantly, Grier was there, helping her to her feet. He pulled her to his chest and held her.

"We have to find Piera," Salena whispered.

"And we will, I promise," Grier said just as quietly as if not to wake Fiora. "I'm already planning it. One of the elders, Lochlann, has old space contacts we can use to get the word out. We'll have everyone looking for her—my aunt's space pirate friends, Prince Jarek of the Var's old space crew, every dignitary we know. We will find her, Salena. We will not stop until we have."

She nodded, grateful. "I almost don't want to leave her side, but we should let her sleep."

Grier lifted Salena into his arms. He carried her toward a long row of curving stairs that led up to a second story which overlooked the area below. "You'll be able to see her from the landing."

The vaulted ceiling of the main living section ended just past the top of the stairs, becoming flat as it cut across a bedroom and beyond. Pushed back where it could not be seen from below was a large rectangular bed. It was placed away from the walls and sat atop a woven rug.

Grier set her on her feet. Salena turned a slow circle as she looked at her new home. It seemed surreal that a girl growing up in the clay pits of Noire would end up the princess of dragons living in a palace carved into a mountain. She smiled at the thought.

"It pleases you?" he asked.

"*You* please me," she answered, still in awe of her new home. "I was thinking how strange life is. I was practically born into a clay pit, even sleeping below our family home in the hand-dug basement, and now I am back to living within the confines of the ground—from clay to stone. It feels..."

"Yes?" he appeared mesmerized by her. His eyes did not leave her.

"Right," she finished, wishing she could think of a better word. Salena covered her mouth and yawned.

There was a small dome over the bed for light. The bedroom also had a fireplace. The arched doorways on the other side of the bed were tall, but then she realized they would have to be for the comfort of her husband's form.

"Do you have a decontaminator?" she asked, not wanting to ruin the comforter on the bed. It looked regal with the golden dragon embroidered on blue material.

"There is a heated water bath downstairs, if you prefer, but yes, I have a decontaminator in here." He walked through one of the archways.

When she followed him, it led to a wide closet, half filled with his belongings and half empty, as if the shelves and hooks had been waiting for a woman to use them. His side had rows of tunics, boots, stacks of pants, and what looked to be a wide array of weaponry.

Grier pushed a button on the wall. A panel opened, and he gestured into the standing unit. "It's an older model."

He sounded almost apologetic.

"It's perfect. Everything is perfect," she assured him.

Salena crossed to the unit and looked in. Suddenly, she frowned. "I take that comment back."

"You don't like it." He joined her by the door and peered inside. "I will have it replaced immediately. You tell me what you want, and I will make sure you have it. This is your home too. I want you to be happy here. I want you to have everything that you desire."

"I was going to say it would be perfect except for the fact that I don't know how we're both going to fit in there at the same time." Salena arched a brow and smiled. She slowly nodded as she waited for her meaning to sink in. She pulled the white shirt over her head and let it drop on the floor. Next, she pushed off the pants and kicked off her shoes.

"You are right, my princess. We must have this replaced at once. It will never do." Grier practically ripped his shirt to get it off. He threw it over her head into the closet. Eager, he pushed his pants down and somehow managed to take them and his boots off at the same time.

Salena smiled at his enthusiasm, thankful to have a husband who wanted her as much as she wanted him. He pulled her against him and kissed her. She didn't care that his face was dirty. His naked body moved seductively against hers.

He pulled back. "But how about we make sure first?"

Salena laughed, surprise when he pushed her into the unit and came in behind her. It was a tight fit, but the door managed to close automatically behind them. The decontaminator activated. The green light of the cleaning lasers caressed them as it sanitized their bodies. There warmth was nothing compared to the heat radiating from Grier's body.

It was difficult to maneuver in the tight space, but Grier managed to lift her up against the wall. Within moments he was inside her, thrusting deep and hard as he feverishly lay claim to his wife. All the tension of the last days, the last years, rolled out of her under the pleasure of his touch.

The dragon made its way into his eyes as he looked at her. She felt the beast just below the surface, primal and impatient. Never had she felt so safe. Grier had done everything he promised. He had protected her. He had helped her. And he would forever love her.

"I love you," she cried as she found release. All that answered her was a hoarse growl as he found his pleasure inside of her and laid claim to what was his.

30

GRIER WANTED NOTHING MORE THAN TO TAKE HIS wife back to their bed so they could be alone. Not just for sex, which was great, but to be with her, kiss her, and marvel at the fact they belonged to each other. He would have easily stayed up all night talking to her. Of course, the gentleman in him required that he let her sleep after such an ordeal. The dragon in him wanted to do more.

As he stared at the ground in front of him, he imagined ways that they could live in the safety of their palace home and never leave. An eternity in her arms was not long enough. But instead of being with his wife, Grier was stuck in front of the mountain palace's barred gates staring into the cold eyes of General Sten.

The fact that the general came with twenty-five highly armed men indicated that he was not here for peace talks. The twenty-five soldiers were just the ones that Grier could see standing in front of them. His dragon senses detected more in the forest beyond. King Ualan had already ordered guards down to the nearby village to warn people to stay in their homes. Coming onto dragon land so heavily armed was an act of aggression that could not be ignored. It did not matter that the general thought he had a right to reclaim his property, which is how he referred to Salena and her sister.

To be honest, the man was lucky Queen Rigan didn't order him killed right then and there. People were not property. Women were not lesser beings. And the queen was not to be messed with when it came to her family or her people. Salena and Fiora were family. Period.

The general glanced behind the royal family as if expecting to be invited in.

Even though he had told Salena to stay in their home, Grier could feel her hiding just beyond the front gate, eavesdropping. He automatically knew that if she felt any of the dragons' lives were in danger because of her, she would run out of the palace and turn herself over to the general in a misguided attempt to save them.

"I'm waiting," the general commanded as if they were soldiers to be ordered about.

King Ualan stepped forward, towering over the

pompous man. He crossed his arms over his chest and did not speak.

"I know you have them. The sisters are dangerous prisoners of the Federation. You will release them into my custody at once." The man lifted his jaw. Several of his soldiers reached for the blasters on their belts in warning.

Still the king and queen did not speak. Grier crossed his arms over his chest and let the threat of a shift fill his eyes. He wanted to claw this man before him. The smug look on the general's face begged to be punched.

Jaxx and Kane stood behind them near the gate, ready to fight.

Grier heard the faint sound of the palace guards moving into position. They waited around the corner of the cliff near the practice fields for the order to attack. All it would take is one whisper from the king and the soldiers would not stand a chance against the fully shifted army of dragons. The general had made a mistake in his calculations. He believed that since the shifters had not fought with the Federation until this point that they were somehow weak and scared of him.

Dragons were not frightened of a fight. Dragons were not scared of death. They lived honorably and knew that the gods would bless them in the end. What was more honorable than defending your family, your people? For all the reasons he had tried to avoid a war, Grier knew he did not want this to escalate if it did not need to. He did not want to see his people die.

However as the tension built, he was not sure how they would get around a war. The air became thick with anger, and fear. Many of the soldiers lifted their blasters ever so slightly from their holsters as if knowing they were going to use them. All it would take is one skittish, untrained idiot and a battle would break out in front of the palace. There was no coming back from that.

When the palace guards were in place, the king finally spoke. "I'm afraid I cannot fulfill that request. If you would like to visit further, please make an appointment through the customary channels. I believe I have time in about four months if you want a meeting."

"F-four months?" the general stuttered in outrage.

"That is how long you made my husband wait for your last meeting," Queen Rigan inserted. "Surely you can understand that he is a busy man. What, with ruling a kingdom and all."

King Ualan shifted his feet.

Grier tried not to laugh, but he couldn't stop the small smirk from curling his lips. His mother was definitely sassy when she wanted to be.

"I will not stand for this," General Sten yelled. "No

one speaks to an official representative of the Federation this way, let alone a decorated general."

The man took an aggressive step forward and balled his fists.

It was one thing to threaten the king. But to threaten the king's wife, Grier's mother?

Ualan and Grier both instantly shifted into dragon-man form. The King roared loudly. The sight of them terrified several of the soldiers who had clearly never seen a shifter before and they backed up.

Within seconds the area had filled with the dragon guards. Jaxx and Kane ripped out of their clothing as they took to the sky.

It was the queen who managed to stop the fight. She lifted her hands and stood in front of her husband. She stared down the general. "No one wants to fight. There's an easy way to settle this."

"What?" The general ground out between his clenched teeth. His eyes moved over the dragon army threatening his own as if calculating his chances of winning this fight.

Grier stiffened, waiting for what was to come. He had no clue what his mother planned but knew enough to trust her.

"As one of the reigning families on this planet I believe we're entitled to see the prisoner documentation as outlined in the temporary settlement clause according to the original agreement between the Federation, the Draig, and the Var. Any off-world prisoner brought to, or captured on this planet by visiting authority, that would be the Federation, must be divulged to the royal shifter families, that would be us, immediately. Since we have not received such documentation of said female prisoners, or any prisoners for that matter, I can only assume that this is a misunderstanding. Otherwise you are in violation of the temporary settlement agreement and must at once vacate this planet. Of course we would welcome those who wish to remain in the settlement known as Shelter City to stay with the understanding that they were no longer under Federation rule, but free to choose whether or not they wish to leave or become true Qurilixen citizens. We would welcome them with open hearts."

General Sten appeared as if he wanted to strangle the queen. His fists clenched and unclenched in anger. His body shook, and his face became red.

"You did read the entire settlement agreement after the dignitaries finished it, didn't you?" The queen kept her voice mockingly sweet. "I did. I memorize the whole thing. I have taken a keen interest in planetary law during my time as queen. My brother, the prince, was very thorough during the negotiations."

The king started to laugh. The sound took away from the intimidation he displayed with his pose, but he didn't seem to care. "You heard my wife. So, what is your response? Is this a mistake? Or is this your notice that you are leaving the planet?"

The general muttered something under his breath.

"I'm sorry, I didn't quite hear that." The queen smiled brightly.

"I apologize," General Sten said through clenched teeth.

"About?" the queen insisted.

Grier began to worry that his mother would push this too far. His father must have had the same concern because the king slipped his arm around the queen's waist and pulled her next to him.

"I must've been mistaken," the general said. "I was clearly given bad information as to the prisoners. I will see to it that the person at fault for this misunderstanding will be punished to the highest degree of Federation code."

"Ah, no need. Take it easy on the inept soldier responsible," the queen said.

"I'm sure it was an honest mistake," the king added. He lifted his fingers and gestured for some of the palace guards to come forward. "I will send some of my men with you to make sure you can find your way off of our land. It is easy to get lost in the forest."

The general stormed away, his feet slamming down on the dirt path like an angry child. When one of his men tried to speak to him, General Sten punched him in the jaw and sent him sprawling back. After that, the soldiers stayed several paces away from the man.

Grier waited with his parents. They watched the general leave and ensured he took his soldiers with him. He focused on the forest, listening to make sure nobody tried to stay behind. After a few minutes Jaxx and Kane came to stand beside him. They were naked from their shifts and held the torn pieces of their clothing over their manhoods.

"I would say that went rather well," Kane said. "Though I don't exactly remember that clause in the settlement agreement."

"It's there," the queen assured him. "Your father asked for it. They had tried to hide it in a small footnote in the middle of all their droning, empty phrasing."

"I guess old habits die hard," Kane said. "Once a reporter always a reporter. Well done, my queen."

"Thank you," she answered.

"Yes, well done, my queen," King Ualan said, pulling his wife close as the shift melted from his body. He kissed her soundly which brought a round of cheers from the palace guards who still waited around the area in case they were needed.

Grier used the moment to gesture at one of the guards to unlock the front gate. When they pulled it open, he slipped past them. Jaxx and Kane joined him, and they walked through the gatehouse toward the door that would take them inside the palace.

"I don't suppose either one of you wants to join me for a meeting with the Fajerkin today?" Kane asked. "I don't know what's going on, but they just transmitted a long apology for their betrayal and offered us more money for the same amount of ore that they have been getting for decades."

Grier chuckled. "Go with it. They were trying to go behind our backs to make a deal with the Federation for the ore."

"How do you know?" Kane asked.

"It is a long story that I will tell you later," Grier said. "And no, I have no wish to go to that meeting with you today."

"Don't look at me," Jaxx dismissed.

Salena waited for him just outside the gate room, wringing her hands in worry. She wore one of his long tunics like a dress with a strap of material tied around her waist. Since she was new to the palace, there had not been any clothes in his closet for her.

When he'd woken up that morning he had honestly thought about it, but there had been no time to send for a seamstress. As a princess, and future queen, she would need to be outfitted accordingly. As his wife, he'd give her anything she desired. He had a feeling if he offered her clothes and jewels she'd turn them down for a chance to help the people of Shelter City. There was a lot of work ahead. They still hadn't figured out what the roaring noise she heard belonged to.

It would seem the gods knew what they were doing after all. They sent him a bride as strong as he was and infinitely more caring.

"Excuse me. I need clothes." Kane hurried past Salena, giving her a slight nod of greeting, before he strode down the hall naked.

"Did I hear correctly? Is it over? Are we really free?" she asked.

"The Federation will not be pleased with this loss," Jaxx said, compelled to answer. "For the moment there's nothing they can do about it. I would advise you not to venture outside the palace without a couple of guards. But yes, I would say you are very free, Princess Salena."

"It still sounds so strange to be called that." Salena moved closer to Grier and leaned into him so that his arm rested over her shoulders.

Grier thought of the sweet kisses she'd been giving

him when the order came that he was to greet the general marching toward their gate. He wanted to go home to pick up where they'd left off.

"How is your sister? Is she adjusting?" Jaxx asked. "I imagine seeing dragons for the first time must've been frightening for her."

"I don't think it was the dragons. I think it was the flying," Salena answered. "I'm sorry about the...other thing that happened. I'm sure my sister is embarrassed by that and would apologize if she was here."

"It's fine," Jaxx said before hurrying to follow Kane.

"Did I say something wrong?" Salena asked.

"Jaxx is always a little anxious when he is at the palace. I think he gets it from his father. Uncle Yusef does not spend much time here either."

"Oh." She nodded.

"How is your sister?" he asked.

"I showed her to the guest suite as you suggested. The Federation pushed her abilities too hard. She keeps mumbling about Shelter City and fighting and other doomsday predictions that are so muddled they sound worse than they probably are...hopefully. It will take her a few days to recover. I think rest and quiet is the best thing for her. It would be nice if she was not thrown into too many family activities right now. In fact, it would be best if she were left alone altogether. I know it might sound strange, but when she's around people, it can be difficult to block their futures. When she is tired even more so."

"Of course," he said. "I will leave her care to your discretion. Anything you need all you have to do is say the word. This is your home now. Fiora is a part of this family and under our protection until such a time as she does not wish it."

"How did I ever get so lucky?"

Grier swept her into his arms and brought her toward their home. Since his hands were full, she opened the door so he could carry her inside.

He kicked the door shut behind him and strode to the stairs.

"You need rest as well, my beautiful wife," he said. "You have had a long journey."

Grier carried her to the foot of the bed and set her down gently. The curtains had been drawn over the ceiling dome to cast the room with darkness. Grier went to a fixture on the wall and pushed the button. A lamp in the shape of a torch lit with fire, creating a soft orange glow over his wife.

"Your mother is an amazing woman," Salena said as she sat on the edge of the bed. "I can't believe she scared the general like that."

"Yes, she is," Grier agreed, not wanting to talk about his mother at the moment.

"Do you think your parents will like me?" she asked, appearing a little insecure. "I know that I'm not easy to be around with my ability. People seem to get annoyed with me very quickly."

"I don't know what the big deal is. Your ability is not hard to be around." Grier pulled her to stand before him so he could hold her.

Salena laughed. "You obviously haven't tried lying to me yet. Give it time. Everyone gets annoyed with it eventually."

"Why would I lie to you?" Grier frowned at the idea. "I will tell you whatever you want to know. I would never dishonor you by—"

"Try it," she interrupted. "Lie to me."

"No." He held her tighter. "You are my wife. I will never try to trick you, or lie to you, or beat you, or hurt you, or make you cry, or—"

Salena laughed. "See. You can't, can you? Trust me. It will get aggravating. The few who've said they could take it always ended up weary after a short time."

"If I am weary around you, it will be for other reasons." His grin said it all, and he nodded that they should return to bed. "In such a scenario, I plan to get very, very weary, every night—*after you have had more rest, of course*—after many hours of—"

"Nice subject change."

"Did it work? Will you rest now?"

Salena arched a brow. "I'll make you a deal. If you try to lie to me just once for my amusement, I'll get in that bed."

"Deal." He grinned and looked around the room. He pointed at the blue curtain overhead. "That curtain is purple."

Salena started to laugh, but then stopped.

"Hold on a moment." She grabbed his face and looked deep into his eyes. "You see purple when you look at that? Maybe we should take you to a medical booth."

"No." He pushed his pants off his hips and kicked out of his boots.

"But..." She glanced up at the curtain. "That curtain is blue."

Grier pulled off his shirt and threw it aside. Once he was naked, he pulled the belt from her waist and dropped it on the floor.

"Grier?"

He tried to pull the long tunic over her head. "I know it's blue. You told me to lie."

She stopped him from undressing her. "Tell me another lie."

"I am sorry I didn't send for proper nightclothes." Since she did not let him lift the tunic over her head, he grabbed the neckline and ripped it open. He grinned now that she was exposed. He moved to kiss her.

She pushed his head back, and he groaned in disappointment.

"Tell me another lie," she insisted.

"I don't like to see you naked." Grier pulled at the tunic again, ripping it further so he could draw it from her shoulders.

"How is this possible?" Salena stared at him as if he'd just told her the secrets to the universes. "Grier, no one has ever been able to lie to me before."

He gazed into her eyes. "Maybe it's different because I'm your mate, and your power doesn't need to work on me, because I will never deceive you."

"Tell me another one." She appeared fascinated with the idea. "All this time, you have been telling me the truth because you wanted to."

Grier went to the bed and pulled back the covers. He gestured that she should get in. "I haven't been thinking of you all morning."

Salena pulled the boots off her feet and moved to the bed. She slid onto the mattress and he covered her with the blankets. Then, walking around to the other side, he joined her.

He drew her next to him, letting her head rest on his arm as he held her. "I don't want to lie like this forever."

He felt the connection between them growing stronger with each passing second, almost as if he could hear her thoughts in his head and feel her emotions. She would be able to feel the same from him.

"I love you," she whispered, her breath tickling his neck.

"There is one lie I will never tell. I will never lie about my love for you." He pulled her closer, hugging her against him.

She pulled back slightly to study his face. "My ability might not work on you, but I feel like there is something else between us, a connection. Is it crazy that I keep hearing that word in my head—*connection*?"

"No. That is what it means to be my mate. My life is now yours. I give you my long years. I give you my thoughts in your head whenever you want them. I give you my heart." He turned to smile at her and reached to caress her cheek. "You are my everything, Salena. You are my soul, my heart, my life. You are the very air that I breathe. All that I am is yours. I love you, Salena. Forever."

Forever.

The word hung between them. Nothing more needed to be said, for their love was all that mattered. It would get them through the times to come, through the battles with the Federation, through Cysgodian hunters, through any number of threats facing them.

"Yes." Salena snuggled into him, and he intended never to let her go. "Forever."

The End

The series continues with
Marked Prince (Qurilixen Lords)
Visit MichellePillow.com for details!

THE SERIES CONTINUES...

Need more Dragon Lords?
The books continue!
Dragon Lords 2: Perfect Prince

Want to see how King Attor's sons turn out,
despite their father's teachings?
Lords of the Var®: The Savage King

Dragon Lords and *Lords of the Var*®
in Modern Day Earth?
Captured by a Dragon-Shifter: Determined Prince

Read all the Dragon Lords and Var books?
Yay, you, keep going!
Space Lords 1: His Frost Maiden

WELCOME TO QURILIXEN

QURILIXEN WORLD - FIRST IN SERIES BOOKS

Keep Reading!

Check out these first-in-series books in the different Qurilixen World series installments!

The Qurilixen World is an extensive collection of science fiction and paranormal romance novels by award-winning NYT Bestselling author, Michelle M. Pillow®.

Note: Each book in each series is a stand alone story.

Dragon Lords Series: Barbarian Prince
Dragon Shapeshifter Romance - The original Dragon Lords series' Anniversary Edition

Going undercover at a mass wedding as a bartered bride, Morrigan Blake has every intention of getting off the barbaric alien planet just as soon as the ceremony over. But the next morning, Morrigan discovers her ride left without her and an alien dragon shifter is claiming she's his wife. It's not exactly the story this reporter had in mind. And to make matters worse, the all-to-seductive dragon-shifter alpha male refuses to take no for an answer.

Lords of the Var® Series: The Savage King
Cat-Shifter Romance

Cat-shifting King Kirill knows he must do his royal duty by his people. When his father unexpectedly dies, it's his destiny to take the throne and all of the responsibility that entails. What he hadn't prepared for is the troublesome prisoner that's now his to deal with.

Undercover Agent Ulyssa is no man's captive. Trapped in a primitive alien forest awaiting pickup, she's going to make the best out of a bad situation... which doesn't include falling for the seductions of an alpha male king.

Dynasty Lords Series: Seduction of the Phoenix

A prince raised in honor and tradition, a woman raised with nothing at all. She wants to steal their most sacred treasure. He'll do anything to protect it, even if it means marrying a thief.

Space Lords Series: His Frost Maiden

Science Fiction Space Pirate Romance

Lady Josselyn of the House of Craven has been betrayed. With her home world on a Florencian moon under attack and her family dead, she finds herself at the mercy of the one who deceived them. There is only one thing left to do—die with honor. But before she can join her family in the afterlife, she must first avenge all that she held dear. Falling in love with a pirate was never in the plan. Evan and his thieving crewmates might have delayed her fate, but they can't stop destiny.

Captured by a Dragon-Shifter Series: Determined Prince

Dragon Shapeshifter Romance

Dragon-shifter Prince Kyran has studied the Earth people and is ready to assimilate. Female shifters are all but going extinct on his planet of Qurilixen, and his people are desperate for mates—so much so they're taking matters into their own hands. What better place to find a mate than Earth? After all, dragon-shifters had come from there centuries ago. Surely a human female would be honored to be selected by one as fine and fierce as himself.

Galaxy Alien Mail Order Brides Series: Spark

Alien Romance

Earth women better watch out. Things are about to heat up.

Mining ash on a remote planet where temperatures reach hellish degrees doesn't leave Kal (aka Spark) much room for dating. Lucky for this hard-working man, a new corporation Galaxy Alien Mail Order Brides is ready to help him find the girl of his dreams. Does it really matter that he lied on his application and really isn't looking for long term, but rather some fast action? Earth women better watch out. Things are about to heat up.

Happy Reading!

MichellePillow.com

New York Times **& *USA TODAY***
Bestselling Author

Michelle loves to travel and try new things, whether it's a paranormal investigation of an old Vaudeville Theatre or climbing Mayan temples in Belize. She believes life is an adventure fueled by copious amounts of coffee.

Newly relocated to the American South, Michelle is involved in various film and documentary projects with her talented director husband. She is mom to a fantastic artist. And she's managed by a dog and cat who make sure she's meeting her deadlines.

For the most part she can be found wearing pajama pants and working in her office. There may or may not be dancing. It's all part of the creative process.

Come say hello! Michelle loves talking with readers on social media!

www.MichellePillow.com

facebook.com/AuthorMichellePillow

twitter.com/michellepillow

instagram.com/michellempillow

bookbub.com/authors/michelle-m-pillow

goodreads.com/Michelle_Pillow

amazon.com/author/michellepillow

youtube.com/michellepillow

pinterest.com/michellepillow

JOIN THE EXCLUSIVE CLUB!

Join the Pillow Fighters' Reader Club to stay informed about new books, sales, contests, giveaways, exclusive content, preorders and more!

michellepillow.com/author-updates

COMPLIMENTARY EXCERPTS

TRY BEFORE YOU BUY!

THE DRAGON'S QUEEN

BY MICHELLE M. PILLOW

Dragon Lords Series

Bestselling Shape-shifter Romance

Mede of the Draig knows three things for a fact: As the only female dragon-shifter of her people, she is special. She can kick the backside of any man. And she absolutely doesn't want to marry.

Mede has spent a lifetime trying to prove herself as strong as any male warrior. Unfortunately, being the special, rare creature she is, she's been claimed as the future bride to nearly three dozen Draig—each one confident that when they come for her hand in marriage fate will choose them. When the men aren't bragging about how they're going to marry her, they're acting like she's a delicate rare flower in need of their protection.

She is far from a shrinking solarflower.

Prince Llyr of the Draig knows four things for a fact: He is the future king of the dragon-shifters. He must act honorably in all ways. He absolutely, positively is meant to marry Lady Mede. And she dead set against marriage.

Llyr's fate rests in the hands of a woman determined not to have any man. With a new threat emerging amongst their cat-shifting neighbors, a threat whose eyes are focused firmly on Mede, time may be running out. It is up to him to convince her to be his dragon queen.

The Dragon's Queen Excerpt

There were three things Medellyn knew for a fact. She was special. She could kick the ass of any boy. And she did not want to marry and have babies.

She was special.

Medellyn was one of the only dragon-shifting females in all the universe, and definitely in all of the Draig. Only once in a thousand births was a female dragon-shifter born. She was rare, or so everyone kept telling her. Her childhood was a strange contradiction. Her very proper mother tried to treat her as if she were some sacred crystal that might crack. Her warrior father tried to make her train like a boy while dressing like a girl.

She could kick the ass of any boy.

Medellyn hated when boys tried to act as if she were weak and to be protected. Her dragon was just as fierce as any of theirs, probably more so. To prove her point, she'd gladly pummel any who had challenged her to the ground...and some who hadn't.

She *absolutely, positively* did not want to marry and have babies.

Being the special, rare creature she was, in the twenty not-so-sweet girlhood years of her life she'd been claimed as the future bride to nearly three dozen boys—each one confident that when they came of the age to marry she would make their crystals glow and they hers.

Glowing crystals wasn't just a metaphor. On the day she was born, her father journeyed to Crystal Lake like all the new fathers did. He dove beneath the waves, swam down to the deepest part and pulled her stone from the lakebed. Like all Draig children, she wore the stone around her neck, and would continue to wear it until the day it glowed telling her which of the dragon-shifting men she was destined by the gods to marry.

Okay, technically she might be destined to marry an off-worlder like most Draig men, but no one on her planet seemed to think so.

Gods bones, she hoped she wasn't destined to end up with any of the idiots on her planet. They had yet to impress her.

When it was her turn to go to the Breeding Festival, the crystal would glow signifying her *curse* for all to see. Well, her "blessing" as her mother called it. Lady Grace did not appreciate her daughter calling marriage a curse. Grace did not appreciate a lot of things that Medellyn liked, such as swords and bows, ceffyl riding, camping alone in the forest, hunting, sparring, smashing arrogant looks off of dragon men's faces.

It was a fight with her mother that sent her running through the mountain forest. Medellyn hated the woman, hated what her mother wanted her daughter to be. Grace was only a human, brought to their planet as a bartered bride. She married Medellyn's father without question and spent most of her days completely in docile agreement with whatever her husband said. Medellyn couldn't imagine taking anyone else's opinions over her own.

Her father, Axell, was a highly praised warrior in the Draig army and carried the title of Top Breeder of the ceffyls. The man's whole life focused on four things: his wife, his only child, and mares and steeds. Her father was a very important man, but his work kept him away from home several nights a week as he slept outdoors with the herd. With a three-year gestation period and only about fifty percent live-birth rate, the animals were not a resource that could be easily renewed. His ceffyls supplied the soldiers with mounts and farmers used them for beasts of burden to help with the fields.

Like Axell, Medellyn was a proud dragon. Had she been born male, she would have been a warrior, too. Instead, she was *special*. How could her human mother begin to understand the wildness than ran in her dragon blood? If she had, Grace would never have asked Medellyn to tame her spirit.

Breathing hard, she came to an abrupt halt and screamed into the trees. Her body shook with rage and she tore at the pretty gown she wore. She hated her body, hated being special, hated being expected to act like a lady when she felt like a dragon. Her taloned finger snagged on the crystal around her neck and she cut the leather strap of the necklace. The crystal flew several feet away.

"I am not some man's chattel," she yelled, knowing she'd run far enough away that her mother could not hear her retorts. Since she was shifted her voice was hoarse and powerful, and she reveled in the fierceness of it. "I am not some breeding ceffyl to have children. It is not my place to give you fifty grandkids. I can't help you only had one child. If you would have made me a boy, I wouldn't be a disappointment to you!"

Tears stung her eyes as Medellyn walked aimlessly, searching the forest floor for the fallen necklace. Finding it, she grabbed the inert crystal into her fist. It was a reminder of all she was expected to be. She took a deep breath, looking at her fist and then to the stones littering the forest floor. A small smile formed on her mouth. Medellyn dropped the crystal on the hard ground and glared at it. Rage boiled inside her, the kind of rage surely only a dragon-shifter could feel.

"This is what I think of your fate," she growled as she fell to her knees.

Medellyn grabbed a heavy rock and smashed it down onto her necklace. The crystal cracked. The noise gave her some satisfaction so she hit it again. Grunting with each strike of the stone, she didn't stop until her future had been ground to dust.

"That is what I think of your destiny."

To find out more about Michelle's books visit
www.MichellePillow.com

THE SAVAGE KING

BY MICHELLE M. PILLOW

Lords of the Var® Book One
by Michelle M. Pillow

A Qurilixen World Novel

Bestselling Cat-shifter Romance Series

Cat-shifting King Kirill knows he must do his duty by his people. When his father unexpectedly dies, it's his destiny to take the throne and all of the responsibility that entails. What he hadn't prepared for is the troublesome prisoner that's now his to deal with.

Undercover Agent Ulyssa is no man's captive. Trapped in a primitive forest awaiting pickup, she's going to make the best out of a bad situation...which doesn't include falling for the seductions of a king.

About *Lords of the Var®* (Books 1-5)

You met their father, King Attor, in Dragon Lords Books 1-4, now meet the Var Princes!

The cat-shifter princes were raised to not believe in love, especially love for one woman, and they will do everything in their power to live up to their father's expectations. Oh, how the mighty will fall.

The Savage King Excerpt

Kirill watched the door to his bedroom open. He'd been sitting in the dark, trying to relieve the stress headache that had built behind his eyes for the last week. The pain started at the base of his skull and radiated up to his temples until he could hardly see straight.

A heavy responsibility had been thrust on his shoulders, a responsibility he really hadn't prepared himself for, the welfare of the Var people. King Attor had not left him in a good position. He'd rallied the people to the brink of war, convinced them that the Draig were their enemy, and even went so far as to attack the Draig royal family.

Kirill wanted to see peace in the land. However, he knew the facts didn't bode well for it. The Draig had a long list of grievances against King Attor and the Var kingdom.

Before his death, the king had ordered an attack on the four Draig princes, all of which ended horribly for the Var. The worst was when Prince Yusef was stabbed in the back, a most cowardly embarrassment for the Var guard who did it. If he hadn't been executed in the Draig prisons, he would've been ostracized from the Var community. Luckily, Prince Yusef survived or they'd already be at battle.

Attor had also arranged for the kidnapping of Yusef's new bride. The Draig Princess Olena had been rescued, or that too would've led to war. The old king had even tried to poison Princess Morrigan, the future Draig queen, on two separate occasions. She too lived. And those were only a few of the offenses Kirill knew about in the few weeks before King Attor's death. He could just imagine what he didn't know.

Kirill sighed, feeling very tired. He'd known since birth that the day would come when he'd be expected to step up and lead the Var as their new king. He just hadn't expected it to be for another hundred or so years. His father had been a hard man, whom he'd foolishly believed was invincible.

"Here kitty, kitty, kitty." His lovely houseguest's whisper drew his complete attention from his heavy thoughts.

Ulyssa bent over like she expected him to answer to the insulting call. He dropped his fingers from his temple into his lap, and a quizzical smile came to his lips. As he watched her, he wasn't sure if he was angered or amused by her words.

"Are you in here, you little furball?" she said, a little louder.

She wore his clothes. Never had the outfit looked sexier. His jaw tightened in masculine interest, as he unabashedly looked her over. All too well did he remember the softness of her body against his and the gentle, offering pleasure of her sweet lips. She'd made soft whimpering noises when he'd touched her, yielding, purring sounds in the back of her throat. Even with the aid of nef, he was surprised by how easily and confidently she melted into him. The Var were wild, passionate people and were drawn to the same qualities in others. He suspected she'd be an untamed lover.

Too bad she'd belonged to his father first. In his

mind, that made her completely untouchable though none would dare question his claim if he were to take her to his bed. Technically, by Var law, she belonged to him until he chose to release her. For an insane moment, he thought about keeping her as a lover. He knew he wouldn't, but the thought was entertaining.

Kirill's grin deepened. Ulyssa strode across his home to the bathroom door with an irritated scowl. It was obvious she didn't see him in the darkened corner, watching her. He detected her engaging smell from across the room, the smell of a woman's desire. It stirred his blood, making his limbs heavy with arousal. And, for the first time since his father's death, his headache relieved itself.

"Hum, maybe I'm looking too high. I'm sure there has to be a little cat door here somewhere. Come here, little kitty. Where are you hiding?"

His slight smile fell at her words. It was easy to detect her mocking tone.

"Where's your little kitty door, huh?" Ulyssa whispered to herself, her blue gaze searching around in the dark.

Kirill grimaced in further displeasure. He watched her open the door to his weapons cabinet. Her eyes rounded, and he thought she might take one. She didn't.

Instead, she nodded in appreciation before closing the door and continuing her search for an exit.

She stopped at a narrow window by his kitchen doorway. Her neck craned to the side, as she tried to see out over the distance. Kirill knew she looked at the forest. From under her breath, he heard her vehement whisper, "Where exactly did you little fur balls bring me? Ugh, I need to get out of this flea trap, even if I have to fight every one of you cowardly felines to do it. I've fought species twice as big and three times as frightening. A couple of little kitty cats don't scare me."

If this insolent woman wanted to play tough, oh, he'd play. Curling gracefully forward, Kirill shifted before his hands even touched the ground. He let one thick paw land silently on the floor, followed by a second. Short black fur rippled over his tanned flesh, blending him into the shadows. His clothes fell from his body, and he lowered his head as he crept forward. A low sound of warning started in the back of his throat. He was livid.

To find out more about Michelle's books visit www.MichellePillow.com

PLEASE LEAVE A REVIEW

THANK YOU FOR READING!

Please take a moment to share your thoughts by
reviewing this book.

Be sure to check out Michelle's other titles at

www.MichellePillow.com

Printed in Poland
by Amazon Fulfillment
Poland Sp. z o.o., Wrocław